~~~~~

# Buried by the
# Boardwalk
## An Ocean Grove Mystery
# Book 2

## Heath P. Boice

~~~~~

Seabreeze Press
Rochester, NY

D1291846

# 2 Buried by the Boardwalk

Buried by the Boardwalk (The Ocean Grove Mysteries) Book 2
Copyright 2012 by Heath P. Boice
Published by Seabreeze Press

ISBN-13: 978-0615661414
ISBN-10: 0615661416

Cover design by Marissa Giambrone
megiambrone@gmail.com

Printed in the United States of America.

For information about film, reprint or other subsidiary rights, please contact: permissions@seabreezepress.com

Seabreeze Press in an independent publishing house.

Seabreeze Press
Rochester, NY
www.seabreezepress.com
contact@seabreezepress.com

Library of Congress Cataloging-in-Publication data available.

Also by
Heath P. Boice
~~~~~

Missing by the Midway
Ocean Grove Mysteries Book 1

Dedication
To Natalie- for falling in love in Ocean Grove.

## Acknowledgements

I would like to thank all of my friends and the special places "down the shore" for your support and inspiration. You provide a never-ending (I hope) stream of muse for the growth of Asbury College.

Special acknowledgement goes to Dr. John Allison, Professor at the College of New Jersey for his guidance, scientific expertise, and creativity.

Also, thank you to Tish for being a good sport, and Mary Anne and Mary-Beth for being my steadfast support. Special thanks goes to everyone in Student Affairs at RIT for indulging me each and every day.

There is a special place in my heart for Monmouth University and all of its wonderful people, past and present.

To my family, all I can say is thank you. I would not be able to write if I didn't have your support and encouragement.

What happens to a dream deferred?
Does it dry up
like a raisin in the sun?
Or fester like a sore
And then run?
Does it stink like rotten meat?
Or crust and sugar over
like a syrupy sweet?
Maybe it just sags
like a heavy load.
*Or does it explode?*

-Langston Hughes
*Montage of a Dream Deferred*
1951

-1-

I'm used to nasty things falling in my lap. Student problems, angry parents, but not unearthed skulls. As the Dean of Students at Asbury College, a small, liberal arts school in the New Jersey beach town of Ocean Grove, I make an unlikely detective. But given the string of events that have happened on-campus in recent years, you wouldn't know it. Last month, one of my students, Jessica Philmore, disappeared. That was where my education in detective-work began, out of necessity. Although the case was solved within a few weeks, the adventure caused me a carnival ride with a dead man, a sprained ankle, and a few more grey hairs. My second foray into the field of sleuthing also just happened upon me one day, but this time the subject wasn't missing persons, it was murder.

I'm Douglas Carter-Connors. I'm forty years old, have a five-year-old son, Ethan, and have been married to my beautiful wife, Barbara, for eight years.  We live in Ocean Grove.  I try to run a mile or two every morning along the boardwalk, I like to walk to work, even in the rain, and I have a penchant for red wine.  Actually, I have a penchant for most wines, but red is better for my heart.

Being a Dean of Students has a lot of similarities with being a dad.  I help establish standards for living, I try to be a role model, I hope to assist in the development of young people, and on any given day I'm never sure if I'm succeeding at any of them.  In many ways, my job resembles that of a circus master.  Students, faculty, and staff are constantly in my office voicing concerns, sharing ideas, or simply venting.  My job is to listen, lead, and direct them for the appropriate support if I can't provide it myself.  I've been at the College for about ten years and I love it.

In my limited experience, strange events seem to pop-up without notice.  Like last month, I walked merrily into my office on a Monday morning to find Jessica Philmore's mother sitting in my waiting area.  In this case, no one was waiting for me, they just barged right into my office while I was checking my e-mail and dumped a skull on top of my desk.  Quite the attention-grabber, I must say.

~~~~~

It was late afternoon on a beautiful fall day.  October at the shore is usually marked with warm days and crisp nights all wrapped-up in a blanket of sea air.  I was sitting at my desk after a long day of meetings, trying to catch-up on my daily e-mail, when I heard a commotion in the outer office.  The Dean of Students Office (DOSO) suite is in the Student Center and comprised of a large waiting area with offices around the perimeter.  The waiting area, or "outer office" as I call it, is guarded carefully by Judy Wessler, Administrative Assistant extraordinaire.  Judy's originally from Brooklyn, never lost her accent, has been at the College for twenty-five years, and acts as mother to five of her own children, and about 1,500 of us at AC.

Now, DOSO is used to varying levels of commotion all day long, consisting of excited students coming to share news, upset students, staff or faculty coming to dump frustrations, or any number of other commonplace disturbances.  Noise and loud voices are not unusual, so I didn't pay much attention from the confines of my back office until I heard Miss Bettie's voice sound a bit more edgy than usual.  Miss Bettie is our resident custodian in the Student Center.  Her voice was so loud in fact, that I could hear every word that she was saying, "Judy!  Where's my boss?  I need to see him!"  Although I wasn't her boss (Miss Bettie works for our Department of Facilities Management), she considers DOSO her personal home base, keeping her lunch and her coat in our office copy room.  I guess referring to me as her "boss" is her way of proclaiming that she is part of

our office staff.  Since Miss Bettie is a tough cookie,
I'm honored by the distinction.

I could hear Judy hushing her, but Miss
Bettie was too riled-up, "This is important!"  Since
Miss Bettie never exhibited such behavior, I knew
something was wrong.  But before I could get up
from my desk to go into the outer office, Miss Bettie
marched in, dragging another facilities worker by the
hand behind her, with Judy right behind him.  They
reminded me of three children, holding hands,
rushing to get to the ice cream truck.

"Doug!"  Miss Bettie shouted (she was just
about the only person on-campus who didn't call me
"Dean Doug").  "You've got to see this!"  She
looked at Arnie, the facilities guy she was holding,
and raised up his right hand as though he had just
won a gold medal.  The motion caused the burlap
bag that he was holding to sprinkle dirt onto the
floor.  He looked shocked and a bit anxious, as
though he had just entered the proctologist's office
for an annual visit.

"What's wrong?"  I asked, standing at my
desk.  Judy piped in, hands on her ample hips,
"Bettie, you can't just barge into his office," she
said, like a dog peeing on her turf.  Miss Bettie and
Judy commonly bicker.  Since they are both strong-
willed women, Judy a tough Brooklyn bitch, and
Miss Bettie a strong black woman, they vie for office

territory on a daily basis. I'm only slightly ashamed to say that I find it amusing.

"Judy," Miss Bettie responded, closing her eyes and putting *her* hand on *her* hip, "I wouldn't do this if it wasn't important, you've got to see what Arnie found! You're not going to believe it!" Never one to dismiss a scandal, which could serve as days of gossip-fodder, Judy backed down immediately and began to scrutinize the burlap bag.

"Arnie," ordered Miss Bettie, "show it. C'mon, show it!" Arnie looked around uncomfortably, he was a soft-spoken man whom I knew to work mostly with the grounds crew and clearly he was more comfortable with plants than people. "Where?" he asked, directing the question toward Miss Bettie.

"Right there!" Miss Bettie said, pointing to my desk. She grabbed a newspaper out of the recycling container in my office and quickly laid it out over my paperwork as though it was a fine linen tablecloth, "You better sit down for this," she said, eyeing me. I sat, and Arnie proceeded to dump the contents of the bag onto my desk. Judy hurried up right next to me near my chair to get a ringside view.

Arnie shook the bag gingerly, careful not to dramatically disturb its contents. "It's not alive is it?" I asked, which elicited a simple, "hrumph," from Miss Bettie's smirking face. Within a few seconds, an object began to roll out onto the newspaper, leaving a trail of dirt behind it. As it rolled, it gained momentum and quickly left the desk and fell into my lap. I let out a yelp, while Judy quickly moved her hand to her mouth to stifle a gasp. Wide-eyed, we looked at the contents of my lap with a great deal more awe than usual. Staring back at us, was a dirty skull. It's clear to me now that my lesson in murder had begun, one that I call, "Buried by the Boardwalk."

-2-

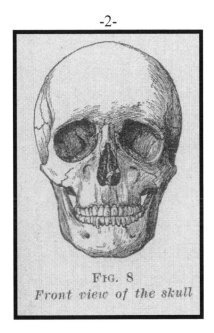

FIG. 8
*Front view of the skull*

I sat, paralyzed in my chair, staring down into the empty eyes of a dead person. A real dead head. As I closed my legs closer together to prevent the skull from falling further to the floor, Judy made the first comment, "My *Gawd*!" she screamed in full Brooklyn style, "Arnie!" He ran around my desk, "Oh!" he said, "I'm sorry, I'm so sorry! It just rolled away from me!" In his haste, he reached right down between my legs and grabbed the skull with both hands. He didn't even offer to buy me a drink first.

"No!" Judy replied urgently, "Where'd you find it?"

"I was planting some tulip bulbs around the Student Center," Arnie said, moving back in front of the desk and placing the skull back on the newspaper. "In one spot I had to take out a dead azalea bush. When I dug up the bush, I hit something hard with my shovel. I did some more diggin' and this is what I found."

"I told you!" Miss Bettie said excitedly, "I told you that you needed to see this!" I finally stood up and brushed the dirt from my navy blue suit pants. Judy immediately rushed to my aid and began helping me. Although I loved her, my crotch had already been violated enough in the previous five minutes, "It's okay, Judy," I said, "I got it." As I moved, something fell from my lap and onto the carpet.

"I'm really sorry, Dean," Arnie said again, embarrassed.

"It's fine, Arnie," I said, looking down to see what fell, "it's not your fault." I saw a dirty object by my feet and bent down to get it. It was an old heavy necklace, the kind of chain typically worn by a man, with a tarnished three inch cross attached to it. I stood up and held the necklace up to the light, eliciting more eager glances and gasps from my audience. The chain was caked with dirt and discolored, so much so that I couldn't tell if it was gold, silver, or something else. I held it as close to my eyes as my bifocals would allow to get a better look and noticed the faint impression of initials inscribed on the back of the cross. I held it closer to my desk lamp to see if I could make out the letters, which appeared to be "ATTN."

"Is that a cross?" Judy asked, cuddling up to me to get a better look.

"Sure looks like it," I responded. "It must have been stuck inside the skull, huh?" Judy immediately shot me a knowing glance, "A skull *and* a cross?"

"Well, it seems to be too much of a coincidence, right?" I knew exactly what Judy was alluding to.

"What are you two talking about?" Miss Bettie piped in, curiously. I hesitated, not wanting to begin a bigger flurry of gossip than necessary, "We're just trying to figure out where this came from," I said. "Arnie, have you told anyone about this?"

"No, sir. Miss Bettie was cleaning the windows downstairs and saw me dig it up." I realized that none of us could verbalize what the discovery was, we could only refer to the skull as "it". Miss Bettie continued, "By the look on Arnie's face, I could see that something was wrong. Arnie, you looked like you saw a ghost! So I ran out to see. I thought he was having a heart attack or something."

"I almost did!" Arnie replied, in his most animated tone of the day, "I couldn't believe it!"

"Well I think that we had better call Sam and Chief Braggish," I interjected, "and probably Chief Morreale." Sam was Samantha Johnson, Vice President for Facilities Management. Chief Braggish was Tina "Quacky" Braggish, head of AC

Security.  Chief Morreale was the Chief of Police in the town of Ocean Grove.  "Judy," I said, "will you call Quacky and the Chief, I better put a call in to Sam."  Dutifully, Judy moved out of my office, escorting Miss Bettie and Arnie alongside of her, "Come with me, you two," she said, "Arnie, you look like you need a cup of coffee."

"After what I found?  I need something stronger than coffee!" Arnie said excitedly.  He had visibly relaxed and he and Miss Bettie were chattering like excited school children once again.  "Well," Judy continued leading them away from my office, "coffee will have to do."

I picked up the phone and dialed Sam, locking my gaze on the skull the whole time.  Sam's secretary, Karen, picked up the phone on the first ring, "Facilities Management, this is Karen, how may I help you?"

"Hi Karen, this is Doug.  Is Sam available?"

"Hi, Doug, she's in a meeting, can I have her call you?"

"No, I need you to interrupt her."

"She's meeting with the sales rep for the carpet distributors.  She's picking out new carpet for the Student Center," Karen said, explaining her hesitation to interrupt.  I weighed in my mind, *carpet or skull?  Carpet or skull?*  And quickly decided that "skull" won.  "No, Karen," I insisted, "I need to speak with her.  Will you interrupt, please?"  Reluctantly, Karen agreed and buzzed me through.

"Doug, I'm with the carpet guy," Sam began abruptly, barely having the receiver to her ear, "What's up?" Samantha Johnson is a woman whose very fabric is woven with contradictions. She's a lesbian and a conservative. She loves big vehicles, but hates mass transit. She's athletic, however drives a golf cart around campus instead of taking the opportunity for exercise. She's tough as nails, yet owns four Pomeranians as her dog of choice. The latter fact is her Achilles heel, the one that reveals her true warm-hearted self. After working with her for three years, I knew the best way to grab her attention was to be direct, "Sam, Arnie found a skull buried under the azaleas next to the Student Center, want to call me back after you look at swatches?" I but couldn't help but play with her a little bit.

"What!" she yelled from the other end, "I'm on my way." I could picture her running out of her office door, leaving the carpet guy holding his swatches while the telephone receiver dangled from her desk with me still on the other end. She arrived at my door in a matter of minutes, not stopping at Judy's desk or being announced. "Holy shit," she said, being welcomed by the muddy skull sitting on my desk in full view, "Where the fuck did that come from?" Did I mention that Samantha has a mouth that could make a sailor cringe?

"Watch your mouth," I responded, "there are students around. And I already told you, under the azaleas next to the building." Sam moved around the desk, examining the skull from all angles. Although I didn't know much about skulls, it seemed average in size and fully intact. It was dotted with mud and slightly pitted all over with a noticeable crack on the back top. "How did you get to be so lucky to be the recipient?" Sam asked, still studying the bones.

"Miss Bettie was washing the windows downstairs and saw Arnie dig it up. I guess that I was the nearest person to tell." Although technically Miss Bettie worked for Sam, she felt much more at home in my office and acted like a member of my staff. It made perfect sense that she came running to me whenever a problem arose. However, I always had to downplay this fact whenever I spoke to Sam, so as not to create a struggle over turf-- the "turf" in this case was Miss Bettie. Sam mulled over my response, and I was relieved when she quickly moved on, "Did you tell anyone else?"

"Judy called Quacky and Chief Morreale who are both on their way."

"Shit," Sam whispered, leaning in close to the top of the skull, "Looks old, doesn't it?"

"It's probably a plastic Halloween prop that we'll laugh about later," I lied.

"I don't know, looks pretty real to me."

"How many skulls have you been in contact with?"

"Well, not many, but it looks real... what's this?" Sam said, pointing to the necklace that I had put on the newspaper next to the cranium. "It must have been inside the skull," I said, "looks pretty old, too."

"Shit," Sam responded again, simply staring and shaking her head.  Sam probably didn't make the connection that Judy and I had regarding the combination of the skull and the cross, and I wasn't going to explain it.  If we were right, it would have some heavy implications.

Within fifteen minutes, Chief Tina "Quacky" Braggish, Director of AC Security, lumbered into my office.  She's a squat woman in her mid-forties with short spiky hair that makes her resemble a porcupine.  As a former police officer, she has the personality of Barney Fife, but the dedication of Andy Griffith which evens out her sometimes overzealous and annoying traits.  People call her "Quacky" not only because she waddles like a duck, but because she's absolutely nuts.  Not many people call Tina by her nickname to her face out of respect, except for Sam, who doesn't care.

"Thanks for coming, Chief Braggish," I said as she entered my office, "here's what we found." Tina, who already had her note pad ready, licked the tip of her pencil and began writing feverishly.  Since she had only just arrived, I had no idea what detail required such copious notes and pictured her writing, 'Dirty skull on Dean's desk.  Newsprint dirty, too. Sam, the bitch who I don't like, standing in corner.'

"I called Samantha over too, since one of her staff members found the skull," I said.  Tina acknowledged Sam with a curt, "Vice President

Johnson." Of course Sam responded with a polite, "Quacky." Tina shot her a dirty look, then quickly moved on to me, "So who found the cranium?"

"Arnie from facilities," I responded turning to Sam, "I'm sorry to say that I don't even know his last name."

"Peters," Sam called from the corner.

"Apparently he was digging next to the Student Center and found it." I continued, "Miss Bettie escorted him directly to my office."

"Why didn't they come directly to the Security office?" Tina huffed. Once again, I needed to swerve to avoid a turf battle, a common occurrence when you work at a college. It seems that many college administrators forget that our reason for existing is assisting students, not building personal kingdoms on campus. However even though this was a common battle, Tina usually wasn't that brash. Obviously, her loathing for Sam was influencing her tone.

"They came to me because I was the closest and I have a phone," I replied quickly, nipping the potential for further discussion in the bud. "We called you, Sam, and Chief Morreale immediately."

"So is Chief Morreale on his way?"

"Yes," I replied, "I was pretty sure that you'd want to call him anyway."

"Hmrffff," Was the only reply Tina could manage. Maybe she didn't want the Chief involved so quickly. She inspected the skull, still writing feverishly, and then said, "I'll need to speak with Arnie and Miss Bettie. Then I'll need to go to the scene, which we'll need to close off." *'Great,'* I thought,' *Just what I need, 'Police line: Do not cross' tape surrounding the Student Center.'* I didn't know if I was mentally or physically ready for the drama that would cause. I was still nursing a sprained ankle from my last escapade of trying to find Jessica Philmore. I ended up hanging off of a Ferris wheel and dropping twenty feet in a lightning storm-- of course, only after sharing a Ferris wheel car with a dead man. But as I said, that was last month's escapade. I wasn't sure if I was quite yet ready for any more excitement.

"Where'd you find this?" Quacky said pointing to the necklace. "Was it with the skull?"

"I think so," I replied, "when the skull rolled into my lap, it must have dropped onto the floor."

"The skull rolled into your lap?" Tina asked, "That could sacrifice the integrity of the evidence." Quacky was known for uttering such important sounding jargon, which I was never sure was real, a product of her imagination, or something she watched on television.

"It wasn't on purpose, I promise," I replied dryly. "And don't worry, I was sure to put on latex gloves before I put it back on the newspaper."

"You did? Good." Tina said, writing again. Obviously, she was too intense at the moment to get my sarcasm. She picked-up the necklace with her pencil, inspected it so closely that dirt fell on her face, and then put it gently back where she found it. "Attention?" she said, now with dirt smudges on her cheeks, "looks like the initials ATTN, attention, inscribed on the back," she wrote feverishly. "Now, where are Arnie Peters and Miss Bettie?"

"They're probably in the back room having coffee with Judy," I said.

"Fine, I'll go look," Tina said, ambling toward the door, "but no one leave. I'll need to talk to you before I go." I suddenly felt as though I was in an Agatha Christie novel. Tina left my office and a few minutes later, Chief Morreale arrived. He's a tall, thin man with white hair on the sides of his head that softens his gleaming baldness. Always congenial, he's the friendliest man I know.

"So, Dean Doug," he said smiling and entering my office, "I thought you'd be tired of detective work after last month?"

"I am," I responded, "but this one literally fell into my lap. I figured that you did such a great job of bailing me out last time, you could help here too."

"So," the Chief said pointing to my desk, "that your latest victim?"

"Part of 'em," I said.

"Just the skull?" The Chief said, walking toward my desk.

"Well, one of our facilities' workers found it next to the Student Center while he was planting bulbs. I'm sure he was too surprised to check for more bones." The Chief nodded. "Chief," I said, "do you know Samantha Johnson, our Vice President for Facilities Management?"

"No, I don't believe I do," he said, taking off his hat, "nice to meet you."

"Same here," Sam said. The Chief got down on his knees and examined the skull as closely as his large nose would allow. "Dean, do you have a magnifying glass?" he asked. I grabbed one from my desk drawer and handed it to him so he could inspect the cranium more closely. After an extended silence, he announced, "*Looks* real." I could hear Sam and me swallow at the same time. "Really?" I asked, "I was hoping it was a Halloween leftover."

"Well, it's old, but I think it's authentic." The Chief said, "Shouldn't be too hard to find out, especially here at AC."

"Why?"

"Because the guy that we often have investigate things like this works here, Dr. Allen Faust. Do you know him?"

"Um, yeah, I've seen him around. I thought that he was a chemistry teacher?"

"He's a forensic chemist, and since he's right here in town, he helps us out. I'll bring it by his office while I'm here. It's already been disturbed, I don't think moving it a few buildings away will damage anymore evidence. He may also want to check out the garden where the skull was found."

The serious nature of our finding was quickly growing, and so was the suspicion that I shared with Judy. I needed to tell the Chief what I suspected, but before I could ask Sam to excuse us, the Chief beat me to the punch, "Ms. Johnson," he asked, "Would you excuse us for a moment, I have some other business that I need to discuss with the Dean." Sam obliged and shut the door behind her. I was so happy that he had provided me an opportunity to spill my guts that I forgot that *he* said that *he* had something to talk to *me* about.

"I'm glad you did that, Chief," I began excitedly, "if this skull is real, I think I may know something about who it belongs to."

"Okay," the Chief began, "and I have to talk to you about a murder. Who should go first?"

I was stunned and wasn't sure if I heard the Chief correctly, "A murder?  Is it related to Asbury?" I asked.

"I think so," the Chief replied, sitting in one of the office chairs in front of my desk, "and you're familiar with the victim."

"I know the murder victim?" I asked with my voice raising in both pitch and volume.

"I don't think that you knew her," the Chief continued, "but you're familiar with her.  Remember the girl who you saw in the morgue last month?  The one that we originally suspected to be Jessica Philmore?" How could I forget.  A body had been found on the beach just as we were beginning the investigation into the disappearance of AC junior, Jessica Philmore.  Keesha Cribbs, the Director of Student Activities on my staff, and I were called to the town morgue to identify the body.  Lucky for us, it wasn't Jessica.  But I felt an immediate sense of guilt now, because I had dismissed the poor teenage body so quickly, never giving her a second thought after we determined that she wasn't mine.

"Sure I remember.  She drowned, right?"

"Well, no, it was homicide, you just didn't see the bullet holes."

"She was shot?"

"Twice.  Once in the abdomen and once in the thigh.  She was also filled pretty good with ecstasy.  The mayor and I didn't tell you any of this, because at the time, we didn't know who she was."

The Chief was referring to Mayor Theodore Carcass (emphasis on the second syllable to distinguish the name from a hunk of dead meat), our town's mayor and resident funeral home director.  The basement of the funeral home also serves as the morgue.

"So who is she, er, was she?" I corrected myself.

"Darcy Green, nineteen.  Lived in one of the old motels over in Asbury Park." I knew that many of the motels in Asbury, formerly for tourists, were either used for low-income housing, or being razed to make room for luxury condos.  The Chief went on, "Originally we thought she was a runaway from north Jersey, which was true.  What we hadn't found out yet is that apparently, she was a part time waitress and stripper, as well as a part time student here at Asbury." I was stunned, "So she *was* one of my students?" was the only response I could manage.  My surprise didn't come from the fact that she was a stripper, but in the fact that she was dead.

"Yes, Doug, I'm sorry.  Even though she was wearing a Asbury College sweatshirt at the time of death, we didn't have any other legitimate connection to AC.  If I had known then, I would have told you.  We just got the positive ID from the ladies at Smoke- it's an exotic dancing club in Asbury." I remembered the day I received the call saying that the body had been snared by a beach fisherman and pulled up onto the sand.  Because of the sweatshirt and physical description, the police immediately concluded that it was my missing student and called us down to the morgue to make a positive ID. At the time, I felt lucky that we couldn't. Now, I wasn't feeling nearly as fortunate. I turned immediately to my computer to look her up, being careful not to knock over the skull in my haste.

"She was apparently a student only for a couple of semesters," the Chief responded, "last spring and this fall."

I punched-up our student database and entered "Green, Darcy." One listing flashed upon my screen and I accessed it with a couple of clicks. It read:

```
     Green, Darcy    UID:   15845-
0034 Major:  Undeclared
     145 Embury Avenue
     Asbury Park, NJ 07712
     Day Phone:  N/A      Evening
Phone:  N/A
```

I immediately went to screen 2 which listed the semesters and classes attended:

```
     Green, Darcy     ID#097127638
     Course            Term
     Grade      Credits
     PSY 101           F10
     B+         3
     PSY 102           S11
     A          3
     PSY 200           F11
     N/A        N/A
               ***END***
```

I took a deep breath, and relayed the information on my screen to Chief Morreale, "According to our records, she was actually here for *three* semesters beginning in the fall of 2010. She took Psych 101 in fall and got a B+, Psych 102 in spring and got an A and is currently registered for Psych 200, which of course, we wouldn't have a grade yet. What a shame." I paused for a second, realizing that the larger question hadn't been addressed, "Do you have any leads on who killed her?"

"No, not yet, but I may need to do some digging here on campus." The Chief and I immediately looked at the dirty cranium on my desk to which he followed-up his comment with, "No pun intended."

"Why here?" I asked, "Are other students involved?"

"I'm not sure."

"Whatever you need, let me know."

"Thank you, I'll keep you posted and I'll talk to Tina. Now let's talk about your skull. You say that you know who it belongs to?"

"Possibly," I said, "just a hunch."

"I'm all ears."

"It could be connected with a secret society that we have on campus, "Skull and Cross.""

"What do you know about this 'secret society?'"

"Well, not too much." I replied, "it's been in existence here on campus as long as we've been a College, since about 1867. It's not unlike any other "secret society," which exists on college campuses all over the country. They have "Cap and Skull" at Rutgers, where I first became familiar with these organizations. "Skull and Bones" at Yale is probably the most famous, both President Bushes are members."

"Are? Didn't they graduate?"

"Of course, but graduation doesn't impact membership. Once a member, always a member. The alumni base is huge with these things."

"So if they're secret, then why do you know who the members are?"

"I think it's an elitist thing, a symbol of high achievement. I guess it wouldn't be as great an honor if there wasn't some level of secrecy. Here at Asbury I get a memo listing the new inductees every year."

"Is it a secret memo?" The Chief quipped.

"Yes," I played along, "written in invisible ink, and after I read it, it spontaneously combusts."

"So you know current members?"

"Sure. Many of them are some of my best student leaders, the president of student government, resident assistants, orientation leaders. I know a lot of them. In fact, I was first introduced to the group at New Student Orientation my first year here."

"How so?"

"I was at the opening Convocation ceremony, which is held on the front lawn, where the President of the College welcomes all of the new students. About half way through the president's speech, I looked past the crowd of new students sitting on the lawn and all of a sudden saw a dozen or so hooded figures dressed in dark robes standing in the back. They appeared out of nowhere and stood in a line in back of the crowd, I don't even think the new students saw them."

"So what happened?"

"Well, it's a little embarrassing. I thought that they were murderers, ready to pull out guns and start shooting. How did I know? They were scary-looking."

"Don't tell me that you stood up on the stage and told everyone to 'get down!'?"

"Not quite, but close. I bolted from the stage in the middle of the President's speech and ran over to Quacky who was standing on the grass nearby. I was shocked to find her uncharacteristically nonchalant. She explained that it was the school's secret society, doing their annual "welcome" of new students. One of my student leaders for New Student Orientation must have seen that I was upset, and he came running over to me and assured me that it was ok. I didn't know at the time that *he* was also a member. He ran over to them and asked them to leave, and they did."

"They dressed in hooded robes?"

"Yes, black hooded robes. And I'm not the only one who found them a little freaky. During Keesha's first orientation, she thought that they were flashers."

"So why you think that there's a connection between the skull and this society of secret flashers?"

"Because the society here at Asbury is called, "Skull and Cross." Seems a bit too coincidental that we find both a skull and a cross together, don't you think?" I replied. The Chief scratched his chin and nodded, "Got it." He continued to look pensively at the skull and then said, "Do you think it could be part of a ritual?"

"What do you mean?"

"Well," the Chief began, "maybe it's not murder. Maybe it's some old skull and an old cross that someone bought at a flea market and they bury it for sport."

"Like a creepy Easter egg hunt?" I replied. Interesting theory, I hoped that it was true.

"Maybe."

"I guess it could be," I said, considering it for a moment, "I tell you, I'd feel a whole lot better if that was true."

"Can you find out?"

"Can I find out about Skull and Cross rituals?" I said, thinking, "I can try. I am pretty close with a few of the members, they might tell me some of their secrets. In fact that's what some of them call Skull and Cross, 'The Secret.' Some of them call each other, 'Secrets', too. It's like a club. In the meantime, are you going to take this?" I said, pointing to the skull still sitting on my desk.

"I was, but it does make an attractive paperweight," the Chief said dryly, following it up with, "I'll take it. Let me go out to my car and get a bag." As the Chief left, I reached for my list of resident assistants and immediately looked-up Jenny

Robins' telephone number.  Not only is she a member of my Residence Life staff, but is a student worker in my office, *and* a member of Skull and Cross.  I knew that she was my closest contact with the organization and my best shot at getting some inside information.  I left a message for her to call me as soon as possible and then proceeded to the outer office to find Quacky, Judy, and the crew.

As I walked out my door, I could hear bickering being moderated by Judy, as usual.  "This is a serious investigation, Miss Bettie, I'm not sure that you realize that," Quacky was saying, all puffed-up like an amorous bird.  She was obviously still agitated by Sam.

"I know that," responded Miss Bettie, eyes shut for effect, "I'm the one who brought it here to begin with, remember?"

"Well you shouldn't have removed evidence from the site, it could damage the investigation."

"I didn't move it, Arnie did.  And it was already *moved* from the site when he *dug* it up."

"Girls, GIRLS!" Judy announced, "This is an office with a lot of students nearby, it's not professional to have you yelling at each other."

"We weren't yelling," responded Miss Bettie, one who always had to have the last word, "we were discussing.  She's just mad that I came here and not to her."

"I am not!" Quacky shot back, to which Judy raised her hand in the air and moved between the two women.  I looked over at the couch in the reception area and found Arnie sitting quietly, sipping a cup of coffee, still looking dazed. I went over to him and sat down, "Quite a morning, huh Arnie?"

"You're telling me! I don't want to go back outside there, I'm afraid what else I'm gonna dig up!"

"Well, I don't think that's a problem because I don't think they're going to let you go back out there anyway. Where's Sam?"

"She left. I think she went out to see where we dug it up." At that moment, Jenny Robins walked into the office, unfazed by the slightly raised voices that Judy was still trying to shush. "Hi, Dean Doug," Jenny said, bouncing through the doorway, "I just got out of class and got your message."

"Hi, Jenny," I said, getting up from the sofa, "I need to talk to you for a minute. Do you have time now?"

"Sure!" Jenny said in her usual perky manner. My office sits in the back of the Dean of Students Office (DOSO) suite, down a short hallway. I escorted Jenny down the corridor and into my office, only to be startled by Jenny's loud gasp upon entering. Jenny moved her hand to her mouth, and looked at me with fear in her eyes. In my haste to speak with her, I had forgotten about the skull that was sitting on my desk in full view.

"Oh, Jenny," I said, moving behind my desk, "I'm sorry, I didn't mean to scare you." Immediately, I could see that Jenny's demeanor had changed. Her look went from fear to calm, as if seeing a skull wasn't so unfamiliar. "You found it," she said, matter-of-factly.  I decided to play along with a simple, "Yes." Jenny looked down at the cranium and then at the floor, "I'm sorry," she said. I chose not to respond and continued to sit silently. The tactic almost always makes 'em crack.

"It's not what you think," Jenny said hastily, to which I responded with a simple raise of the eyebrow.  That usually causes 'em to spill their guts as if they had a case of food poisoning.  "We do it every year.  We hide the skull and have one of the new members find it."

"You *hide* a skull?  Why?"

"It's tradition… for Skull and Cross.  We've always done it," Jenny responded matter-of-factly. Whenever a student says this, I know that it could mean that the tradition is either a century or five-minutes old.  "Where'd you find it?" Jenny asked.

"Where'd you hide it?" I responded, not sure if I should give the specific location.

"I'm not sure," she hesitated, "I wasn't in charge for hiding it this year."  We stared at each other for a few moments in silence.

"Where did you get the skull?" I asked.  This elicited a big shrug from Jenny, "I don't know," she replied innocently, "we've just always had it." Finally, she asked, "Are we in trouble?"  The question struck me hard.

"Not yet," I responded immediately, "as long as what you've told me is true.  You've been a big help, Jenny.  I know that you aren't supposed to share your "secrets."  I promise not to reveal my source."  Jenny smiled, "Thanks.  Now what?"

"What do you mean?"

"Do we get our skull back?" she asked, indifferently. Now I never thought that I'd be asked *that* question during my career.

"Well, I don't think so just yet. We need to do some more checking. In the meantime, you may have to play 'hide the something else.'" As Jenny pondered this thought, Judy appeared in the doorway, "Doug, VP Johnson's on the line for you. She says it's important."

"Where is she?"

"She didn't say, why don't you pick-up the phone and ask her?" Good advice, indeed. I reached for the phone and hit the line that was flashing, "Sam?"

"We've got a problem."

"*More* of a problem?"

"Literally," Sam sounded tense.

"What's wrong?"

"There isn't just a skull. I think we have a whole body."

-4-

I sat, frozen for a second.  I guessed that we hadn't actually found Jenny's skull used in the scavenger hunt- but the one on my desk was a new one.

"Doug, did you hear me?" Sam called over the phone.

"Yes," I said, shaking off disbelief.  A body? Did she say a "whole" body?  I needed to ask Jenny to leave so that I could get the details, "Jenny, I need to take this.  I'm sorry, you've been very helpful, I'll let you know if I have more questions."

"Okay," Jenny said.  She must have sensed that I was shaken, and practically ran out the door.  I wasn't going to let on that her skull was probably still hidden somewhere.

"Where are you?" I asked immediately.

"Downstairs outside of the Student Center, near the bushes where Arnie was digging."

"How'd you find a body?"

"Come down here!"  Sam's voice seemed to be built by a mixture of disbelief and panic; I knew that I needed to go immediately.  I would know the answers to my questions soon enough, since I only had to go downstairs.  "I'm on my way." I said, already moving from behind my desk.

I hurried past Judy, mumbling that I'd be outside as I went.  I ran down the stairs and out the back entrance of the Student Center.  I saw Sam immediately, trying to act as casual as one can after finding a dead person.  She was leaning against one of the Facilities Management golf carts that she often drives around campus to meetings. On such a small campus, I never understood this lazy practice, but it was just one of Sam's idiosyncrasies that I was used to. Another one of her idiosyncrasies was sitting in the golf cart next to her, barking feverishly.

Ralph, a ratty looking border collie, is Asbury's resident goose-chasing dog. At least that's what Sam says. Actually, he's nothing more than a furry figurehead with a dubious job and a ridiculous name. Sam purchased him for the College a couple of years ago after an incident between a student and some goose poo. In New Jersey, a state known for its multiethnic society, Canada Geese run rampant. Along with new residents from all over the world, these geese take-up residence and become contributing members to communities all over the state. However these residents don't contribute anything but poop.

After a student slipped on some fresh goose poop on the sidewalk near one of our academic buildings and broke her leg in three places, Sam took it upon herself to take action. She purchased a $5,000.00 dog trained to chase away the geese at Asbury College. In actuality, what she purchased was an example of how to waste $5,000.00. Also what she purchased was a very expensive pet who she named after one of her pre-deceased former pets. It's not that Ralph isn't capable of chasing geese… he is. But he's just not usually required to. On a daily basis, he rides shotgun in a Facilities Management golf cart and barks at every living creature in his path.  Today, he was barking in the direction of a pile of dirt.

"Ralph!" Sam shouted as I approached, "Stop it!"

"What's wrong with him?" I asked.  Sam grabbed Ralph' muzzle and pointed to the adjacent flower bed, "That," she said, directing my attention to the ground near an azalea.  Laying exposed near the shrub was a dirty, grey bone.  Although I'm not an expert, it looked like a femur; a large, thick leg-bone with bulbous ends.

"That's too big to be an animal," was the intelligent, almost scientific, detective-like response that I managed.

"So are they," Sam said, pointing behind the azalea.  I took a few steps into the flower bed and could see at least three other bones, worn and partially exposed.  Although I could identify one as a rib (I watched a lot of the Flintstones, growing up), the others were indiscriminant to me.

Since it was the middle of the day, there were people walking around everywhere.  I moved next to Sam to be as discreet as possible.  "How'd you find them?" I whispered, keeping my gaze straight ahead.

"I didn't.  Ralph did." Sam said through pursed lips not looking at me.  We acted as if we were making a drug deal.  Sam continued, "When I came out of the Student Center, Ralph was digging in the azalea bed.  He had the big bone in his mouth and was trying to dig-up the others."

"Hi, Dean Doug," said a student as she passed by, "What're you doing?"

"Just admiring the shrubs," I responded with a fake smile, "Have a great day." Believable. *Very believable, I'm sure.*

"What do we do now?" asked Sam, still trying to calm Ralph who was frantically pawing at her trying to get out of the cart to finish his snack.

"Well first," I said in an exasperated tone, "You should get that mutt out of here- he's attracting attention!"

"And the pile of bones isn't?" Sam responded, "And for the last time, he's not a mutt, he's a purebred border collie."

"Sam," I responded just like Abbott or Costello in one of their bad "horror" flicks, "This is no time to discuss canine genealogy."

"Hey, Dean Doug!" called a student from across the walkway, "What's wrong with your dog?"

"Fleas!" I shouted, grinning broadly. Gosh I'm a comedian. "Sam," I said trying to hush myself, "You've got to get him out of here, he's drawing attention to a potential crime scene. I don't want *everyone* on-campus to see it!"

"Fuck," Sam uttered, running her hands through her shaggy hair, "What are we going to do?" Sam asked, obviously over the hurt that I had insulted her dog.

"I'm going to call Quacky and the Chief."

"Quacky? You're calling *her* again?" Sam asked. Perhaps it was the stress of the situation that was causing us to keep falling into a slapstick sort of banter, "Sam, she's the head of security," I replied, "who would you like me to call? I hear Columbo's out of town."

"Can I help?" Came a deep voice from behind us, causing both of us to jump. Sam and I looked over our shoulder to find Chief Morreale leaning into the golf cart to pet Ralph.

"Chief!" I said in the elated tone of a doting teenage girl, "We found more bones." The Chief raised an eyebrow and looked toward the azaleas, "So I see," he said casually. "Let me guess," he continued, "the pooch here found his lunch?"

"When I came out here after meeting you, he had dug 'em up." Sam replied, "I stopped him as quick as I could."

"Well, chances are that there's no harm done. By the looks, those bones have been here awhile. Why don't you take the dog out of here and we'll rope this area off." I forced myself not to give Sam a big-fat-hairy-I-told-you-so look and turned to the Chief, "How'd you know we were here?" I asked.

"Judy showed me out the window. Apparently, you've drawn quite an audience." he said, pointing up to the huge plate glass windows of the second floor of the Student Center. Looking down on us, was a group of at least ten people, including Judy and Miss Bettie, both of whom were waving and smiling enthusiastically. I gave a brief, royal-type wave and quickly turned from their gaze. I hate having an audience.

Sam jumped into her golf-cart, strapped Ralph in with a makeshift seatbelt, and sputtered away. Before she left, she promised to be right back.

Arnie and Jerry Ricardo had come out of the Student Center to join me. Jerry is my Assistant Dean for Residence Life and perhaps the closest thing to a best friend that I have at AC. "What's happening, boss?" he said, half-mocking, his tall frame casting a shadow on the scene, "You looked like you were having quite a discussion out here."

"Yeah, skeletons have that effect on me," I said sarcastically.

"What?" Jerry said, immediately impotent. Standing beside him, Arnie's face dropped. I continued, "Arnie started with a skull, but it looks like Sam's dog has dug up more." All Arnie and Jerry could manage was a collective, "Holy Shit", which seemed appropriate.

"Doug," interjected the Chief, holding a spool of yellow, plastic tape in his hands, "I'm going to need some stakes to wrap this tape around, can you get some?" Arnie jumped to the task without further prompting, "I'll be two-seconds!" he said, bounding away in nearly a run; The Chief was already bending down to inspect the unearthed bones as Jerry and I looked on.

"Who do you think it is?" Jerry asked, fidgeting with his tie.

"Was," I responded flatly.

"Who do you think it *was*, then?"

"Well thank God we know it's not Jessica Philmore," I responded, referring to the recently finished investigation of our missing student. It was turning out to be quite an academic year already. I thought about telling Jerry about the cross that was in the skull, but decided against it at that public moment in the middle of campus. As the Chief continued to survey the area, it occurred to me that Quacky was conspicuously absent, "Wasn't Quacky upstairs in the office?" I asked Jerry.

"Yeah, but just before we came out she got a call that she said was important." Of course we both knew that to Quacky, a call about missing linens in the dining hall is an emergency; she takes her job very seriously. Joe Friday has nothing on her. As we continued to watch Chief Morreale do whatever it was that he was doing with his hands on his hips and his outsized nose nearly rooting in the dirt, Jerry decided to update me on work-stuff.

"We had another transport last night," he said, matter-of-factly. This meant that we called an ambulance to transport a student to Jersey Shore Medical Center for an alcohol or drug-related issue. "Another one? This makes the third this semester, right? Drinking or drugs?" I asked. Unfortunately, both are common on most college campuses, but three emergency transports in a couple of months was extremely rare for us.

"Based on what we found in the room, probably both. I'll know more by this afternoon- but he's fine."

"Who was it?"

"Bryan Rivers, sophomore. I don't know him too well, but always seemed like a nice kid. I'm on my way to the hospital to see him now, they should be releasing him soon."

"Did you call his folks?"  Although students are considered to be adults at 18 and are afforded certain confidentiality rights under the national law, FERPA (Family Education Rights and Privacy Act), we reserve the right to call parents in a medical emergency, and other activities involving drugs or alcohol.  As a private institution, Asbury College has this latitude and in my opinion, the responsibility to do so.  "Yes," Jerry answered, "But they live in Washington D.C.  Since he's fine, they're coming up this morning.  I'll see them there.  Have you got everything covered here?"

"Uncovered is more like it," I said, looking at the exposed skeletal remains and nervously making an attempt at humor, "But I'll be alright."  I looked at Jerry and smiled, "Go take care of Bryan.  I don't think my person here is in any more immediate danger."  As Jerry walked away, Chief Morreale approached.  Arnie had returned with some wooden stakes and had already begun to cordon-off the area. Butting-up against the brick Student Center was now a ten by ten patch of azaleas and mulch framed in yellow, "Work in Progress- Do Not Cross" tape.  To me, it looked as though the work had already been done.

"So, where do we go from here?" I asked, as the Chief removed his hat and wiped his mostly-bald head.  "Well," he began as if ready to begin a very long story, "this one's a little more than we can handle by ourselves.  I'm going to call the State Police and they'll call a team in to investigate the area."

"What kind of team?" I asked.

"CSI, probably."

"CSI," I responded, surprised, "Like the TV show?" The Chief chuckled, "Yup, it was a real thing long before it was a show.  We need a Crime Scene Investigation team to excavate this area, dig-up what's here, and not lose any evidence."  Crime Scene.  It was sinking in now.  "So," I stated, hesitantly, "You think a crime was committed?"

"Well," the Chief chuckled again, "I doubt this person died of natural causes in the middle of your azalea bed."  Just then, Quacky emerged from the Student Center and ambled toward us, her squatty frame struggling to build-up speed.  She reached us, hiked-up her pants and reached for her steno pad again, "Sorry, folks.  Hope I didn't hold up the investigation, but I got an important call that I had to take."  We indulged her self-importance and the Chief filled her in on the latest.

"Good, good.  Sounds good," she affirmed, nodding vigorously, "And we'll need to keep this area secure."  This was a good point that I hadn't yet reached.  Quacky is nothing if she isn't thorough. She continued, "I'll have one of my officers posted here around the clock."  Although this seemed like a good idea, even necessary, I immediately wondered how she would make this happen.  On our small campus in the middle of a sleepy shore town, security isn't exactly a problem.  Our security staff only consisted of four, including Tina "Quacky" Braggish herself.

"Do you have the staff?" I asked.

"Sure!" she said, with a growing look of intensity, "We don't have a choice.  This is a crime scene, Doug.  It's my responsibility to keep it secure so that evidence isn't destroyed or removed.  I'll bring in more men if I have to."  She was so earnest that if I hadn't known her, I would have thought she was joking.  "That's great, Tina." I responded, "thank you."

"And if you run into staffing shortages," Chief Morreale interjected, "Just let me know and I'll have someone come over."  To this, Quacky responded as if she had just been slapped in the face, "Not necessary, Chief," she said, waving her hand dismissively, "but I appreciate the offer.  We'll be fine and cover the area as necessary.  Al is coming over right now to take the first shift."  Al Towers is Quacky's second-in-command, a mid-twenty-something, handsome, police officer in training.

As we all prepared to disband our unfortunate meeting, the sound of Sam's sputtering golf cart approached like an oversized mosquito.  She wheeled-up right next to us, this time, dogless, "What'd I miss?" she said, putting her foot on the brake and turning the cart off.

"We were just about to leave," I said.

"You can't leave!" Sam responded, "What about the bones?  We've got to watch the area to make sure nothing happens to it."  Quacky, the Chief and I glared at her in unison.  Sam had a way of trying to take control of a situation, even when control was already taken.  Quacky took the opportunity to set Sam straight, "Already taken care of. We've secured the area and will man it around the clock." The look of satisfaction on Quacky's face reminded me of the one that Ralph had a little while earlier, chewing on a bone. Sam looked embarrassed for a second and then replied, "Oh. Just making sure. So what now?"

"We leave it to the experts." I responded, "A team will come in to see what else is buried here. Until then, we wait." Since patience wasn't common to Sam, I knew that this would be a problem.

"Wait?" she said loudly, "Until when?" The Chief took the opportunity this time, "Until we collect the evidence and figure out what happened."

"How long will that take?" Sam followed-up.

"Depends. Probably a day or so," the Chief replied.

"Sam, we need to let the experts handle this one," I jumped in, which on the second time around, seemed to disarm her.

"Oh," she said, looking around, "Sure, I was just trying to see if I could help, that's all. Anything I can do?"

"You've done enough already," the Chief joked, "Your dog found the bones. We'll take it from here." Just then, Security Officer Al Towers sauntered up, ready to keep watch over the crime scene, thus giving us license to leave. We disbanded like a group of awkward middle-schoolers at a dance, all eager to exit, but not wanting to appear too enthusiastic. "Well," I started, "It looks like we're in good hands. I think I'll go back to my office. Thanks for your help Chief," I said, reaching out my hand to Chief Morreale, "I assume you'll keep me posted?"

"Of course. I'll give you an update tomorrow, once I hear from the State."

"Great. Chief Braggish, Al, thanks for keeping the place safe." Both nodded, then moved toward the police tape and began discussing their staffing plan. "Sam," I said smiling, "Keep that pooch of yours locked up. If there are any more bones buried on-campus, I don't want to know about them, huh?" Sam chuckled, started-up her golf cart and sputtered away.

I stepped back into my office just after lunchtime. Usually eager for my midday meal, I wasn't feeling hungry. I was received excitedly by Judy and Ronnie Branch, Jerry's secretary who worked in the office next door. Ronnie, a stately woman who vaguely reminds me of an edgier, hipper June Cleaver, immediately showed her concern, "Doug, is everything alright?" Judy, never one to be outdone, spouted, "Did you have your lunch? Do you want me to get you anything?" In some office circles, a doting support staff would seem hierarchical, here, it just seems motherly.

"Everything's fine," I said looking at both of them, "And I'm fine. I'm not really hungry."

"What'd they say?" asked Ronnie, "was it awful?"

"They're bringing in a team to figure out who it is. I suppose that's when it gets awful." Judy took this opportunity to get her daily gossip fix right on cue, "Do they have any idea who it is? It's got to be old, right?"

"Right now, we don't know anything. We won't know how old or who until they can do some tests."

"How are you going to keep people away from the area? You know, *these kids* will want to take a peek." Judy said, licking her lips.

"Quacky and her staff will keep watch until the investigation is over."

"How long will that take?" asked Ronnie.

"Not sure, a day or two according to Chief Morreale. Any messages?" I asked, anxious to change the subject and resume normal operations.

"R.I.P called twice," Judy responded taking the hint, "He's stopping by. I told him that you were busy, and he said that's why he's stopping by." R.I.P stands for Reginald Ichabod Preston, an ancient professor and head of the faculty council. I hate him. Well, perhaps hate is too strong a term. I loathe him. Fortunately, the feeling is mutual. "Did he say why?" I asked.

"No, he wouldn't say, and believe you me, I pressed. That man is nothin' but a bastard, if you'll excuse my French." That's what I like about Judy, she has her politics straight.

"Well, let me know when the old codger arrives," I said, resigned to the fact that R.I.P. was known for appearances with little notice. "You sure I can't go downstairs and get you a sandwich or something? You can't argue with that man on an empty stomach," Judy asked, "Ronnie can man the

phones until our student staff arrives." I had to
admit, the thought of going down to the food court in
the Student Center made me cringe. By now, the
scene in the roped-off and secured azalea bed right
outside was assuredly causing a stir. I wasn't in the
mood for a barrage of questions just yet.

"Maybe that is a good idea," I responded
pensively, "You don't mind? It seems awfully 'gal
Friday' of you."

"Let me tell you," Judy said, assuming her
typical stance with one hand on her hip and the other
moving in the air like a traffic cop, "Back in the day
when I used to work in corporate, I was asked to
give a whole lot more than a sandwich, if you get my
drift." It was moments like these when Judy's
Brooklyn accent really took hold, her ample bosom
heaving up and down for emphasis, "I could tell you
stories…" she took off her half-specs which now
hung around her neck by a silver chain and looked
longingly in the distance. By the look in her eye, I
couldn't quite tell whether or not she was reliving
the old days with contempt or ardor. Ronnie, the
June Cleaver look-alike immediately piped-in, "I
know what you mean. When I worked for the law
firm, one of the lawyers grabbed my breast and
asked me to give him a bj!" As I said before, an
edgier June Cleaver.

"Oh!" Judy continued, hushing her voice
"That ain't nothin'…" I couldn't bear to hear any
more. It was like hearing about Beaver's mom and
an older, bustier Mrs. Brady discussing former
sexcapades. Any other time, the outer office would

be filled with students and commotion, but today, the coast was clear for story swapping galore. I reached for my wallet and interrupted, "Let me leave you two to reminisce without me." I grabbed a ten and handed it to Judy.

"What, too spicy for you?" Judy asked, taking the money.

"Yes," I responded, matter-of-factly. Judy just rolled her eyes and winked at Ronnie, "OK, fella," she said, "what can I get you?"

"Anything as long as it's boneless." I replied with a smile.

"It's a do." She said, making a circular motion with her hand and moving away from her desk, "Ronnie, you get the phones. I'll be back in ten." I walked back to my office and sunk down in my chair. Miss Bettie had removed the dirt-laden newspaper and left a note on my desk, written on my memo pad, "Cleaned your desk. Gave paper to Chief of Police before he left. Your desk's a sty. If you clear it off, I'll dust it for you! Have a nice day." I smiled and felt like a kept man as I turned to my computer screen to check the emails that had piled-up while I was gone. My homey glow, however, didn't last long. Within seconds, I could hear the shrill, crackly voice of R.I.P. in the outer office, "Where's Connors!" he cawed. What was so urgent? I was about to find out.

-5-

"I need to see Connors, Miss!" R.I.P. cackled to unsuspecting Ronnie in his usual high-pitched voice, "Where's he hiding, in his office?" As I got up the energy to pry myself from my chair to save Ronnie, I heard her ask politely, "Do you have an appointment?" Although to strangers, Ronnie's tone sounded genuinely sweet, I could tell that she was already primed to put this prima donna professor in his place if need be.

"No, I don't have an appointment! I told the other lady here earlier this morning that I would be stopping by to talk to Connors and that's what I'm here to do!"

"Do you mean Dean *Carter*-Connors?" Ronnie asked in a saccharine voice. This caused R.I.P. to pause, "What?!". He had never acknowledged my full name, which I wasn't sure was out of disrespect or ignorance. Ronnie continued her lesson, "This is Dean Doug *Carter*-Connors' office. Is that whom you mean?" I was now standing in my office door jamb eavesdropping and was having a great time.

"Whatever his name is, I'm here to see him! Where is that other lady that I usually speak to, the bigger one? She never gives me the run around like this."

"May I have your name?" Now with this, I could tell that Ronnie was simply toying with the old codger. R.I.P. is infamous around campus.

"Don't you know who I am? I've been associated with this college for over fifty years. I went to school here before I became a professor!"

"I'm sorry sir, I was barely born and not an employee back then. I've only worked at Asbury for three years. Your name?"

"Professor Preston!" he cackled.

"I'm sorry, Pres… Pres… Presson? I want to make sure that I get it right."

"Preston! Preston! For someone who claims to be so young, you sure are hard-of-hearing!" Ouch. I knew that I needed to stop hiding and save them before someone drew blood, and I wasn't sure who would strike first. I popped from my office as if playing hide-and-seek, "Professor," I continued Ronnie's syrupy tone, "to what do I owe this unexpected pleasure?"

"I called the other one earlier and told her that I was coming! I don't know who this one is," R.I.P. said, pointing his cane in Ronnie's direction for emphasis, "but she doesn't even know who I am!"

"Your royalty here is omnipresent, I assure you Professor." I said, turning my back to R.I.P. and heading back toward my office. I knew that the move would cause the cranky old coot to follow. At seventy, Reginald Ichabod Preston's once 5'8" frame has shrunk to a stooped-over 5'4". I'm not taller than many men, but proud to say that R.I.P. is one of them. His shocking white hair and sallow, gaunt face always make the man appear to be closer to the grave than probable. As I said before, he and I have a history at Asbury College; of hating each other.

"Are you turning your back on me, Connors?" he called behind me. I turned on my heels and looked at him like an insubordinate student, "I am going back to my office so that you and I can talk in a more private place, which is what I assumed you were asking for." He replied with a "Hrmphhhh," and began ambling behind me, ramming the carpet with his silver-tipped cane all the way. As R.I.P. told Ronnie, he was an alum. Class of '57, I believe, and rumor has it that he was just as difficult back then as he is today. He majored in history, went on to graduate school immediately following his bachelor's degree, and received both his master's degree and doctorate in record time. A talented scholar, he was hired back at Asbury College as an assistant professor in the history department and never left. Now, he tortures me as the head of the faculty council.

I walked into my office and sat down behind my desk to face my accuser. Although I wasn't sure what I had done, R.I.P. always produced the aura of an executioner. "What can I help you with, Professor?" I began. True to form, he lashed out immediately, "You can stop harassing my students, that's what!", his high-pitched screech reaching record decibels.

"Who am I harassing?"

"Members of The Order, and I want it to stop immediately!" Ah, yes. The Order of Skull and Cross. Although I considered Jenny Robins to be a student leader with whom I am close, clearly not close enough to supersede the secret order of Skull and Cross.  Not only is R.I.P. a member dating way back to his days as an undergraduate at Asbury, but he's their advisor and staunchest supporter.  Once a member of a secret society, always a member, and allegiance runs deep.  I decided that the best way to handle this line of persecution from R.I.P. was to be straight-forward, but not give away any information, "Why?" I asked.  The question caused a line of red to well-up from the top of R.I.P.'s navy blue ascot to the top of his forehead.

"Why!" he shouted, more like a statement than a question.  I sat calmly at my desk and leaned toward him, folding my hands, "Yes.  Why?".

"Because it's harassment, that's why!"  It was this weak explanation that made me realize that good ole R.I.P. didn't have much ammunition.  I was confident that I could beat him in his game.  "Asking a student some questions is not considered to be harassment, Professor," I responded.

"Tracking a student down like a criminal is! She said that you called her in her room!  That's harassment at the very least, and inappropriate, I'd say.  You might be up on sexual harassment charges, Connors!"  I could see that since he had nowhere to go with his platform, he was eager to play dirty to try and intimidate me.  I wasn't going to let him win.

"Jenny Robins is a member of my staff, Professor." I replied, "Her room number is listed on my Resident Assistant roster."

"Connors, you're shady!" R.I.P. barked. Although I hated him, you had to love a person who speaks their mind so clearly and without reserve. He continued, "You're trying to pin this thing on us and trying to get information from innocent young ladies. You've crossed a line, Connors, and I'll see to it that something's done!" Although I wasn't bothered by the fact that he was challenging me, his threats were getting annoying. "Are you threatening me, Professor?" I asked, as unaffected as possible.

"I'm telling you to leave us alone!" I found his use of "us" not only elitist, but creepy. I had been fascinated with the culture of secret societies on college campuses ever since I wrote a research paper on the topic in graduate school. I knew that they use secrecy and coercion to meet their objectives. Historically at Yale University where secret societies all began, the objectives were almost always political, members considering themselves "Patriarchs" of society. Some past accounts even contend that Yale's "Skull and Bones" was responsible for the creation of the Soviet Union. Although I wasn't confident that the motives of Skull and Cross on the Asbury College campus could be quite as political in nature or world-altering, the desperation to conceal information and continue the secretive nature of the organization seemed comparable. I decided to play with R.I.P. a bit, "Leave who alone?"

"You *know* who!" R.I.P. shouted. I found it odd that we had not yet mentioned the organization's name once, as if it was unspeakable in public.

Again, I threw caution to the wind, "You mean Skull and Cross?" R.I.P. nearly gasped at the utterance, clearly shocked by my brazen disrespect. He caught his breath and said, "We were part of this campus since the College began, long before you were here, Connors, and I won't have you implicating us in nonsense."

"You call a skull 'nonsense'?" I asked. Although I hadn't planned on discussing specifics, R.I.P.'s superior air annoyed me into it. "You don't understand, Connors," said R.I.P., "and you never will. You're making something out of nothing. Nothing! And you're harassing my students in the process."

"They're my students as well, Professor." I knew that the remark verged on the fringes of a pissing contest, but I couldn't help myself. "You have no right to delve into matters that don't concern you," he spat back, "And I want it to stop immediately!" With this, he stood from his chair, and stamped-down his cane on the floor. R.I.P. was being more defiant than usual and it was having a negative impact on me. I must admit, although it doesn't happen very often, I was livid. I was also done with the conversation. How dare he come into my office and tell me about the parameters of my job.

"This is none of your business!" R.I.P. shrieked.

"Professor," I said through nearly gritted teeth, "I'm going to make something perfectly clear- when I find the remains of a human being on my campus, it certainly is *my* business!" I paused to inhale and then concluded, "This conversation is over. Thank you for your time."

"You're throwing me out? I have a lot more to say, Connors!"

"And I don't have the patience to hear anymore. This investigation is under my watch and I will talk to whomever I need, regardless of their affiliation. Your permission is not necessary, contrary to *your* opinion." R.I.P. stood up, "You don't know what you're dealing with, Connors!"

"That's exactly why I'm pursuing this investigation." With this, I also stood and walked to the door, "Have a nice day, Professor." R.I.P. stood silently for a brief period before moving. For a second, I thought (or hoped?) that maybe he was having a stroke. Finally, he moved slowly toward the door without a word, the only sound being the dull thump of his cane hitting the floor. As he walked passed me, he paused inches from my face, so close that I could smell his scent: a mixture of hair oil and liniment. He looked me in the eye, and then turned his gaze and lowered his voice, "You'll make a fool of yourself, Connors," he whispered in passing, "a very big fool." R.I.P. took his exit as the smell of Ben Gay lingered in the air. I remained standing in the doorway, contemplating his words. *Was* I blowing this out of proportion? After all, we weren't just talking about a random skull anymore... now, there seemed to be a whole body attached. Didn't R.I.P. know about that piece?

As I stood daydreaming in the doorway, Judy came-up behind me, "Are you okay?" she asked, holding a sandwich, "What'd he want?"

"To annoy me," I said, coming out of my contemplative stupor, "and to threaten me." Although after the words were out of my mouth, I realized that Judy would now have water-cooler fodder for days, perhaps weeks. Nonetheless, it felt good to get it out.

"Threaten you?" she said, walking into my office and putting the sandwich and a coke on my desk, "About what?" Well, the barn door was open and the horse was long gone, I decided to continue confiding in Judy, my trusted assistant.

"The skull, I guess. He wasn't very specific."

"Does he know about the entire graveyard outside of the Student Center?" I knew that she was becoming heated when her Brooklyn accent turned "Center" into, "Centah". She continued, "What does he think, that they're *sparah* ribs from an old *gahden pahty*? That man has a lot of nerve. A lot of nerve!" Although Judy was gossipy at times, she was faithful to the core. And right now, I needed that. She continued, "Why did this get him so fi-ahed-up? Sounds like you hit a nerve. That's what I think. I wondah what old R.I.P.'s hiding. Hrumph!" She left me with my lunch to give me some peace and quiet. I'm sure that she was also eager to begin heating-up the phone and computer lines, communicating the afternoon's events in play-by-play fashion.

I ate my lunch and half-heartedly did some of the paperwork piling-up on my desk. Just as I was finding a rhythm in my work, Judy buzzed me, "You have an Ivory on the phone for you?" she said, hesitantly.

"Who?"

"Ivory. That's her name, I asked her twice. She won't say what it's regarding, she just says that it's very important. Should I take a message?" Although I wasn't in the mood to talk to anyone, the name piqued my interest. If someone named "Ivory" needed to speak with me, I needed to meet them. "No, Judy, It's ok. Put her through, please." A couple of clicks later, I could hear loud music in the background, "Hello, this is Dean Doug."

"Is this Dean Carter-Connors?" came a woman's voice, stuck in the middle of a hush and a yell, trying to be heard over the background noise on her end. "Yes, it is.", I answered, "Who's this, please?"

"It wasn't easy to find you! I didn't know where to start, so I called admissions. Finally, I got your office."

"Who am I speaking with?"

"Ivory. You don't know me."

"Ivory." I repeated, "What's your last name?"

"Nope, just Ivory. I need to talk to you."

"Ivory, what is this about?"

"I don't want to get into it over the phone. I shouldn't even be calling you from here, but I grabbed the phone between sets."

"Who are you, Ivory?"

"I'm a friend of Darcy's... was a friend. I need to talk to you." Darcy, Darcy, did I know any Darcy? Then it struck me. Darcy Green, my first dead person. I had been so preoccupied by my other dead body that I nearly forgot for a minute.

"You knew Darcy?"

"Yes," she said, lowering her voice even more. I could hear thumping music and yelling in the background, so loud that I could hardly hear her, "Ivory," I said fighting the urge to shout, "I can hardly hear you. Do you want to come to my office?"

"I can't... that wouldn't be good. You could come here and we could talk."

"Where's 'here'?" I asked.

"The club," she said as if I should have known, "Smoke. It's on Ocean and Asbury Ave. in Asbury. You know the place?" Oddly enough, I did. Although I had never been to a strip club, Smoke was right down the street from my favorite restaurant, Moonstruck, in Asbury Park. Although the city had been nearly decimated by the race riots of the sixties, and shotty business management in the eighties, it was a resilient town on the verge of a revival, especially near the waterfront. Slowly but surely, dilapidated hotels, homes and warehouses were being bought and renovated into upscale condos, restaurants and shops. I didn't think that Smoke was part of the rejuvenation, but it was a shorefront landmark known for the smoke that came from its pink neon sign.  "Yes, I've heard of it," I said.

"Ooh, I'm almost on, I gotta run.  So tonight, say ten o'clock?"  I didn't want to let on that I liked to be snug in my bed by ten o'clock, snoozing with the latest Sue Grafton or Janet Evanovich open on my chest.

"You work at Smoke, Ivory?"

"Yeah, I'm a dancer.  So I'll see you tonight?"  I needed to think about this one a bit and didn't want to rush into anything.  "Tonight's not good for me," I said stalling, and wanting more time to consider her request, "How about tomorrow?" I asked.

"That's fine, this is just really important."

"Tomorrow at, um, are you working at eight?"

"Eight's no good, it'll be too slow here.  Someone might notice.  It's gotta be 9:30 at the earliest."

"Fine, I'll be there.  Do I ask for you?"

"Oops, I'm on… gotta run.  Just ask for a dance from Ivory.  See you tomorrow!" Click.  The raging rhythms of Smoke went dead.  I turned to my computer to look at my calendar for the next day.  Not that I typically had many commitments at 10pm, I wanted to make sure that I wasn't blowing off a guest lecture or PTA meeting to go to a strip club.  As I opened my calendar, I saw that the administrative computer screen for Darcy Green was still open from earlier in the day.  I had been so distracted by the skull that I nearly forgot about the other dead person on my campus. Shot to death. High on drugs and shot to death. One of *my* students.

I could only assume that Ivory and Darcy worked together at Smoke. What did Ivory know that was so important? And why did she need to tell *me*? How did she even know me? I guessed that I would find out the following day-- when I would lose my virginity and go to my first strip club. I must admit, I was a little nervous. I couldn't do it alone, I needed to bring a seasoned professional along with me. I immediately thought of Jerry. He was just about the closest person to Casanova whom I knew. He probably had a personalized bar stool at Smoke.

I got up from my desk and walked next door to Jerry's office. Ronnie was back at her desk getting ready to pack it in for the day. "Hello, Doug," she said sweetly, "I'm sorry about today. I hope that I wasn't out of line, but that Professor is maddening!"

"You were right on target, Ronnie, and I appreciate the support. Is Jerry in?"

"No, he went to the hospital earlier in the day and hasn't come back yet. Do you want me to call him for you?"

"No, that's ok, I'll give him a call, thanks. Have a nice evening. Have a nice glass of wine, you deserve it."

"Forget the wine," Ronnie said, plumping the bow on her frilly blouse, "I'm having a scotch on the rocks."

I walked back into my outer office to find Judy going through the same packing-up motions. "Have a good night, Judy," I said. "Thanks for all your help today."

"Oh, it wasn't nothing," she said, her jet-black hair and half glasses still glistening in the afternoon light, "You should go home, too. You don't have anything on your calendar." I was dying to tell her what I had on my calendar for the following night, but resisted the urge. "I'm going shortly," I said. "I'll see you tomorrow."

"You got it," she said, straightening her skirt as she got out of her chair and walked out the door. I went to my office and dialed Jerry's cell phone. His voice mail picked up on the first ring. Was he *still* at the hospital? I left him a message to call me and decided to succumb to peer pressure and leave for the day. I dutifully put some files in my briefcase, with no intention of looking at them, locked my office, and started my fifteen-minute walk home.

~~~~~

I love my walk to and from work every day. I consider it to be free therapy, allowing me to clear my head and relax without having to write a check. My normal route home is to go out of the main gates of the College then straight down Pilgrim Pathway to my house.  That day, however, I felt like taking the scenic route along the beach.  So, I took a left onto Surf Avenue and walked the three short blocks straight to the boardwalk along the beach.

I have always loved the ocean.  From the time when I was a kid and we used to go to Kennebunkport, Maine every summer.  Since I grew up in upstate New York, Maine, or "Vacationland" as their motto says, was only a short four hour drive.  I remember the water being so cold that your feet would become numb on contact, but I didn't care.  I scoured the beach for shells, buried my cousin in the sand, and soaked in the salty air.  For me, the Atlantic saturated my being and never left.

While I walked, I could feel that the well-intentioned sun of the fall afternoon was easily diminished by the cool breeze coming off the water, and it made me glad that I was wearing my sport coat.  The gardens that framed many of the homes on Surf Avenue seemed to be welcoming the autumn respite, and languished under a thin blanket of newly fallen leaves.  As I approached the boardwalk, lost in dichotomous thoughts about tired gardens, skeletons, and murdered students, I heard my name being called from behind, "Hello, Dean Doug!"  From the raspy characteristic of a two-pack a day smoker's voice, I knew that it was none other than Malificent Brown, our town's most quirky  spiritual leader.

Malificent runs our town's popular church, the Grove Unitarian Church on Heck Avenue (no pun intended, I promise).  A savvy preacher, she draws in her congregation from Ocean Grove's traditional Methodist crowd, with a mixture of Gospel and popular culture. Not only are her Sunday sermons upbeat and full of religion, but she hosts monthly sushi suppers to encourage a constant flow of hip blood into her community. If she wasn't a woman of the cloth, I would swear that she was a business mogul. Well, except for her appearance. A tall and painfully thin woman, Malificent always wears black to match her dyed-black pageboy haircut. Paired with her round dark-framed eyeglasses, she always reminds me of a praying-mantis. That afternoon, she was looking particularly bug-like in black leggings, black socks underneath her size ten Birkenstocks, and a black, form-fitting sweater.

"Hi, Malificent," I said, standing still as she approached. She moved with the subtle dexterity of a feline, not necessarily walking, but flowing toward me. "Doug," she purred, "I haven't seen you in quite a while and wanted to say hello. How are you?"

"I'm fine," I lied, "what are you doing down here?"

"I was just stopping by Bonnie Burton's place, she's been ill and I wanted to spend some time with her. I'm heading back to the church now, going my way?" I wasn't going her way, but how do you tell a minister that you'd rather go to Sunday service than spend ten minutes making small talk? Malificent and I had a fine relationship and I truly liked her, even though I found her to be slightly pushy at times. She wasn't a religious zealot, but as the self-proclaimed and unlikely religious leader of

Ocean Grove, she often felt it necessary to involve herself in every kind of situation.  Since she also served as one of the campus ministers for Asbury College, I was used to telling her, nicely, to butt out.

"Sure," I said, "I'd love the company." Lying to a minister, now that's gotta mean some hell time, "So, what's new at the church?"

"Well, we're trying something new that I think you and the students will be interested in," she paused dramatically, and then huffed, "Video Game Night!"

"Video game night?"  I replied, trying my best to stifle a laugh.

"Yes, it'll be wild!"  I hadn't heard that line since Mr. Freeze on the old Batman series.  "It will be on Thursday nights.  That's the night that the students tell me is the heaviest party night.  Is that true?"

"It's one of them," I responded.  As a Campus Minister, Malificent was actually a part-time member of my staff and sat on several campus-wide committees.  I assumed that this was where she derived most of her reconnaissance.  She looked at me closely and grabbed my arm, "I think this will help."  I didn't want to admit that it probably couldn't hurt.  We've tried many on-campus activities and interventions to distract students away from sitting in their rooms with a case of Old Milwaukee or a bottle of Popov, none of them overwhelmingly successful.

"After the video games will you be studying the Bible or the Koran?" I joked. Since it was the Unitarian church, I knew that they followed many religious doctrines. Although I was being flip, Malificent didn't pick-up on it, "That's the beauty of it, we won't be doing any ministering, only video games... and snacks of course. We just want students to come and enjoy themselves. If they become comfortable and happen to find a spiritual 'home', then the ministering will come later." She smiled, and looked toward the sky. I looked-up too, hoping that a seagull wasn't primed and ready to shit on my head. Thank God that we were nearing the church, so my penance with Malificent was almost over. "I think it's a great idea," I said, even though I wasn't exactly sure, "are the students excited about it?"

"Oh, yes. I think it will be big. We're going to do the first one on-campus, and then bring it home to the church after we get people involved. It's the involvement that's important. Once they find a spiritual home, they usually stay in that spiritual home." As Malificent continued talking about better homes and spirits, or something, my cell phone rang. I grabbed it and saw that it was Jerry returning my call. Damn, I couldn't exactly invite him to go the strip club with me with a Holy woman standing right next to me. "Excuse me, Malificent," I said, answering the phone. "Hi, Jerry, how'd you make out at the hospital?"

"Fine, Bryan's going to be fine. His parents are okay, too. They're going to take Bryan home for the rest of the week, and bring him back next week. Then, we can work with him and the counseling center. Is that why you called?" I paused for a moment and thought, 'Well actually no, Jerry, I want to know if you will join me to go look at naked women tomorrow night.' Instead, I settled on, "Yes and no. I'm on my way home, but with Malificent right now. I'll give you a call right back?" As I hung-up the phone, I felt compelled to share with Malificent, "We had another student transported to the hospital last night, Jerry was with him and his family all day."

"Is he alright?"

"Yes, he's going to be fine."

"See Doug, this is why we need Video Game Night. We need to show the students that there are other avenues to explore, beyond drugs and alcohol." Although I wasn't sure if a game of Tetris was going to do it, I still couldn't argue with the sentiment. As usual, Malificent continued, "There have been a few transports this semester, right?"

"Three so far. Yes, we're only half-way through the semester… normally we only have a couple the entire year." I neglected to tell her about the fourth, Darcy Green, who never quite made it to the hospital.

"All drug related?"

"Yes." I said as we reached the front steps of the church. Ironically, the church looked more like a bar than a church, perhaps because it used to be a brothel in the late 1800s. Malificent touched my arm and moved in close, so close that I could smell her nicotine laced breath, "A spiritual home, Doug," she said, "the students need a spiritual home."  I obediently agreed, and left Malificent on the steps of the church.  Hell, she had created a "spiritual home" out of a former house of ill-repute, in fact, she made the former bar into the altar.  If she could make that transformation, maybe she could do it again on the Asbury College campus.

I decided to forego my walk, and with only a couple of blocks to go before I reached my house, I called Jerry back, "Hey, sorry about that." I said.

"Was she bending your ear about Video Game Night?" Jerry chuckled.

"Yeah, you knew about Video Game night and didn't tell me?" I laughed.

"I was going to, but didn't have a chance today."

"Will you go to a strip club with me tomorrow night?"  I blurted it out like an adolescent on a first date.

"What?" Jerry asked, shocked.

"It's a long story," I said, "I can fill you in tomorrow, I'm not going for me, it's work related.  I was asked to go."

"What!"  Jerry was in hysterics.

"Is it so funny that I would want to go to a strip club?" I asked.  He laughed, "Yes, you've never even been to Hooters!  Where do you want to go, Smoke?"

"As a matter of fact, yes."

"Are you kidding me!  Sure, I'll go, but you can't make me wait until tomorrow for the details. Spill 'em."  As I approached my four-bedroom cape, I stared at my house wrapped by its white picket fence, and relayed the story of Darcy Green.  As I spoke the new details about Darcy's demise and Ivory's invitation to her place of work, I could practically see the paint peeling from the pickets as I spoke.  We hung-up and I thankfully walked in my front door, relishing in the scent of home.  Barbara and my five-year-old son, Ethan were in the family room playing on the floor with an assortment of toys.

"Daddy!" Ethan said, dropping a red car and running over to me.  It was my favorite part of the day.  Barbara stood to join him, and I soaked-in the icky-sweet family portrait.  I had clearly found *my* spiritual home.

~~~~~

At 1:57am, the telephone rang.  I picked-up the receiver to find Jerry on the other end.  "Boss," he said shakily, "I'm sorry to bother you, but we've got another one.  This one is bad."

"What?" I asked, groggily.

"Another transport.  Drugs again," Jerry explained urgently, "it's worse this time, Doug. They don't know if he's going to make it."

-6-

    The news was like a splash of ice-cold water-
- so was Jerry's quivering voice.  As soon as I hung-
up, I whispered to Barbara what little I knew and
jumped out of bed.  I threw-on a pair of jeans and a
sweatshirt, not even stopping first to put on
underwear.  I quickly brushed my teeth, threw an AC
hat over my messy hair and I was out the door.

    The inside of my red Mini Cooper was cold,
and for the first time in the season, I cranked-up the
heat.  Although I walked to work, and do not
consider myself a "car-guy," I fell in love with the
Mini as soon as it arrived in the US.  I consider it a
luxury that is about as extravagant as I get.  Barbara
reserves a mini-van for her own luxurious driving
pleasure.

Jersey Shore Medical Center is in Neptune, New Jersey, barely two miles from my house. I was there in five minutes, parked, and ran into the Emergency entrance. Since Jersey Shore is a nationally respected trauma center, the waiting area was busier than I expected at 2am. Gurneys rushing by, doctors and nurses moving swiftly and worried-looking people sitting restlessly in metal, institutional chairs-- one of them was Jerry. His willowy legs extended far beyond the confines of the chair and swayed nervously like tent-poles in the wind. He was staring into space, with his head resting on his left hand. He jumped up as soon as I approached and nearly hugged me, clutching my hand.

"What's the latest?" I asked.

"I'm still waiting. He's unconscious, Doug. He's been that way for at least two hours. When he got here, he stopped breathing." I grabbed Jerry's arm, and walked away from the main seating area in order to get a little privacy. "Who is it?" I asked, since I hadn't even heard the student's identity yet.

"Jeffrey Jordan."

"From the basketball team?"

"Yes, he's a junior. Lives in Hoosick." Hoosick was one of our residence halls. "Do we know what happened?"

I got the call around eleven-thirty from Al," Jerry began. "He was just ready to go off-shift. He'd been guarding the skeleton all day. Jeff's roommate got to the room after being at the library and found him on the floor. He called the RA who

called security immediately. He was still
unconscious when the paramedics arrived, but still
breathing."

"When did he stop breathing?"

"Apparently on the way here. When I got the
call, I ran over to Hoosick and saw them rushing him
out. He didn't look good, boss. He didn't look
good."

"What is it, alcohol? Drugs?"

"They think drugs. Jeff's roommate said he
had just seen him a half-hour before... he says that
they were both in the library. Jeff apparently got
tired, and said that he was going home."

"So on the way from the library to his room
he got so high that he passed out? Are we sure that
he doesn't have some sort of medical condition?
Heart? Something else?"

"No, we're not sure. But the paramedics
treated it as an overdose. I don't know why."

"Did you call his parents?"

"Yes, I just got off the phone with them
before you came. They only live in Red Bank, so
they're on their way." At this time of night, I knew
that Red Bank would only be a twenty-minute trip.
"Jerry," I asked, "who's Jeff's roommate?"

"Marcus Woods." Jerry answered. I knew
Marcus to be another basketball player. I didn't
recognize either name, however, as ever being in
trouble. "Have they had any conduct issues?" I
asked.

"No problems at all."  At this point, I was trying to make sense out of a senseless situation, so I decided to stop interrogating Jerry.

We waited for another ten minutes, pacing back and forth without speaking a word.  Shortly after 2:30am, two more people rushed into the ER reception area, looking around frantically.  Since I had seen them at basketball games and some other College functions, I knew that they were Jeff's parents.  I looked at Jerry, and then approached them immediately, "Mr. And Mrs. Jordan, I'm Douglas Carter-Connors, Dean of Students at Asbury."

"How's our boy?"  Mr. Jordan asked immediately.

"He's still in there.  We're waiting to hear."

"But he's going to be alright?" Mrs. Jordan asked with beseeching eyes.  I tried my best not to hesitate before I responded, "We're still waiting.  When he arrived he wasn't breathing.  But he's in there now."  Mr. Jordan shook his head, and Mrs. Jordan gasped.  After she recovered, she spat through gritted teeth, "He was *fine* until he went to that college!  I never wanted him to go there.  He could have gone anywhere.  Rutgers wanted him, Rider University wanted him, The College of New Jersey, he even had a tour at Princeton.  But no, he wanted to go to little Asbury College, and look where it got him?"  She stopped, and stared directly at me while her husband held her shoulders.  I could feel the searing heat of her eyes as they bored holes through my own pupils. "Well?" she began again, "what do you have to say for yourself, Dean?"

"I'm sorry that you feel that way." Was all I could manage, and clearly it wasn't enough for an emotional parent, "Sorry? You're sorry? That's it? Well you will be sorry, I promise you that. You're going to be very, very sorry." At that point, Mr. Jordan pulled her into him and escorted her a few steps away. I wasn't sure if it was out of deference to his wife or to me, but I didn't care. I turned around and almost walked into Jerry who was standing right behind me. Beyond him, already anxious people in the waiting area were craning their necks to get a better look, thankful for any distraction.

"Whew," Jerry said, "I've never heard a parent like that."

"Well," I responded, "unfortunately it could get worse." I looked at my watch. It was 2:45am and I wondered how much longer we would have to wait to find out if Jeffrey was going to live or die.

~~~~~

At around 3:30am, a haggard young doctor emerged from the maze of glass doors and curtains and called, "Jeffrey Jordan?" Immediately, the four of us waiting in the reception area rushed to his side. The doctor, obviously too fatigued to be phased, looked at Mr. and Mrs. Jordan holding each other and said, "You're his parents?"

"Yes." They responded in unison.  He then turned to Jerry and me, "And you are?"

"Jeffrey's a student at Asbury," I said. "We're from the College."  The doctor shook his head approvingly, and motioned for us all to step inside the glass doors.  "How's my son," Mrs. Jordan asked urgently.  "How is he!"  The doctor stroked his stubbly chin.  He didn't look like he'd shaved or even had a shower in days.  He glanced down at his blood-spattered blue scrubs and quickly covered the stains with folded arms.  "Well," he began, "when he arrived, he wasn't breathing.  They began CPR in the ambulance and we continued it here."  Mrs. Jordan's hand rushed to her mouth, but remained silent, listening intently.

The doctor continued, "We got him breathing again, but he still hasn't regained consciousness. We're doing a tox screen and other tests to see what's going on.  We'll know more when the results come back."

"Tox screen?  What is that?"

"It's a test to see what toxins are in his body-- drugs, medications, things like that."

"Drugs?"  Mrs. Jordan nearly shouted, "My boy's not on drugs.  He's never been on drugs!  Not since that college!"  She again turned her attention to me, pointing in my direction, "So help me God, you and your precious college will pay for this.  I give you my word on that-- you've never felt pain like you're going to feel!"

"Well," the doctor began again, giving me a sympathetic look, "we'll know more when we get

the results back. Would you like to see your son?"
He ushered the Jordans behind a curtain, and shot me
a tiny smile as he went, "Sorry," he said, "family
only." With that, he winked. "Sure," I said, "we'll
go back to the waiting area."

It was after three in the morning and Jerry
looked exhausted. After all, at least I had some sleep
before I was woken-up, Jerry had not. "Jerry," I
said, "why don't you go home."
"No, I'm alright." He said, practically falling
asleep standing-up. "No," I insisted, "go home.
There's no reason for both of us to be here. I'm just
going to wait for the Jordans to come back out, say
my goodbyes and go home myself. There's nothing
we can do… except be Mrs. Jordan's scapegoat, and
you don't need that. Go."
"You sure?"
"Yes."
"Okay, thanks, I think I will." He headed
toward the sliding doors, "You call me if you need
me though, huh?"
"Sure, but I won't," I said.
"But call me if something… changes." Jerry
stopped, evidently not wanting to finish the thought.
"I will, don't worry," I replied. We went
through the doors and then immediately popped his
head back through, causing them to open again, "Oh
and Doug?"
"Yeah?"
"I'm not sure that I'll be up for Smoke
tomorrow, er, I mean, tonight." A couple of heads in

the waiting area turned, I tried to cover quickly, "Yeah, no more Marlboros for you, I'll see you later." Jerry looked at me curiously, and then left. I knew that he was too fatigued to understand that I had just tried to cover for the fact that he announced to the entire Emergency Room that we were planning on going to the locally famous strip club. As I turned and made a move toward one of the waiting chairs, I was pretty sure that a middle-aged woman gave me a disapproving look, so I felt compelled to explain myself once again. "My friend's trying to quit smoking-- can't seem to get that monkey off his back." She clutched her purse closer to her, and turned her attention to the television resting on the wall, ignoring me.

It was a little after 4am, when the Jordans emerged from the sanctity of the inner-ER. I stood immediately, but didn't move. I simply stared as they approached. Mrs. Jordan had been crying and much to my surprise, walked right past me and out the main entrance doors without saying a word. Mr. Jordan stopped to meet my stare, and I moved toward him. "How is he?" I asked, walking toward the entrance.

"He's still unconscious. We just have to wait. Do you know where they found him?'

"In his room. Marcus found him. He said that they were at the library, Jeff left, and a half-hour later, Marcus found him on the floor in their room. He called for help immediately." Mr. Jordan nodded, "Drugs. I can't believe it. Pauline's

brother's an addict, but Jeffrey? He's always been a
good boy." I shook my head in agreement and was
thankful to know why Mrs. Jordan reacted with such
hostility. Clearly it was much easier to blame
Asbury College than family demons for her son's
drug use. "Are you going home?" I asked.

"No, no. We don't want to leave him. I'm
taking Pauline out to get some air and then coffee in
the cafeteria. We'll be back. You're not staying, are
you?" I felt awkward and torn with this question.
Although, as the Dean of Students, I felt a
responsibility to Jeffrey and wanted to see him
through this, he wasn't my child. I had other
responsibilities besides Jeffrey, both at home and at
Asbury. Finally, I responded, "No, I think I'll go
home for now. I'll come back later today." I paused,
looked at Mr. Jordan, and then said, "Unless you
need me?" He seemed touched by this comment and
replied, "No, but thank you. I can handle Pauline."

I reached for one of my cards to hand him,
but quickly realized that I was wearing a sweatshirt
and jeans. "Oh," I said patting myself down, "I
don't have a card on me, let me give you my
numbers in case you need me." I walked over to the
reception desk, asked for a pen and a piece of scrap
paper and quickly scrawled both my office number
and the number for security. "Here, Mr. Jordan," I
said, handing the pen back to the nurse at the
reception desk, "here are my phone numbers. The
top is my office during the day, the bottom is
security after hours. They'll get in touch with me if
necessary." He took the paper and shook my hand,

"Thank you, Dean," he said, "we appreciate your coming out this morning" He looked out of the doors, "She's not really mad at you."

I nodded and walked with him as the automatic glass doors sprang open. We walked into the night, immediately gripped by the chilly fall. The wind was still, waiting impatiently for the dawn-- waiting for light, warmth, and new opportunities. Just like us.

~~~~~

I woke-up at 10am feeling like a truck hit me. On my way home at 4:30 I called and left a message for Judy that I would be in late to the office and explained, in little detail, what had happened. God, I was exhausted. As I rolled over, snuggling into the covers, I immediately thought of Jeffrey Jordan and sat straight-up in bed. I reached for the phone, dialed information and asked for Jersey Shore Medical. I was connected to the hospital, transferred a couple of times, and finally was able to ask about Jeffrey's condition. After a moment, the woman got back on the line with one word, "Serious." That was all she could tell me, "serious." No shit. I hung-up the phone, and dropped back into my pillow. It was one of those days when I wished I never had to leave my bed.

As I closed my eyes again, I began to think about the office. I considered what nasty things R.I.P. had planned for me. I wondered how the skeleton was doing. I worried that there was a major drug problem raging through campus. I wondered if I ever needed to leave the security of my bed. I sat-up again and called Judy.

"Good Morning, Dean of Students Office, Judy speaking."

"Hey," I said in a voice lower and raspier than hers, "what's shakin'?"

"Doug, how's the boy?"

"He's still in serious condition, I just called the hospital."

"What time did you get home?"

"Around 4:30 this morning… I haven't gotten out of bed yet."

"Well I'm sure you need your sleep. You should stay there and come in after lunch."

"Why then?"

"Mary has called an emergency Wellness Task Force meeting for 2 o'clock to talk about all of the drug transports lately. I figured that you'd want to be there." Mary Mumford was our Director of Health Services. The Wellness Task Force was a group of campus individuals who met regularly to assess the wellness climate on campus. The group, however, was also convened as necessary to discuss various emergency health risks. The last time we had an impromptu meeting, we had to discuss a plan for dealing with a suspected case of meningitis. Luckily, that was a false alarm. I knew that this time we wouldn't be so lucky.

"Great, I'm glad she did that," I said, "I'll be there. Anything else?"

"No, a few messages, but nothing urgent. Stay in bed, I'll take care of everything until you get here, don't you worry." I wasn't, with Judy at the helm, I wasn't worried at all. I thanked her, we hung-up, and I pulled the covers up around my neck again. This time, I was trying to think happy thoughts, and as luck would have it, Barbara came into the room right on cue. "Hey," I said with closed eyes.

"I thought I heard you talking?" she said.

"Yeah, I called the hospital and Judy."

"What time did you get home last night? I didn't even hear you."

"4:30," I said, eyes still closed.

"Oh, Doug. Are you staying home today?"

"No, I have an emergency meeting this afternoon and an appointment at the strip club later tonight."

"What?" Barbara said, clearly amused, " strip club? You've never even been to Hooters."

"I know." I said, realizing that I hadn't given her the details yet, "Sink or swim, that's my motto."

"What's going on?" Barbara asked, lying on the bed next to me. Since she is a freelance writer and part time staff at the Grove Guardian, Ocean Grove' hometown paper, Barbara works out of her home office. This was especially nice on days like this.

"I didn't tell you about Ivory?"

"Ivory?"

"Yeah, Ivory the stripper?"

"Is that like Jack the Ripper?"

"No, stripper's not capitalized. She called me the other day, and asked me to go to Smoke."

"But you don't smoke."

"Not smoke as in smoking, Smoke, as in the strip club."

"A strange stripper invited you to a strip club?"

I stopped teasing and explained about Darcy Green and Ivory and their connection to Smoke. After hearing my explanation, Barbara asked, "So why you and not the police?"

"I don't know," I answered, "But I think I'll have to wait until tomorrow to find out, I'm going to be too tired tonight."

"Remember the last time you did something without the police you ended-up hanging off of a Ferris wheel in a thunder storm." Again, referring to the incident that happened a couple of months before when I took it upon myself to find Jessica Philmore. "I didn't do it alone, Chief Morreale drove me. I just did some investigating on my own while he was checking things out."

"Exactly." Barbara said, part scolding, part musing.

"I'll be fine, this is just a strip club, not…"

"A scary carnival?" Barbara interrupted, laughing.

"Exactly." I laughed, and reached out to hug her. In mid-hug, she asked, "So how's your student."

"Serious condition. Apparently drugs, we should know more today." She hugged me again, and then kissed me on the cheek, "Sorry," I said, pursing my lips, "I haven't brushed my teeth yet."

"That's ok, you smell like roses."

"Shit-covered roses, maybe." I said, covering my mouth. I looked at the gleam in her eye, and suddenly wasn't tired anymore. "Maybe I should go brush my teeth, and we can investigate this further?" I said.

"If you're up for it, I think that's a great idea." I jumped out of bed and raced naked to the bathroom. With Ethan at school, and me home unexpectedly, Barbara and I simply had to take advantage of the situation, and thus each other. I brushed and rinsed, decided to forgo the floss for later, and dove back into bed with Barbara, who had conveniently removed her clothes.

We made love and then lay in bed, catching-up on the daily details of our lives that we had been too busy to share. Barbara got another article accepted by Parenting magazine, Ethan had a class field trip to the Philadelphia Zoo next Thursday, R.I.P. accosted me in my office, the important tiny details that impacts day-to-day living.


"So do you expect to hear any word about the skull today?" Barbara asked.

"I'm not sure, it's actually still on-campus."

"What do you mean? Isn't it in a lab somewhere?"

"Yes, right on-campus. I didn't know this, but apparently we have our own resident forensic scientist at Asbury College. His name is Dr. Allen

Faust. I've seen him around, but never had any dealings with him."

"And the police use his services regularly?"

"Evidently. I think that, normally, Dr. Faust gets called out to the field or goes to other labs around the state, but since the skull was found right on-campus, Chief Morreale brought it right to him."

"Well that's convenient."

"Very."

"And what about the rest of the skeleton?"

"I'm not sure. I guess the Chief has to get someone to dig it up, or maybe Dr. Faust is helping with that too. I really don't know."

"Who do you think it is?" Barbara was unconsciously moving into her investigative reporter mode. "I don't know," I said, not really contemplating the question, "it's sort of secondary on my list right now. I have more recent bodies to think about."

"Bodies?"

"Okay, bad choice of words. One dead body and another lying in the hospital trying to stay alive." I could immediately feel that "hit by a truck" feeling flowing back into my body, likely caused more by stress than exhaustion.

It was after eleven, and I felt compelled to get moving and get to the office. I swung my feet over the side of the bed and suddenly felt old. As I paused to reflect on my place in the world of the middle-aged, Barbara must have sensed my trepidation, "What's wrong?" she asked.

"I feel old," I said, trying not to notice that my six-pack had turned into a 2-liter bottle. "You're only forty, Doug. That's not old."

"Yeah, but I'll be forty-one in a few weeks."

"December… that's a couple months away."

"Which is *only* a few weeks. I'm a middle-aged man."

"You are not."

"If I live 'til 80, I'm middle aged, if I live to 90, which I doubt, I'm very close."

"I think this talk of bodies has really gotten to you," she said, rubbing my back.

"It's not the talk that's bothering me, it's the actual bodies themselves."

"Body, Doug. You only have one body." Forever the optimist, Barbara was always looking on the bright side and at the moment, I needed that. I leaned back to kiss her again, and then hopped out of bed and went to the shower. I couldn't help but catch a glimpse of myself in the full-length mirror as I opened the shower curtain. I certainly wasn't a heavy man, but at 5'6" or so, a couple of extra pounds really showed. I had always been a three or four times a week runner, but since my fall from the Ferris wheel the month before, I had been forced to retire my Adidas for a while. However, my doctor said that my ankle had healed nicely and that I could resume normal activity-- that was a few weeks ago. Tomorrow, I'd get back to my running routine.

I showered, shaved, got dressed, and kissed Barbara on my way out the door in about twenty-five minutes. Since it was nearly lunchtime, I dispensed with breakfast and chose to grab something in the Student Center. On my walk to work, I thought about my impending visit to Smoke. Since I had decided to postpone until tomorrow, should I let Ivory know somehow? What was I supposed to do, call-up the strip club and ask for Ivory? Leave a message saying, "Doug can't make it tonight"? Since Ivory seemed insistent on not telling anyone, I didn't want to jeopardize her situation, whatever that was. I decided that I would call Smoke later and try my chances at getting Ivory on the phone. I had never stood-up a date before, and I wasn't about to start.

On my way into the Student Center, I passed Quacky, loyally guarding the skeleton. "Good afternoon, Chief Braggish," I said, "how's our friend?" She seemed taken aback by my attempt at humor, "All secure," she said, "I spoke to Chief Morreale this morning. They're going to begin uncovering the remains this afternoon. Dr. Faust has already been by to assess the scene." I thanked her for being a great sentinel, and walked up to my office where I was greeted by Judy, Ronnie, Keesha, and Jerry.

"Welcome to work, sleepy-head," Jerry joked.

"Hey, I was there later than you."

"Judy said you left at 4 o'clock?"

"Yeah, about that."

"Anymore fireworks from Mrs. Jordan?"

"Fireworks?" Judy chimed-in, looking at me, practically drooling, "you didn't say anything about fireworks!"

"It was no big deal. She's just an upset parent."

"Yeah, so upset that she threatened him," Jerry shared with the group, which I wished he hadn't.

"She *threatened* you?" Judy said anxiously, and Keesha joined the conversation with, "What'd she say?" I shot Jerry a disapproving, 'thanks a lot' look, and said, "She didn't threaten me… well, not really anyway. She was just upset. I spoke with Mr. Jordan, it will be fine." At that point, a couple of students came into the office, one looking for Keesha, another occupying Judy with a story about multiple parking tickets. I took this as an invitation to go to my office. Jerry followed.

"Sorry about that," Jerry apologized, "I didn't mean to share sensitive information."

"Don't worry about it," I said, sitting down at my desk, "it's not that it's so sensitive, it's more about the fact that I didn't want to get into it."

"Got it. Are you going to grab lunch before the meeting?"

"Yeah, just let me do a quick check of my e-mail first," I said, logging in. Jerry sat down and said, "So, Smoke tomorrow night?"

"Yes, don't let me forget to call Ivory and tell her of our change in plans."

"Oh, I forgot, you're on a first name basis."
Jerry smirked. I chuckled and we headed out of my
office. As we approached the stairs to go down, I
heard Judy calling for me, "Dean Doug! Dean
Doug!" I turned around and saw her motioning for
me from behind the plate-glass windows to our
office. Jerry and I made our way back to the office
and found Judy holding the telephone receiver
impatiently. As we entered, she said, "It's Mr.
Jordan, he's at the hospital and wants to speak with
you."

-7-

"I'll take it in my office, Judy," I said running past her. I picked-up the phone as though it was a cockroach, barely wanting to touch it. "Hello, Mr. Jordan," said. Normally I would have said, 'How's Jeffrey', but I was afraid to ask.

"Hello, Dean. Did you get any sleep?" Mr. Jordan's voice sounded tired, but he was making an attempt at small-talk, which put my nerves at ease just a bit. "I got a little, how about you?" I asked.

"No, we've been here all night. We didn't want to leave his side. I was calling you just to let you know that there isn't much progress, he's still unconscious."

"What's the prognosis?"

"Not good if he doesn't come out of it soon, there's not really anything they can do. We've been praying." Mr. Jordan paused, "Dean, I'm not sure if you're a religious man, but prayer's all we've got now. We'd appreciate any prayers you can offer, too." I was not a particularly religious man, but his words struck me. I was sure to say a prayer later. "I will," I said, bowing my head involuntarily. We ended the conversation pretty quickly thereafter and I went back out the outer office to join Jerry for lunch. I gave everyone the update, or lack thereof, and we went downstairs.

The Student Center food court has many healthy options: Wrap sandwiches, veggie quesadillas, sometimes even broiled fish. True to form, I headed straight for the fryer and loaded my tray with chicken fingers and french fries. Although a brief glimpse of my naked self flashed across my mind as I moved the fried yum yums from the warming area to my tray, it was quickly erased by the luxurious scent of hot grease. I sometimes think that fried food is the ultimate mind-eraser. Who would have thought that only a few hours earlier I was lamenting both my age and my weight? Hell, I didn't even get a Diet Coke and reached for the good old Coke Classic. Sugar and Grease-- a famous combination surely surpassing even Lucy and Desi.

Jerry and I ate in a booth and had very few interruptions by students and staff. The questions, always beginning with, 'I'm sorry to bother you, but...' ranged from how to get a roommate change to reserving a room in the Student Center for events. Although sometimes annoying, and often making even simple conversations cumbersome, I rarely squelched the interruptions. I guess it's because of a professor that I had in my own undergraduate years who once made me feel two inches tall when I knocked on his office door. I still remember it distinctly, his door was open and he was meeting with another student. As a shy, and not so socially aware undergrad, I knocked quietly, wanting to ask if I could make an appointment for the next day. I knocked softly, and asked, "May I interrupt?" The professor looked directly at me, deadpan, and said, "You just did." That experience left me forever traumatized. I still remember the feeling of wanting to erase the time preceding the ill-fated knock.  Not only did I get a "D" in that class, but I vowed never to shun students like that if ever in a similar position. I still do my best not to.

After lunch, I responded to e-mails and telephone messages and then Jerry and I headed to the Health Center for the Wellness Task Force meeting.  On the way, we picked-up Francesca Marconi, one of the psychologists in AC's Counseling Center.  As the three of us approached the Health Center, which is actually an old, Victorian house on-campus converted for modern conveniences, we mostly chatted about nothing.  We talked about the cool nights, rough surf, as well as the newest movie playing at the Cheap Theater that is down the street.

We walked up on the white, wrap-around porch of the Health Center and passed several students milling about holding tissue boxes, and snuggling into their AC hoodies.  Some were clearly sick, others were just there for moral support.  When mom's not at school, I guess a good friend has to do. As we entered the slate-grey double doors into the lobby and reception area, we were quickly greeted by Mary McElroy, one of the two staff nurses.  "Hi, guys!" she said, holding a handful of charts, "Mary's in the conference room, you know the way."

We went down a dark hallway, typical of homes of the era, and into the former sitting room that had been converted into a conference room. Although dark wallpaper and heavy red drapes still lined the perimeter of the room, a large conference table and chairs took the place of settees and cushioned ottomans.  Mary was busily fussing with a potted fern, one of the many plants resting on the old window seat, "Hello, hello!" she said, grabbing a fist full of dead fronds, "Good thing this plant lives in the Health Center, because it's very sick!  Poor thing, I always forget to water it."  Mary is a slight, attractive woman, with kind features and a personality to match, "Can I get you anything?  We have coffee, tea, hot chocolate?"

Jerry and I declined a beverage, but Francesca asked for hot tea.  "Are you sure that you boys don't want anything?"  Mary asked again, and this time we both felt pressure to accept something from our gracious host.  Mary made three cups of tea from a station at one end of the room and placed them for us at the table.  As we all took seats, Mary pulled out a canister from the fireplace mantle, "And here," she said, "is some candy to keep you awake."  Mary always had candy, pocketfuls of Jolly Ranchers in her cardigans, batches of butterscotches in her white coat.  Good thing she didn't run a dentist's office.  Next to Judy, Mary was the biggest mom on-campus, always trying to mother everyone, students and staff alike.

We continued our small talk while the other members of the committee filed-in.  Anu Datta, Professor of Political Science, Patti Acola from Athletics and Quacky, all arrived within ten minutes. Always one to make an entrance, Quacky entered saying, "I hope I'm not late, folks, I had to get someone to baby-sit the skeleton." I was shocked that she shared the information, but I was happy in the fact that she had finally found a hint of humorous irony in the situation. Patti quickly responded, "Is that what's going on? I saw the tape and wondered. The kids have been saying everything from a body to buried treasure. Of course, I didn't believe either."

Quacky shot me a quick look and I quickly scolded her with my eyes. Once the word got out, it wouldn't be her who would get the barrage of panicky calls. Just as she started to speak, I found myself talking over her to drown her out. It was pure self-preservation, "It seems that Facilities was digging near the Student Center and found a few bones. We're having them and the scene analyzed to see what they are and where they came from." Quacky's eyes widened and she quickly took a seat, getting the hint that I didn't want to discuss the topic.

"So it's a human skeleton?" Professor Datta asked, sounding more intrigued than shocked.

"We won't be sure of anything until the investigation is complete," I responded, again shooting Quacky a look, I really didn't want panic over a dead body taking over the campus. I looked over at Mary, who graciously took my cue, "Well," she began, "Thank you for coming today. I'm sorry that the circumstances aren't better, but in light of the recent events on-campus involving drugs and alcohol, I thought that I had better convene a meeting." Everyone began to shuffle papers and make notes on notepads. With the soothing voice of a librarian, Mary continued, "So far this year, we've already had three medical transports to the hospital. We usually only have two or three an entire academic year. I wanted to get us together today to update you on these events and try to come up with ideas for interventions."

Mary updated us on Jeffrey Jordan, relaying pretty much the same information that I had. Professor Datta asked about activities on-campus that would occupy idol young minds, Patti talked about a new program that she was coordinating in the Athletic department to educate athletes about the dangers of steroids. We bantered back and forth for nearly an hour, coming up with a few well-intentioned ideas, but not any real plan or solution. In my experience, this is usually what happens in most meetings on a college campus. Jerry offered to look into developing a poster campaign, deterring students from drug use, which he admitted would probably be futile. I informed the group about Malificent's video game night, since Campus Ministry fell under my jurisdiction.

Professor Datta asked about the source of the drugs, to which everyone gave a collective shrug, except for Quacky who began a diatribe on Columbia, street gangs, and rich white housewives. Although I still have no idea what she said, she uttered the word, "Cartel" six times-- I counted, making little tick marks on my notepad. Francesca disclosed that students coming to the counseling center with drug-related issues were increasing, but as professional ethics dictated, didn't share any specific details.  We ended on that happy note and I grabbed a handful of peppermints for the walk home. Mary thanked us for coming and we scheduled another meeting in two weeks.  I hoped by that time, things would settle down.

By the time Francesca, Jerry, and I returned to the Student Center, the taped-off crime scene was buzzing with activity.  Al, the security officer, was still standing guard, watching Professor Allen Faust and another man picking at the bones.  Chief Morreale was also standing by.  "I'll catch-up with you later," I said to Jerry and Francesca as I stopped to get an update.  "What's new?" I asked, not quite sure how to begin conversation over a skeleton. Beginning a conversation over drinks, I can do.

"Well," began the Chief shaking my hand, "They just started.  Dr. Faust?  Do you know Dean Doug?"  The man had a shaggy grey beard and wore half-spectacles.  He was wearing a floppy canvas hat that tied around his neck, khaki cargo pants, a tee-shirt and Birkenstocks.  Tied around his waist was a raggy denim shirt.  He looked more like a haggard rock star than a PhD.  He glanced-up at me quickly, squinted to get a better look, and responded, "Yeah, sure man.  How ya doin'?" and then quickly got back to his work.

"The other guy is from the State Police," the Chief said, not bothering to introduce us since the man was engrossed in brushing away pebbles from what appeared to be a rib.  Dr. Faust was anxiously looking over the man's shoulder like an expectant father, bobbing up and down with excitement. Every now and then he'd come out with, "Oh man, would you look at that. Beautiful. That is fuckin' beautiful!" I looked at the Chief, who looked back at me enough to say, 'he's one of yours.'

"When do you think they'll be finished?" I asked.

"They think by sometime tomorrow."

"And when will we have some answers?"

"In a day or two, I would think. As you can see, Dr. Faust is pretty excited. They've already found something... clothing fibers. Looks like the victim was wearing something black at the time of death." A wave of dread suddenly poured over me... Skull and Cross members wore black robes during all of their ceremonial functions. This wasn't going to be good. Not good at all.

"Okay," I said, "then we can take down the yellow tape?"

"Yup," said the Chief, scratching his bald head, "you can keep it as a souvenir."

"I'll pass, but thanks anyway," I said as I turned to walk away. "Nice meeting you," I said in the direction of Dr. Faust and the other guy, who were both too busy to notice that I was even there. I ran upstairs to find Judy surrounded by a gaggle of chattering students. As I entered the office, they all stopped immediately and turned toward me. Judy stood immediately, as if I were royalty and motioned at the students, "Kids, now sit down. Let me fill Dean Doug in on the situation and I'll be right back."

The four students sat immediately, without a word as Judy led the way to my office. I followed like any good boss should.

We entered my office, and Judy shut the door behind us, "We've got problems," she said, hand on her hip. "They say that they're from SAFE, a new student organization working for the safety of our campus. Have you heard of them? *I haven't.*"

"What does 'SAFE' stand for?" I asked.

"You're asking me? Who knows. Anyway, they want to meet with you about campus safety, one of 'em is that squirrelly little Mike Gordon from the campus newspaper. Shifty fella if I ever saw one. Another is that Taylor boy, the one who was protesting a couple of months ago? He should spend more time finding a girlfriend, if you know what I mean. Then did you notice who else?" I merely shook my head, since Judy wasn't going to give me an opportunity to speak anyway, "The Borden girl… Sarah. You know, the witch from a couple of months ago? And finally Emily Boyd, the RA. What she's doing hanging around this pack, I have no idea. She should spend *her* time trying to find a *boyfriend.*" That said, Judy stood in silence, this time with both hands on her hips-- her case rested.

"Would you like to send them in?" I asked, chin on my hand.

"Not really," she responded, "I don't like pushy students to think that they can just waltz in here and see you any time they want."

"But that's what I'm here for, Judy," I reminded her, "I'm the Dean of *Students.*"

"And we need to teach them that life isn't immediate. They can't just snap their fingers and get what they want. Life is about making appointments."

I mulled over her retort and decided that we were both right. But in this case, I decided to go with *my* argument. I worried that if I didn't meet with them now, they would begin spreading more rumors about campus safety. I explained myself to Judy again, like any good boss should, and waited for her approval, "Since you put it that way," she said, "I'll send them in." On her way out, she leaned back into my doorway, "But I still don't like that Mike Gordon... I tell you, he's squirrelly."

"What does 'squirrelly' mean?" I asked.

"You know," she said, bouncing her hands up and down under her chin and making little clicking noises with her teeth, "sneaky. Squirrelly like a little rat."

I sat at my desk and shuffled papers until the foursome appeared. The 'squirrelly' one appeared first and knocked quietly, "Dean Doug?" he asked.

"Hi, Mike," I said standing up from my desk, "nice to see you. Come in, please." The group cautiously entered and took seats on the small couch and chairs that I have in front of my desk. I moved to join them. "So," I said, "SAFE? Is this a new student group?"

Mike spoke again, "Yes. Well, actually, we're not an official organization yet, we haven't received approval from Student Government, but we're working on it. We're pursuing campus safety.

SAFE stands for:  Safety Allowed For Everyone.
We want to work on safety issues around campus,
especially in light of recent events which are of
momentous concern."  Mike was the star reporter for
the *Asbury Word*, our campus newspaper.  He was
known for using particularly large and unnecessary
words, as well as sensationalism, which I suppose
can be the same thing.

"To what events are you referring?" I asked.

"The grave for one, and then there's the
missing student case that happened in the beginning
of the school year."  I found it interesting that they
weren't concerned about the recent hospital
transports.  Emily Boyd, one of our campus Resident
Assistants, piped-up, "We want to help so that
students feel more secure."

"What about the grave, Dean Doug," Mike
interrupted, "it is a grave, isn't it?"

"Is this an informational meeting, Mike, or an
interview?"

"Oh!" he said, shocked at my candor, "it's a
meeting, but I thought that since I was here…"

"You'd get a scoop?  Doesn't that seem like a
conflict of interest to you, Mike?  You're here
representing SAFE, not the Word, right?"  I didn't
usually challenge students in front of their peers, but
I found Mike particularly annoying.  I had to give
him credit, though, he didn't back down, "If there is
a mass grave on-campus, the students have a right to
know about it!"  Funny how we went from grave, to
mass grave in under two minutes.  I knew that if I
waited any longer, we'd move into genocide or

weapons of mass destruction, so I looked to the entire group and said, "I'm not prepared to speak about what's happening outside the Student Center until I have all the facts."

"But the security guard already confirmed that there is a body," Mike continued.

"Well," I said, "That's great, you can quote the security guard, then. I'm waiting for all of the facts before I speculate."

"Students are just upset," Josh Taylor interjected, "they don't feel safe."

"Why do you think that is?" I asked, "we actually have very little crime that occurs on campus."

"What about the missing student a couple months ago?" Mike began again. This kid was a barracuda for sure. Although I couldn't breach any confidentiality, the "missing" student was alive and well and back on-campus-- everyone knew that. She was also the former roommate of Sarah Borden, who shifted uncomfortably in her chair. "Mike, I'm sure that you know that the 'missing' student to whom you're referring is back on campus and safe."

"But she was abducted, can you verify that?"

"I'm not verifying anything," I said, not feeding into Mike's jabbing, "What I will verify is that we have a safe campus and we have the statistics to prove it. You can see them for yourselves, they're right on our website. We have an ethical responsibility, and are required by law, to share those data freely. This doesn't, however, mean that we don't need to be careful and use common sense

around here.  Students should lock their doors, not
walk alone at night, things like that.  Now, if you
have legitimate concerns that we can discuss, let's
discuss them, if you want to continue to chase
rumors, I'm not willing to do that.  In fact, perhaps
the best thing that SAFE can do is begin to squelch
gossip."  The silence in the room was almost
deafening.

"So," I began again, "What can I do to
support SAFE?  When you are an official student
organization, you should select one of your members
to be on the College wide Safety and Security
committee.  Just give the name to me, and we'll
invite them to the meetings.  That seems like the best
way to help us help students.  What else?"  They
continued to stare like zombies.  Even Mike Gordon
had nothing to offer.

"Anything else?" I asked.  Each of them
shook their heads, Mike finally spoke, "No, uh, I
think that's about it."

"Okay, then" I said, "just get me that name
and I'll see you soon."

I stood up and the foursome followed like
little dejected ducklings out the door.  This was
always one of the difficult parts of working with
college students.  It was often difficult to get them to
understand that disagreement, or differing
viewpoints, didn't necessarily mean rejection.  In
this case, it simply meant that we needed to work
harder to find common ground.  Although I wasn't
sure about the motives of SAFE, brand new student
organizations cropped up all the time, often after a

3AM, post-bar chat.  I really did want to help them, that was my job.

The rest of the afternoon I read and responded to all of my e-mail, wrote a memo or two, and called it a day.  Even though I had arrived late, 4am was catching up with me and I was tired. Before I left, I called the hospital to check on Jeffrey Jordan's condition and found that he was still listed as "serious."  I walked out of the Student Center and past Dr. Faust and his crony still picking away at the skeleton, which I was surprised to see was becoming clearly evident now.  There were a number of students standing-by, watching, sipping sodas, and totally mesmerized.

The bones of one full arm were now fully visible, parts loosely covered by moldy, black material which certainly looked to be an old robe.  I stopped and found myself staring, too.  Even headless, I could see one of the skeleton's ribs jabbing the earth out of protest.  The hand of the exposed arm, palm up, seemed fully intact, craggy fingers curled as if in pain.  The grey, pock-marked bones screamed with age, embarrassment, and humiliation.  Looking on, I truly realized that we weren't dealing with a carnival sideshow, but the death of a human being.  The novelty of finding a skull in my lap was wearing-off.  We had another murder on our hands.

Since I was disturbed by the sight, I knew that having the scene visible to the entire campus could lead to disastrous results, mostly more rumors.

I approached the site, ducked under the yellow crime tape and got Dr. Faust's attention, "Excuse me, Professor?" He ignored me at first, lost in his work, until his buddy nudged him to acknowledge my presence. He didn't say a word to me, simply looked up as if he had never seen me before. "Hi," I said, "I'm Dean Doug, we met earlier this afternoon?"

"Yeah, yeah," he said impatiently and gave me a look prompting me to continue quickly. "Would you have any objections to us concealing this area? I want to avoid unnecessary attention and get you out of the spotlight." I looked to the students who were watching a few yards behind me.

"Uh, no, no. It doesn't matter to me. Just as long as it doesn't harm the site."

"Well, I'm going to call Facilities Management now and see what they can come up with. You'll be here to make sure that they create a barrier that doesn't affect the site." Dr. Faust nodded, and turned back to his work. I walked away, past the onlookers, and called Sam on her cell phone.

"Are you still here or on your way home?" I asked.

"I'm still here, why what's up?"

"We need to barricade the site of the skeleton somehow, it's becoming pretty clear what's buried there, and I don't want hundreds of students getting freaked out."

"What kind of barricade?"

"I don't know, I'll leave that up to you, you're the fixer-upper facilities people. It doesn't have to be substantial, just something to block the view around the area. Old room dividers might work, hell, a curtain might work."

"Okay," she responded, "I'll go take a look and we'll do it tonight."

"Yes," I joked, "it's the least you can do, your mutt's the one who got us into this in the first place!" Sam laughed begrudgingly and hung-up. I approached Al the security guard informed him that Facilities would be coming by to build some sort of screen, and then headed home.

~~~~~

From the moment that I stepped into my house, I was comforted in my family routine. Barbara had prepared an excellent Chicken Cattiatore which Ethan and I gobbled-up with gusto. We all took an evening stroll to the beach, letting Ethan run out some of his five-year-old energy before bed. Back at home, Ethan and I jumped into the tub for a water fight and some baby shampoo Mohawks. Stories and kisses goodnight followed, and then it was time for Barbara and I to spend our last hour of consciousness together as a couple.

Just as I was settling into my favorite chair next to Barbara and a glass of Shiraz, I remembered Ivory. I had forgotten to call her. Although the thought crossed my mind to attempt a call at that moment, I figured that by 9:15pm she'd be on the stage dancing. I surmised that it probably wasn't easy to talk on the phone while mounted to a pole.

'Hell,' I thought, 'I'll just see her tomorrow night.'
That was an error that still haunts me.

-8-

I got up at 5:45am, slithered out of bed so as
not to disturb Barbara, brushed my teeth full-monty
and walked down the stairs to get dressed for my
first run in many weeks.  I felt like a little boy
getting ready for my first day back at school.  Even
though I'm not a great runner, or even a good runner,
it's the running that counts.  If I can, I try to push out
a mile or two and then consider myself exercised for
the day.  I keep my running clothes, usually dirty and
sweaty, in our downstairs guest room so that I don't
wake Barbara at quarter to six with either getting
dressed or the stench.  As I grabbed my clothes that
day, I discovered that it was a banner day—Barbara
had washed my gear and they were waiting for me
clean and ready.  What a partner.

I walked out the front door, hid my key in my
usual key-hiding-place and stretched my way to the
boards.  The air was chilly and I was glad that I had
grabbed a sweatshirt.  I inhaled the morning air,
relishing its salty sweetness.  As I made my way to
the boardwalk, I took in all of the sights along the
way: Mrs. Hollister's yellow mums lining her
walkway; the climbing red roses on the yellow house
nearby that looked as if they needed a sweater; and
the pumpkins sitting in between the rockers at the
Misty Dorm by the Sea Bed and Breakfast.  I
reached the boardwalk and found it deserted, only a
couple errant seagulls resting on the railings eyeing
my intrusion.  I hadn't realized how much I missed

this morning ritual—not only the exercise, but the bonding with my little town of Ocean Grove.

I took a deep breath and set out south toward Bradley Beach.  That's one of the many neat things about the boardwalk on the Jersey shore,  it often continues from town to town with little regard.  One minute you're in Avon-by-the-Sea, the next you're in Belmar and on into Spring Lake.  It's a great way to travel.

Even though I was ecstatic to be running again, my ankle didn't seem to share my exuberance.  About five-minutes in, it started a dull ache that quickly turned into a nagging pain.  I continued, nonetheless, for another five minutes trying to work through the pain, then quickly decided to walk instead.  Since I wasn't training for the New York City Marathon, there was no need to suffer.  I walked as briskly as my ankle would allow for a few more minutes and then turned back toward the Grove.  Just as I was crossing "the border" into the village of Ocean Grove, I immediately knew that I was back in my hometown when I saw Cruzer, our resident vagrant.

He was walking up from the boardwalk, pushing his wheelbarrow as usual.  A strapping man of over six feet, Cruzer traverses Ocean Grove on a daily basis, always pushing a wheelbarrow full of junk and treasures, usually wearing work boots and a gown of some sort.  This morning, he had chosen an ensemble that included a peach ball gown (cut off at the knee to expose his hairy legs), a plaid work shirt (because it was chilly), and some pretty white gloves (just because, I suppose).  I wasn't about to tell him that white anything after Labor Day is considered gauche.  Cruzer lives in an apartment under the Unitarian Church and performs odd jobs around town for Malificent and others in lieu of rent.  He is truly a fixture of our community.

I waved to him, and he nodded in return since it's impossible to wave and push a wheelbarrow at the same time.  He continued on his merry way, not giving me a second glance.  Jilted, I turned to look at the ocean before heading home.  The grey water beat the shore with blasts of white surf and reminded me of newly shoveled snow.  The ocean was beginning to take on the dark, aloof tone of winter, even though it was only October.  I stretched-out my ankle, which was beginning to feel better, and with a sigh that lamented the passing of the long days of summer, I walked slowly home.

It was nearly 7:00am when I walked in my front door and I could hear Barbara and Ethan upstairs preparing for another busy day of Kindergarten.  I went up, gave kisses all around, and hopped in the shower.  Afterward, I stood at my closet contemplating my day, which usually dictates what I wear.  No meetings that I could remember meant khakis, shirt (no tie) and blazer.  Perfect.  Just what I was in the mood for.  As I grabbed my loafers, I suddenly remembered that I was going to see Ivory later that night.  What does one wear to a strip club?  Loose pants for easy access, or tight pants to hold everything in place and avoid awkward moments?  I'd have to ask Jerry.

I ran downstairs, and found that Barbara was making pancakes for Ethan, and I hoped, me as well. "Mmmm," I mumbled, "pancakes."

"They're almost ready." Barbara said, armed with a pancake turner the size of a small plate.  As I sat next to Ethan, he asked, "Daddy, did you run today?"

"Yes, as a matter of fact, I did."

"You haven't run in a long time, right?"

"Right.  Today was my first in a while."

"How'd it go?" he said, nonchalantly grabbing the funnies from the morning paper.

"Um, it went ok," I answered, chuckling at the question.  "My ankle started to hurt a little, so I cut it short… but I'm sure it'll get better and better."

"Can I run with you someday?"

"Sure, you let me know when you're ready," I said, never sure when a five-year-old's whim might strike.

"Tomorrow?" he asked, looking up at me.

"Well, I'm not sure if I'm gonna run tomorrow, how about this weekend so you don't have to get up so early?" I asked.  Ethan mulled this over for a bit, moving pancakes around in his mouth as if they were fine wine.  After a great deal of consideration, he gave me a, "sure," and went about his business.

I ate my pancakes, took my dishes to the dishwasher, and kissed Ethan and Barbara goodbye.

"Remember," I said to Barbara, "I've got Smoke tonight."

"When are you going?"

"I'm not sure, I have to ask Jerry, my consultant."

"Well I can't wait to hear all about it," she winked and gave me another kiss on the cheek.

On my walk to work, my ankle didn't give me any trouble at all. 'Figures,' I thought. I entered campus and walked past the crime scene on my way to my office, only to find that the area had been concealed with large sheets of plywood. There must have been seven or eight sheets, nailed onto two by fours. Stenciled on each sheet, were the words, "DANGER: KEEP OUT." Just what I wanted-- inconspicuous. I nodded to the security guard as I passed and peeked inside to see if Dr. Faust had begun digging for the day; he hadn't.

I went inside the Student Center and made my way up the stairs only to find Miss Bettie waiting for me, hands on her hips, shaking her head. "*What* did they do?" she asked.

"What are you talking about?"

"That," she pointed out the window to the plywood shanty town. "It looks worse now than it ever did."

"Well, it's really my fault, I asked them to put up a screen to hide the area. I have to admit, that's not exactly what I was expecting."

"It looks like an outhouse, if you ask me," she laughed. "A *toxic* outhouse that you're not supposed to use."

"It really looks that bad, huh?" I asked, confirming my own opinion.

"Bad?" she said with a roll of her eyes. "More people are gonna notice it now,  wanting to know what the 'DANGER' is.  You know these kids!"

She was right.  My attempt to hide the skeleton had made it worse.  I had essentially put our skeleton in a proverbial closet with a neon sign hanging on it.  I shook my head, looking out the plate-glass window alongside Miss Bettie in disgust. "A toxic outhouse, huh?" I asked.  Miss Bettie only shook her head, "And you asked them to do *that*?"

"Well, not *that*," I said defensively.  "I just asked them to hide the area somehow.  I never said anything about a 'DANGER:  KEEP OUT' sign."

"Doug," Miss Bettie said, gearing up for a lecture, "you know that those people in facilities don't know *shit*."  Present company excluded, I assumed.  She continued, "They don't have the sense to know that it's sensitive, and they don't know how these kids think.  They might as well have painted, "FREE DRINKS" on those boards.  It would draw the same amount of attention."

Utterly dejected, I left Miss Bettie and walked into my office, only to be met by my next worst critic, Judy.  "Did you see what they did?" she asked.  "Who told them to build a shed?"

"I did." I answered, which caused Judy to look at me over her half-glasses.  "You told them to build a shed?"

"No, I told them to conceal the area."

"Hrumph," she responded, "they concealed it alright.  All they have to do now is put spotlights out they-uh and it will look like they're selling Christmas trees."

"I better give Sam a call."

"I'd like to be a fly on the wall for *that* one."

"You are a fly on the wall every day, Judy," I said. "You know *all* of my business."  Although I said it with a hint of sarcasm, Judy took it as a complement, "that's my job," she said, primping her jet black bouffant.

I walked into my office, put my briefcase on one of the easy chairs, and sat at my desk where Judy had already laid out a stack of morning chores. Memos and purchase orders to sign, the newest copy of the Chronicle of Higher Education , and a couple of voicemail messages were among the pile.  I picked-up the phone and called Sam's direct line, which she didn't pick-up.  Within four rings, Karen, answered, "Facilities Management Vice President's Office, how may I help you?"

"Hi, Karen, it's Doug.  Sam's not in yet?"

"She's on her way, can I help you with something?"

"Do you want to buy a Christmas tree?" I joked-- a funny that was clearly lost on Karen. "Excuse me?" she responded.

"Never mind," I said.  "Can you just have her give me a call?"

"And the message?"

I thought for a moment as Jerry stepped into my office and I waved him in.  "Ask her if *she* wants to buy a Christmas tree."  Karen paused, and hung up, obviously annoyed.


"So, is tonight the big night, boss?"  Jerry asked, practically drooling.

"Remember, it's business."

"Oh, yes, it always is for me at Smoke. *Strictly* business."

"When should we go?"

"What time did your 'friend' ask you to be there?"

"I think by 9:00pm."

"9:00pm?  They still have most of their clothes on then!"

"I think that's the point, so Ivory doesn't have to talk to me in the buff.  Could be awkward."

"Well, can we stay later once you talk to her?" Jerry asked with the innocence of a child going to an amusement park.  I thought for a moment, and then figured that it was the least I could do.  "Sure," I said, "but not too late, remember it's a school night."

"Don't worry, I'll have you home by midnight, Cinderella."

"Thanks," I said, "but I have one more question… what do I wear?"  Jerry looked at me like I was crazy, "You're kidding, right?"  The sad part was that I wasn't. Was I supposed to go dressed-up or low-rent? How was I to know the dress code of a strip club. "No, it's a legitimate question," I responded.

"Anything goes, brother. I usually go with jeans. Not like the guys who get all pimped out or the ones who wear sweats." Although I had pondered the same question, sweatpants seemed a little too casual to me, even for a club-for-ill-repute, "Sweats, huh?" I asked.

"Yeah," Jerry said, "You know, for easy access." As I suspected. "Okay," I said, "I'll figure it out, but I think I'll leave my sweats at home. I'd rather not give anyone access to anything."

"Suit yourself," Jerry said. "So, I'll pick you up at quarter to nine."

"You'll drive?"

"Of course, there's no way that I'm stuffing myself into your Mini and your only other alternative is Barbara's minivan. You don't see too many of those parked outside of Smoke." Just then, my phone rang. "Hello?"

"Doug, it's Sam. What's this about Christmas trees?" I chuckled to myself and then said, "Yeah, do you want to buy one? I know a great place."

"What are you talking about? It's October?" Sam was not finding any humor at all. "Sam," I said, "I appreciate the effort, but I hate to break it to you, the barricade that your guys made…"

"Yeah, it looks great, doesn't it? They did a great job."

Crap.  She actually liked it.  "It looks great, don't you think, Doug?"

"Well," I muttered, "actually, Sam, it looks like a shed."

"What do you mean a shed?  You asked for a screen and that's what we gave you!"  She sounded much more hurt than angry, which made me feel worse.  "I know, I know, you did exactly what I asked, but I didn't expect it to be so…"

"What?"

"So…"

"So, what?"

"Shed-like."  I finally said with wisdom clearly pouring out of my every orifice, "I think it brings more attention to the area instead of concealing it."

"Fuck," Sam mumbled under her breath.  "So you need us to take it down?  Is that what you're saying?"

"Maybe," I tried to sooth.  "It might just be the *DANGER* stencil."  I was backtracking.

"Shit," Sam responded, "that was my idea."

Damn.  Sam with hurt feelings was not pretty.  I had to backpedal some more.  "Let me talk to Dr. Faust," I responded, "to see how much longer he's going to be.  Maybe we'll just leave it if he's going to be done soon."

"Alright," Sam said dejectedly.

"Sam, I'm sorry.  You did exactly as I asked, and I appreciate that.  It's just not exactly how I expected it.  I should have explained it more clearly." I took the responsibility, which was only right, and we got off the phone; while I was thinking about it, I looked-up Dr. Faust's on-campus number and dialed. His secretary said that he was in the field, which I took to mean outside the Student Center. I got up and went down the stairs to see if I could find him, passing Miss Bettie along the way. She was still standing at the window shaking her head.

As I got outside and approached the shed, I heard mumbling. As I leaned in closer to the structure, I could hear Dr. Faust inside saying things like, "That's a good boy… yup, just like that." And, "Nope, nope… just a little bit more to the left… almost there, almost there…" His voice was breathy, and I almost didn't want to invade on such a private moment. Not knowing how to announce myself, I knocked lightly on the shed wall. I heard a brief rustle, and then Dr. Faust's shaggy head popped out from behind the plywood, exposing nothing below the neck. I hoped to God that he had his clothes on.

"Yes?" he said, still giving me the deadpan stare of a stranger.

"Dr. Faust, I'm sorry to bother you, do you have a moment?"

"Well," he said glancing behind him, "I'm in the middle of something."

"I know, but I came to see how much longer you'll need this barricade?"

"The what?"

"This!" I said, tapping on the shed.  I felt as though I was talking with the wizard from the Wizard of Oz who kept disappearing behind a curtain.

"Oh, well, I'm nearly done, here, I'm just finishing up, actually," he was decidedly distracted, as if he was being tugged from behind.  As he looked over his shoulder one more time, he said, "Oh come in, come in."  And his head disappeared from the shed.

Although invited, and even curious, I wasn't sure that I wanted to see what was hidden in "the shed."  I already had intimate knowledge of this person's skull, and frankly, I wasn't impressed.

I squeezed behind the barricade and found Dr. Faust already hovering over the body's remains which were now fully exposed,  and I was shocked at the sight.  Although I expected to see a fully intact skeleton lying in the dirt, what I saw instead was a few piles of bones scattered around the hole.  Interspersed among the heaps, were a few bones that appeared to be in natural order-- the hand and forearm that I saw before; a few ribs in succession; the majority of a leg.  Conspicuously missing, was the cranium that had landed in my lap.

"A little freakin' freaky, huh?" asked Dr. Faust.

"The whole skeleton thing?" I asked.

"Yeah.  I remember being fascinated the first time I saw a dead body.  Utterly fascinated.  I was ten. It was at my aunt's wake." Dr. Faust's voice was brimming with excitement and I realized that this was the most engaged I had ever heard him. He continued, "my mother kept having to shoo me away from the casket because I couldn't keep my hands off the body."

I must have shot him a subconscious disapproving look, because he snapped out of his dreamlike state briefly to acknowledge my presence. "No," he chuckled, "it wasn't like that. I didn't even know my aunt all that well. It was simply the fact that I was seeing a lifeless human. A vessel, really, who had stopped all life functions, except for farting of course, which is involuntary even after death. I kept wanting to touch her hand. Something about the cool, lifelessness captivated me. I wanted to know how she died, the scientific reasons for death, not simply the explanation of 'heart attack.' That wasn't enough for me, I wanted to *see* it. I wanted to *see* the causes of death."

I wasn't sure what prompted this purging of Dr. Faust's soul, but I was enjoying getting to know his human side a little more. "Even at such a young age," I asked, "you were interested in the causes of death?"

"Yes, yes," Dr. Faust said pensively. "I was."

"Why didn't you become a medical doctor?"

"Because I wasn't interested in saving lives," he laughed. "Only with figuring out the science of death." He looked at me over his half-glasses, "sick bastard, I know."

"Any idea about the cause of *this* death?" I asked, pointing to the remains.

"I haven't looked thoroughly, and I won't know for sure until I do some tests, but from the look of the skull in my lab, I would say blunt force trauma is a good place to begin.  It looks like this old boy took a pretty good whollop."

"So, he was hit over the head?"

"Or he fell and hit his head… but if that was the case, I don't see any evidence of it happening here."

"Are you suggesting that he was killed somewhere else and then buried here?" I asked.

Dr. Faust cocked his head and smiled, "Well, you can't murder then bury yourself, now, can you?"

-9-

I left the crime scene and headed back up to my office. Judy greeted me, waving a pink phone message, "Mr. Jordan called, he said to call him on his cell. How's the shed?"

"The shed's fine. I think they're going to need it for a little while longer." I intended to ask Judy whether Mr. Jordan gave any indication about Jeffrey's condition, but she cut me off.

"Did you see it?" Judy asked, nearly panting.

"What?" I asked, merely playing with her.

"The body!" she said, hands resting fully on her hips.

"Yes."

"And?" she demanded intently.

"Ghastly. Simply ghastly," I said, trying to think of a word that would provoke Judy's imagination even more, if that was possible.  As I walked away, Judy's hand was already dialing one of her on-campus cronies to fill them in.


I sat at my desk and immediately dialed Mr. Jordan who picked up on the second ring.  "Mr. Jordan?  This is Dean Doug."

"Oh, Dean, thanks for calling me back, I wanted to give you an update on Jeffrey."

"Any change?"

"Well, he woke up this morning, thank God."

"Oh that's great news!" I said, feeling a surge of excitement.

"Yes, it is.  The doctors are doing more tests, but preliminary results show that he is going to be fine."

"I'm so relieved.  Thanks for letting me know."

"Sure, but there's one more thing that I wanted to tell you.  It's about the drugs."  I wasn't sure what Mr. Jordan was going to tell me, but he certainly had my interest, "Drugs?"  I asked.

"Yes, from the lab report.  The drug that was found in Jeffrey's system was Oxycodone, a prescription drug."

"Did you know that Jeffrey was on a prescription drug?"

"No, that's what I wanted to tell you.  He wasn't.  The doctor said that this is a drug used for recreation these days.  Jeffrey's not in a position to talk about it right now, but when he's a little stronger, he's got a lot of questions to answer."

"Well, I hate to add to his list of interrogators, but before he returns to campus, Jeffrey will have to speak with someone on my staff, too. If this was drug related, he'll be facing some on-campus disciplinary charges, but we don't have to focus on that just yet"

"Where would he get those kind of drugs?" Mr. Jordan asked vacantly, not looking for an answer from me.

"Why don't you give me another call when Jeffrey's released, okay?" I responded and we hung-up. Although I was disturbed about the drug information, I was relieved that Jeffrey was going to be fine. On some level, I was also relieved that the drugs involved weren't street-drugs. Even though I knew intellectually that any drug can be used for recreational purposes, something about stealing a prescription bottle out of your parents' medicine cabinet seemed better to me than a drug deal on a street corner. I knew that I was being naïve and for the moment, I was going to go with it for the remainder of my day. Maybe I would even have a drink at Smoke to celebrate.

~~~~~

It was twenty to nine, and I waited on my porch for Jerry to pick me up for our adventure to Smoke. The air was crisp and laced with the sweet scent of wood smoke. Ethan was in bed, Barbara was in her home office banging away on a new magazine article, and I wished for nothing more than to stay at home with a nice glass of merlot. Although I was never considered to be a party animal, as I got older, I was becoming much more of an introvert. I imagined that an introvert in a strip club was like a vegetarian at a pig roast, just a tad out of place.

I sat in one of the white wooden rocking chairs on our porch, and without much effort, my mind drifted to the skulls. Before I left the office earlier in the day, Dr. Faust called me to say that he would be a day or two more outside the Student Center. I decided that I wasn't going to worry about the conspicuous nature of the shed, and save Sam some distress by leaving well enough alone. I was throwing caution to the wind-- I'm crazy like that.

As I rocked, like any good type-A personality should during a relaxing moment, my mind shifted to the task before me: Smoke. I reminded myself that I was actually supposed to visit Ivory the night before, and hoped that she was working again. If not, I would have to make *another* trip. Jerry would be thrilled. Why hadn't I taken two seconds to call her and confirm?

I wondered what information she had for me. She must have worked with Darcy Green, did she know more about *her* death? Why would she tell me and not the police? Did my jeans look too new? Did I have any singles in my wallet? I guessed that I would find answers to these questions during my dance with Ivory. Was it going to be a *lap* dance?

As my mind raced with a flurry of insightful and ridiculous questions, Jerry pulled-up in his Cadillac.  He was the only person I knew under sixty who drove a Caddie—in fact, he was the only person I knew who had one, period.  He attributed his affinity for the luxury vehicle to his growing-up in the family business:  A funeral home on Staten Island.  His summer job had always been transporting clients and families from their homes, to the funeral home, then to the cemetery and back again.  Jerry once told me, "You can't fit a family of six in a Toyota."  Given Jerry's 6'5" frame, I supposed it wasn't very easy to stuff one of those in a Toyota either.

I walked to meet him as he pulled to a stop.  Jerry rolled down his window, and a puff of cigar smoke wafted out, "Hop in, boss!"  I got in and said, "Doesn't that smoke ruin your interior?"

"All leather, brother, all leather.  Just wipe it clean."  He took another puff and shot me a devious grin, "Want one?"

"No, thanks.  I'd prefer that my heart attack come from fried food, not smoking."  We laughed and chatted about nothing during the short drive to Smoke.  Jerry discussed the latest blonde that he was courting, as well as the previous blonde that, "just wanted too much" from him.  Equally as provocative, I discussed the latest Cabernet/Shiraz that I wanted to try, as well as the next project on my homeowner to do list (which included re-grouting the upstairs bathroom and fixing a running toilet).

At times like this, our ten-year age difference was painfully evident, at least to me.

In under ten minutes, we were a world away from my porch and white picket fence, and standing in an expansive parking lot littered with beer cans. Straight ahead of us was Smoke. It was once a beachfront hotel, but fell into disrepair after the race riots in Asbury Park in the sixties and seventies. Like many places in Asbury, developers were beginning to buy cheap real estate and turn them into million dollar homes and businesses.

Although Smoke resembled a Days Inn, there were some distinct differences. For one, the awning that covered the front entrance was hot pink. For another, there was a hot pink neon silhouette of a shapely, ten foot woman, fixed above the awning. At regular intervals, the hot pink outline of her hand clutching a cigarette in a long holder, moved in jerky motions toward her mouth. After each "puff," quick bursts of smoke emanated from the area above her head. How clever. Magic like you might find at a seedy Disney world.

The area surrounding the parking lot was dim and sprinkled with uncertainty. Boarded-up hotels and motels not yet gobbled-up by developers were uncharacteristically juxtaposed with the beachfront only steps away. One long-closed storefront, missing a roof, boasted a sign above the door, "Cold Drinks! Ice! Best Pizza in Town!" Amidst the tattered landscape that resembled Baghdad more than a seaside resort were a couple of conclaves of people who I assumed to be hookers and dealers. Once a vacation wonderland, the scenery showed how sadly Asbury Park had fallen.

"What's the matter, boss?" Jerry asked, clearly sensing my discomfort. "It's hard to believe that this is ten minutes from my house," I said.

"What're you talking about? Asbury's on the comeback! In a couple years this place is going to make your house worth a mint!"

"I've been hearing that for years. It looks to me like there's still a lot of work to do."

"Sure, but it's coming back, believe me. New businesses are coming in, and people are coming back. We're here, right?" I didn't want to mention that the purpose for our visit to Asbury Park was to see women in stilettos hump a pole, not urban renewal. "Ready to see your friend?" Jerry asked, patting me on the back.

"Let's go," I said, walking toward the entrance.

"You seem nervous?" Jerry asked curiously. "C'mon, boss, let's have fun."

"You have all the fun you want," I said, "I'm here to see what Ivory has to say about Darcy Green."

"Buzz kill," Jerry said with a smirk, and I smiled a little.

We approached the entrance to Smoke, walking on a well-maintained pink carpet under the pink awning. Although I expected to be greeted by a beefy guy named Dirk, I was surprised to be welcomed by two very attractive women in Tuxedo shirts and black miniskirts. "See, brother? This is a classy place," Jerry offered.

"Welcome to Smoke," the women both sung in unison, and then one said, "IDs, please." Jerry eagerly pulled out his wallet, I hesitated, which prompted one of the greeters to say, "Sir, we card everyone who looks under 35." Was she trying to charm me? Maybe this was a classy place after all.

I handed over my license and the greeter looked at it closely, "I would have never guessed," she said demurely while sticking out her breasts in my direction, "Enjoy your Smoke, Mr. Carter." Since we had just met, it seemed awkward to correct her that actually it was Dr. Carter-Connors. I didn't want to ruin the moment, I had already been accused of being a buzz-kill once.

"Thank you," I said, and the greeters opened two oversized frosted doors for us and we walked in.

I thought that we would walk into the bar and dancing area, but I was wrong. Our next step toward "the ladies" was another room that resembled a coat check area. In fact, there was an area for coats, staffed by another tuxedo-clad vixen, and this time, a very large man who I suspected was named Dirk. "Welcome, guys," Dirk said to us as Tuxedo-girl smiled cutely. "Step right this way. Do you have any controlled substances or weapons on your persons?"

"No," Jerry said, and I shook my head following his lead.

"Fantastic," Dirk said, getting up from the stool he was sitting on. "Please remove any items from your pockets," Dirk held out a yellow plastic bin, and before I knew it, Jerry had raised his arms out from his body, and Dirk was patting him down. Within seconds, Dirk was all over me, too.

I was startled when he paused at my right cheek—not the one on my face. "What do you have in your back pocket, sir?" Dirk asked in a serious tone. "I need you to remove all items from your pockets." I curiously reached around, and realized that I had put a corkscrew in my pocket earlier in the evening after opening my bottle of wine, and forgot about it. "Oh, I'm sorry," I said, pulling the corkscrew out of my pocket, "I didn't realize that I had this."

"Didn't I ask you to remove all weapons?" Dirk asked sternly.

"Yes, you did." I said, deciding not to argue that in my casual circles, a corkscrew was a coveted tool, not a weapon. "I'm sorry, I forgot I had it. I don't usually carry a corkscrew with me." Dirk looked at me suspiciously, took the corkscrew from my hand, and continued to pat my legs, paying particular attention to the area around my socks. Finally, he stood, "Thanks. That will be ten dollars each." So now I was being charged for this harassment? Again, I decided not to complain and handed Dirk a twenty. "Enjoy your Smoke." Dirk said, and directed us to a ramp down a hallway.

As we walked away, Jerry said, "Nice job, troublemaker."

"You didn't tell me that we were going to be molested!"

"It wouldn't have been a problem if you weren't concealing a weapon," Jerry laughed.

"It was worse than airport security."

"There have been some problems with people getting loaded and then getting into fights; this is just a precaution to keep everyone safe."

"I'm not getting my corkscrew back, am I?" I asked.

"I doubt it," Jerry responded, "I hope you have a spare."

"Many." I said, and we walked down the hallway into the bowels of Smoke.

~~~~~

The hallway led to an expansive room that had the feel of an old seventies discotheque with hints of speakeasy. Closest to us was a black lacquer horseshoe shaped bar, fit with pink-vinyl cushioned barstools. On the opposite side of the room was a stage joined to a ten-foot catwalk. As I suspected, there were two gold poles on the stage and one on the very end of the catwalk. On the main sections of the floor sat black tables for small groups of two to four, and high-backed pink booths for larger groups of six to eight lined the outer walls. The room had a misty feel, with "smoke" emanating from various corners of the room at regular intervals.

At that moment the stage was empty, and jazz music was playing while the audience, mostly men, laughed and drank. It wasn't nearly as seedy as I had anticipated, in fact, despite the hot pink textures and the stripper poles, it almost had a classy feel. Although I was expecting a dingy warehouse with sticky floors and horny men, I found a softly lit, warm nightclub—probably still filled with horny men. As I continued to survey the room, something brushed-up against my back and I heard, "Drinks, boys?" The scent of jasmine invaded my nostrils. I turned around and got a face full of blonde, curly hair. A very attractive woman, wearing a slinky white evening gown was standing so close that it felt as if we were dancing. I immediately saw what was poking me in the back. They weren't real, but they *were* nice.

"Jerry, do you want a drink?" I asked, always the gentleman and answering the nice lady's question. "We're gonna sit at the bar," Jerry replied over me. She smiled and walked away. "What are you doing?" Jerry asked.

"What?"

"If *she* gets you a drink, they cost double… plus the cost of one for her."

"Oh," I said a little disappointed, "I thought maybe she just thought I was cute."

"Maybe she did, but unless you wanted to drop forty bucks right here, we better head to the bar." Jerry led my inexperienced self to two hot pink empty barstools and got the bartender's attention. "What will you have?" Jerry asked me. I figured I would look like too much of a newbie if I asked what their house Cabernet was, so I simply said, "Bud." Jerry gave me a funny look, ordered me a Budweiser and then said, "I'll have a Bay Breeze." As the bartender went about her business, Jerry turned to me and said, "You're drinking Budweiser?"

"You're having a Bay Breeze?" I asked in retaliation.

"Doug, we're in a strip club. No need to be macho," Jerry responded. I considered this, and wondered if it was too late to change my drink order, but before I knew it, a tall bottle of Bud was sitting in front of me. "Need a glass?" the Bartender asked me. I looked at Jerry and smirked, "Yes, please."

Six-dollar Budweiser in hand, I surveyed the room for the first time looking for Ivory. Of course, I quickly realized that I had never met the woman. I would have to ask someone, maybe the bartender, or that nice lady who approached me earlier. Ivory's instructions were to ask for a dance with her, and I intended to follow her directions to the letter. As I continued to look around, the house lights became dimmer, and two spotlights turned our attention to the stage.

"Gentleman and ladies," came a booming game show host voice from nowhere, "Welcome to Smoke! Please turn your attention to the stage and take a long drag on Sissy. She's smokin' hot!" As the audience burst into fits of applause and cat calls, I wondered why I never heard of a stripper named "Maggie", or "Ida". Could a stripper named "Ida" still be "smokin' hot?"

Sissy emerged on-stage through one continuous puff of smoke. She was tall and thin with very large breasts that seemed to sit on her chest like volleyballs. She was dressed like a nurse, a slutty nurse mind you, and her red hair cascaded half-way down the back of her uniform. For the occasion she dispensed with the standard white, thick, hospital shoes and instead chose a pair of six-inch white stilettos. I couldn't really imagine her running down a hospital corridor in a "code blue" medical emergency in those shoes, but hey, this was entertainment.

As "Doctor, Doctor" boomed loudly over the sound system, Sissy playfully listened to her heart with the stethoscope she had hung around her neck. She clearly had trouble finding it because she kept having to touch various parts of her bosom to listen. Although I had never seen any of my doctors listen for my heart beat through my nipple, this is where Sissy paid a great deal of attention. I couldn't help but think, however, that it must be difficult to hear a heartbeat through loud music blaring and eight inches of artificial liquid.

Sissy used the stethoscope to listen to nearly every part of her body, again, a medical practice that I was unfamiliar with. From time to time she went to the edge of the catwalk and tried to listen to some of the patrons' hearts, too-- medical outreach that Mother Theresa would have been proud of. I hoped that if she pulled out the blood-pressure cuff next she would come my way, since I hadn't been diligent about performing my daily readings as I should.

Nurse Sissy danced, listened to heartbeats, and stripped down to only her stilettos and a white thong that had a red cross on the front. I wondered if the Red Cross had approved this type of undergarment, but Sissy *was* a medical professional providing a service. As she collected dollar bills held tightly in her thong, she gyrated to the beat and occasionally spun around on the pole at the end of the cat walk. Was there no limits to Sissy's talents? After a few minutes, the music faded, and so did Sissy, exiting the stage in another burst of smoke, still trying to listen to her heart. Dedication to the very end.

I looked over at Jerry, who had sucked-down his Bay Breeze and ordered a second, "You want another drink?" he asked, still slurping his finished beverage through the tiny straw it came with.

"No, thanks," I said, "remember, we're here on business."

"You're here on business. I'm just your guide."

"Then I think it's time that you guided me to Ivory."

"I told you, I don't know who she is!"

"She said that I should ask for a dance with her. Who do I ask?"

"I don't know, chief, I've never gotten one."

"*You?*"

"I'm a good boy," Jerry smiled.

"Some guide you are," I said with a smirk, "I'm going to ask someone."

I turned to the bar, and caught the bartender just as she was dropping-off Jerry's Bay Breeze, "Excuse me," I said, "but do you know if Ivory's working tonight? I need a dance." The moment it came out of my mouth, I knew how pathetic it sounded-- a middle-aged man *needing* a lap dance.

"Who?" The bartender asked through the din of talking, laughter, and music. "Ivory!" I repeated. She gave me a quizzical look, and said, "Uh, just a minute." She walked over to the opposite end of the bar and consulted with a male counterpart. They whispered a little bit, and then she returned to me, "Um, I'm not sure," she said, "why don't you ask that woman over there." She pointed to my friend who had approached me earlier in the evening about a drink. At that moment, she was sitting down at a booth full of men enjoying a tall beverage.

"She looks busy," I said, "you don't have a schedule of who is dancing tonight? Ivory told me to tell you that I'm an invited guest." She thought a moment, it was obvious that what I had said changed things, and then responded, "Go over there, and someone will meet you." She pointed to a dimly lit doorway in a nearby corner of the room.

As excitement began to build in my stomach, I leaned over to Jerry and said into his ear, "I've got to go over there to meet Ivory." Without flinching, Jerry responded, "Call me if you need me, you know

where I'll be."  He didn't even glance at me since
Nurse Sissy's friend the Police Woman had taken the
stage.  I got up from my barstool and headed over to
the empty corner of the room.

Although I hadn't thought much about it until
that second, I was beginning to get anxious about
what Ivory had to tell me.  I still couldn't figure out
why I was the target of information about Darcy
Green and not the police, but I wasn't going to
argue.  As I stood in the corner, still nursing my first
beer, I began to nervously peel-off the bottle label.  I
was sure that to the other patrons of Smoke, I
probably looked like an inexperienced strip club
virgin waiting for some action in the back room,
which wasn't far from the truth.

I waited for at least ten minutes, but who was
I waiting for?  Finally, my question was answered
when a short, Danny Devito-type, wearing all black
and a great deal of bling approached me.  "I hear
you're lookin' for Ivory?" he said, puffing on a
cigar.  Evidently no one had told him that despite its
name, smoking was not allowed in Smoke.

"Yes," I said, clutching my empty, torn beer
bottle for comfort.  He looked me up and down.
"Why do you want to see her?" he asked, speaking
through his cigar clenched teeth (a very talented
man, indeed).  I felt like I was in the principal's
office, "She told me to say that I was an invited
guest."  With that, his demeanor changed, now I was

getting somewhere. He raised his eyebrows and said, "Oh, she did? When did she say that?"

"Um," I thought, "a couple of days ago. I was supposed to come by last night, but I got held up, so here I am tonight." I was becoming a bit more relaxed, and beginning to speak to the man as if he was a neighbor who I met on the street corner. "What's your name?" he asked, and I hesitated. I hadn't thought about this. Should I give him my real name? Could that get Ivory in trouble? "Doug," I said finally, "My name's Doug."

"Do you have a last name, Doug?" the little man asked, "We've got to know for our records. You know, we like to keep our ladies safe." Just as I started to say, "Cart…" I was interrupted by my friend, the sociable, nice-smelling blonde, "Is this the son-of-a-bitch?" she yelled from half-way across the room. Suddenly, I could see that all eyes were on me. Where was Sissy when I needed her? My friend, who didn't seem so friendly anymore, raced toward me, repeating, "is this the son-of-a-bitch?"

Danny Devito turned to her, his grip loosening on his stogie, "Hey, hey, what's this? Calm down." As my friend got close to me, I felt a sudden surge of pain. Dazed at first, I didn't realize what happened until I found myself holding one side of my face. My friend had slapped it so hard, that she had knocked my glasses off my head. As I crouched on the floor, I felt around for my glasses, feeling like Velma from Scooby-Doo. I could still hear her screaming, "What? A friggin' piece of ass? That's what we are to you? A friggin' piece of ass?"

What was she talking about? I recovered my bent glasses and stood-up, swiftly greeted by blondie in my face. Although I could still smell her scent of jasmine, for some reason, it didn't smell as sweet anymore. "Get out of here, you horny bastard!" she continued to scream. "Just get the hell out of here, now!"

I was pretty sure that blondie didn't think that I was cute anymore. In fact, she was drawing quite a crowd of patrons more interested in us than in the boobies on the stage. Luckily, I saw Jerry push his way through the interested crowd, Bay Breeze in hand, of course. By the time Jerry reached me, Blondie was hitting my chest regularly and shouting, "We're not pieces of ass, you asshole! That's all you think about!" She was sobbing now, and Danny Devito was doing his best to get her off me. As he finally ripped her away from me, doing my best to cower against the wall, her motive became clear as she yelled, "Isn't bad enough that she's dead, asshole? Isn't it bad enough that Ivory's dead?"

As I tried to digest what she was saying, through her raging and hitting, a hand grabbed my shoulder and pulled me in the direction of the exit. Before I knew what I was doing, I was being pushed up the ramp toward the lobby of Smoke; Jerry had finally dropped his drink and rescued me. As we walked out the main doors, I could still hear my friend screaming from below.

The greeters opened the main doors as Jerry led me out and onto the sidewalk. "Sorry, ladies," I vaguely remember Jerry saying, "this one's had a little too much sauce." Dazed, disheveled, and still trying to affix my broken glasses to my face, I surely felt as though I had been on a bender for sure. Jerry put his arm around my shoulder directing me to the car and sat me in the passenger seat. My face still stung from the first slap, and my chest hurt from her repeated punches. I had been beaten-up at Smoke.

Jerry got into the Caddie and turned it on, "Well, that was fun," he said sarcastically. "What happened?" I asked, rubbing my chest.

"You tell me, boss!" Jerry snickered. "I was minding my own business at the bar, you were the one causing a scene."

"I went to the corner like the bartender said, the little Danny Devito guy started asking me questions, and then my friend the blonde attacked me!"

"What'd you ask for, chief?" Jerry asked smiling, "something illegal?"

"I didn't ask for anything!" I said, feeling defensive, "I just asked for Ivory and said that I was an invited guest. That's it. Then she started screaming that Ivory is dead!"

"Well this may help clear things up," Jerry said, pulling a folded piece of paper from his shirt pocket.

"What's this?" I asked, taking it.

"I'm not sure," Jerry said, "but while your friend was beating you up, another girl slipped this into my hand.  I think you were set-up, boss."

-10-

When Jerry dropped me off, it was only 10:30pm, and Barbara was up watching television. "Hey," she said as I walked into the family room, "you're home early?" I hobbled onto the couch in a heap, still holding my chest where I had been repeatedly punched by a girl. Barbara took notice and said, "Honey, what happened? Were you mugged!"

"Naw," I said, "just beaten up at Smoke."

"Beaten up? What! Did you call the police? Who was he?"

"*She* was a striking blonde with big guns."

"You were held up?" Barbara asked excitedly.

"Not those kind of guns," I responded.

As I filled Barbara in on the few details that I knew, I realized that my vision was fuzzy. Was I going to have to go to the emergency room for my injuries? When they asked me what happened, what would I say? That a beautiful blonde woman worked me over? "I'm having trouble focusing on you," I said to Barbara through squinted eyes.

"That's because you're missing one of the lenses in your glasses," she said, "and you have a cut on your face. She must have really slapped you!" At least now I knew the cause of my vision problem. Barbara continued, "Why did she do this to you?"

"Jerry suspects that it has something to do with this," I responded, pulling the note out of my pocket.  Barbara took the note and read it.  She hesitated, "So what do you think it means?"

"I don't know exactly, but Jerry thinks that blondie started the fight as a distraction."

"Because the woman who called you is dead?"

"Ivory.  Yes.  Apparently… that's probably why people were being so weird when I was asking for her.  Jerry thinks that blondie and the woman who handed him the note might have really saved me from something bad.  I just wish she would have done it without hitting so hard."  Barbara touched my wounded face, "Poor baby," she said with only a hint of a smirk on her face, "You should take a bath and then go to bed, it's way past your bedtime anyway."

I agreed and made the trek up the stairs and into the tub.  Before I got into the bath, I looked in the mirror and saw my wounded face.  Even with my compromised eyesight (due to my now broken glasses) Barbara was right, I had a bloody gash (at least ¼ inch in length) where I had been slapped and the whole left side of my face looked swollen.  I would need to put some peroxide on it after my bath to avoid a severe infection.  I checked my chest for bruises, but they hadn't appeared yet.  I was sure that by tomorrow, I would be all black and blue.

I sank into the tub and steered my thoughts away from myself and turned to Ivory.  Poor woman.  I had never even met her.  If only I had made it to Smoke the day before when she asked me-- would

that have saved her?  I then thought about the note.
The cryptic note that had been slipped to Jerry.  He
was right, the fight became too overstated, too
quickly, to be real.  Blondie really *was* my friend,
trying to save me from something.  But what?  Was
Ivory's killer right there at Smoke?  Were they the
same person who killed Darcy Green?  Instead of
washing away my thoughts, the tub encouraged me
to drown in them, soaking into every pore.  I went to
bed thinking about all of these questions and don't
think I stopped until morning when I woke up,
feeling exhausted.

~~~~~

Despite my restless sleep, both my mind and
body welcomed my alarm at 5:30am.  I suppose I
needed a break from obsessing about Darcy Green,
Ivory, and the other women of Smoke.  I got out of
bed and went downstairs to put on my running duds,
which consisted of nylon running pants and a
sweatshirt to match the 40 degree temperature
outside.  I grabbed an old pair of glasses that had
both lenses intact, remembering that I would have to
stop by the Ocean Grove Optical Shoppe on my way
to work.  Before I dressed, I examined my beaten
body, which to my surprise, was only a little bit sore.
Still no bruises on my chest.  Hmmmmmmm.
Maybe blondie didn't hit me as hard as I thought.

I went outside, stretched by leaning on my
picket fence surrounding our house, and set out for

the boards.  The air was refreshing and renewed my
lungs with every step.  Although still dark, I could
see signs of life beginning a new day in Ocean
Grove.  Secretly a voyeur at heart, I enjoy catching
glimpses of people going about their daily lives as I
run by; and that morning was a banner day.

Mr. and Mrs. Strickland had put out their
recycling bins a day early, the yellow containers
sitting idle, overflowing with vodka bottles (perhaps
the reason for the wrong day).  A house on Asbury
Avenue seemed to be experiencing a sprinkler
malfunction, the ground spikes hissing to life as I ran
by, spraying the brown, cold grass with icy water.
And then over on Jersey Avenue, I saw the piece de
resistance, an overweight man standing in his dining
room sipping coffee and reading the morning paper--
buck naked.  I thought that he should really invest in
some drapes, and maybe a good waxing.

Once I reached the boardwalk, there was
much less spectacle; only the boards, the beach, and
the ocean escorting me as I ran.  I let the cries of the
seagulls drown-out my thoughts about Ivory, Smoke,
drugs, and dead bodies.  I ran, pounding the boards
as hard as I could, racing as though someone was
chasing me.  I sprinted for nearly half a mile, turned
around, and raced my way back.  I didn't think of my
ankle or Asbury College; I just ran as hard and as
fast as I could.  I ran until my lungs felt like they had
been sliced with a kitchen knife and been exposed to
the frosty air.

I stopped abruptly and leaned over the boardwalk railing, finally giving in to the fatigue. I could hardly breathe and it felt wonderful. I kneeled and stretched out, gasping for breath but exalted by the thought that I had pushed my body to the limit. As the pain subsided, I stood and stared at the churning ocean. My thoughts again turned toward Smoke and what had happened the night before. Darcy was dead. Ivory was dead. But if the note that had been slipped to Jerry was true, another brave soul was putting herself in danger by trying to tell me something. Someone named Lacey.

The note was to the point:

*DD- See Lacey. Shore Thing Motel, room 104. Don't call police...*
*To dangerous.*

Not exactly an inviting (or grammatically correct) note. Who was Lacey? Given the name, I suspected that she was probably another dancer. But how was I supposed to contact her, just show up at the motel and knock on the door? I figured the motel to be one of the many rundown flop-houses near the beach in Asbury Park, but I'd have to check that out too. The word, "dangerous" was the most alarming, yet obvious, declaration in the note. Two women were dead, and by the looks, there was the potential for more bodies. "Dangerous" might have been an understatement.

The piercing cry of a gull overhead snapped me out of my self-induced daze, and I snapped myself straight. The ocean churned in front of me, repelling me from its frigid and complex temperament. Given the mood, I turned my back to the sea and headed to the more welcoming surroundings of home.

It was 6:45am. Fog hung over the town in sheer ribbons. All was quiet, and the only person I met was Cruzer—that day in a royal blue gown that he had layered over navy sweatpants; he had also donned a fluorescent orange down vest. The sight made me wonder how easy it was to find formal wear in Big and Tall, and where Cruzer got the fashion moxy to mix Bloomingdales with E.M.S. Only he could pull off such a fashion faux pas. I waved to him from across the street, he sullenly lifted one finger off his wheelbarrow in return. Maybe under his ball cap he was having a bad hair day.

I got home and found Barbara sitting at the kitchen table having coffee. I handed her the newspaper that I had found inconspicuously in our shrubs on my way in. "How are your wounds?" she asked, with only a hint of sarcasm.

"I'm still waiting for the bruises to appear. Everything else seems okay."

"Your run was okay, too?"

"Yep… pretty good, given my current condition," I said, finally ready to make fun of myself a little bit.  Barbara smiled, but then turned serious, "So, what are you going to do about Lacey?"

"I don't know.  I'm a little leery to just show up at her motel room."

"Not that you're not a hunk and all," Barbara said with a smile, "but why you?"

"You mean aside from my dashing good looks and obvious sexual prowess, why would a stripper invite me to her motel room?"

"Yes," Barbara said with a wink.  "Why have people been contacting you and not the police?"

"I don't know, maybe I should go and find out."

"Maybe you should call Chief Morreale and give him the heads-up?"

"But the note says not to call the police."

"You've gotten into trouble like this before, Doug," she reminded me again. "Maybe if you had called the Chief last month, you wouldn't have had to climb out of a moving Ferris Wheel to save your own life."  Barbara was being cheeky, but she was serious.  She was also right.  As I've said before, that adventure was no fun.  "You may have a point," I said.  "I'll call him later."

We chatted about nothing for a few more minutes including Barbara's latest idea for an article, the fact that we needed to get our gutters cleaned, the latest tribulations on General Hospital, and then I went upstairs to take a shower.  I inspected my naked body once again for bruises, gashes, and miscellaneous bumps, but still came up empty for the most part.  I guess the scars would mostly be in my memory.  Maybe that was better anyway.

By the time I finished showering and getting dressed, Ethan was up and I joined him for breakfast.  He didn't even notice the wound on my face, which I must admit, had almost disappeared after my shower.  "Hey, buddy," I said, kissing him on the top of his head.  His dirty-blond hair partially hid his eyes as he looked up at me, spoonful of Cheerios in hand, "Hi, Daddy," he said, casually.  "Where were you last night, work?"

"Um, sort of," I lied to my five year old, which seemed far better than explaining that daddy went to a gentleman's club and got beaten-up by a stripper.

"What were you doing?" he asked.  Wow, this kid had a knack for interrogation and I was worried that I might crack.  "Um," I started explaining, grabbing the newspaper from the table, "there was a program last night that I had to go to."

"What kind of program?"  Ethan questioned, milk dripping from his chin.

"Um," I responded, "A program about dancing."  The pressure was on, and I was doing my best to hold it together.

"I like dancing." Ethan replied, taking another bite and then turning his attention to a toy car that was sitting on the table next to him.  I thought that the potential catastrophe of me spilling my guts to my son had been successfully averted, until he stared at me and then asked, "Why are you wearing your old glasses?" I fought the urge to panic, and lied again, "Oh, I dropped them this morning on the boardwalk... while I was running... I ran again this morning... and I dropped them... so I have to get them fixed on my way to work today." This either appeased the child, or bored him to tears. Either way, he again turned to his toy and ended the conversation. Whew.

~~~~~

On my way to the College, I took a detour down Main Avenue and stopped-by the Ocean Grove Optical Shoppe. For years, the plate glass window in the front of the store was known around town for its displays. Sometimes museum-like, other times cutesy, people waited for the exhibit to change with the anticipation of a groupie. That day in particular, the window exposed a graveyard display of famous, bodiless heads wearing a variety of eyeglasses. The heads rested on the window's shelf which was covered in astro-turf and sprinkled with fallen leaves from outside. The illusion offered that the heads were poking from out of their graves, wearing the latest in optical trends.

In back of each head, was a gravestone bearing the name of the deceased. There was Richard Nixon wearing a rimless style, Marilyn Monroe donning playful pink cat eyes, Elvis with black horn-rimmed, Lady Diana sporting dainty gold wire frames, and E.T. showing off a monocle. A dingy white sheet was draped behind the stones as a makeshift banner, and scrawled in red was the caption, "Styles so Great, You'll want to take them *Everywhere*." I'm not sure that the disembodied display highlighted eyeglass frames, but it certainly caught attention. The exhibit proved educational too, since I wasn't aware that monocles were back in vogue, or that E.T.: The Extraterrestrial had passed.

I entered the store and was immediately greeted by resident owner and optometrist/optician, Dr. Harold Farrow. "Good morning, Dean Doug," he offered without hesitation. Dr. Farrow is a good-natured, portly man in his late fifties with a grey handlebar mustache. Whenever I see him, I always think that he should be wearing red and white stripes and singing, "Sweet Adeline" with three of his best friends.

"Hi, Dr. Farrow," I replied, closing the door behind me, prompting the attached bells to jingle wildly.

"To what do I owe this honor?"

"I'm wondering if you can fix these," I said, pulling my broken frames from my sport jacket pocket. The doctor collected the specimen with the care of a professional, "Had a little mishap?" he said, inspecting my frames.

"You could say that," I responded without offering any more.

"Do you have the lens?"

"No…" I stuttered. "I lost it."

"Not a problem," Dr. Farrow said. "Give me a minute, and let me pull your prescription."

"Great, thanks."

"Lots happening at the College, I see."

"Always, always." I responded, used to this common small talk and therefore surprised by his next comment, "So, find any more bodies?"

I stood and looked blankly at him for a moment. Although I shouldn't have been shocked, I wasn't aware that our skeleton had walked out of the closet and into the mainstream of town gossip. I quickly ran through my response choices, and settled on, "It's still early."

Dr. Farrow chuckled, and turned his attention back to my frames and his metal file cabinet. My subsequent silence must have pointed to the fact that I wasn't going to offer any more details, so he started again, "Don't you think it's probably just a prank?" Now he was getting specific, and a bit judgmental; was this a ploy to get me to say more? "Well I guess we'll soon see," I responded, and followed it with, "will you be able to make a new lens? Would you like me to come back later to pick those up?" Without being rude, I wanted him to know that this conversation was not going to happen.

"Oh, Dean... I didn't mean to pry. It's just not every day that you find an entire skeleton in your backyard, or in your case, on-campus. It's a wolf's shame." He looked up at me for acknowledgement, and again, I stood as stone-faced as one of the heads in his window display. Indeed it was a shame, even a wolf's shame, whatever that meant. He turned back to tinkering, and then said, "I'll have to call the lab for a new lens. I'll rush it and it should be here by this evening."

"Great," I said, "I appreciate that."

"It's the least I can do.  Courtesy to the community."

"Thank you," I said, and walked past the dead stares of the graveyard characters and out the door, bells heralding my exit.

On my short two-block walk to campus, I was preoccupied about the gossip on the street; even if those streets weren't exactly "the hood."  Although I was used to town chitchat, I am always amazed by how quickly it travels.   Before I even got to my office, my cell phone rang.  "Where are you?" came Judy's rarely harried voice.

"I'm walking onto campus right now,  I had to make a stop first."

"Have you gotten any calls?"

"No, why?" I asked, wondering what was going on.  Judy rarely seemed flustered.

"Well, I've been here for five minutes, and the phones have been ringing off the hook.  Sam Johnson, Quacky, even R.I.P. who, p.s., called from home.  Word on the street is that they found another one."

"Another one-- what?"

"A skull.  Or a body… I'm not sure which. You better get here fast."

-11-


I entered the DOSO office suite expecting lots of fanfare, but what I got was Judy sitting impatiently at her desk like an expectant mother. She jumped up the second she saw me, "There you are!  Turn right around, I put everyone in the conference room."  She rushed me like a linebacker, turning me on my heels.

"What's going on?"  I asked.

"I'm not sure, but I don't think it's good. Sam, Quacky, R.I.P., and Jerry are all in the Skull and Cross conference room waiting for you.  I had to put them in they-uh, all the others are booked.  The calls started coming in at quarter to 8 this morning."


The Skull and Cross (S & C) conference room was not to be confused with the four other conference rooms located on the second floor of the Student Center.  It was named after a former S & C member who donated a pile of money.  Lavishly decorated with cherry furnishings, heavy burgundy drapes, and vintage photos of Skull and Cross members, the room looked out of place and more familiar to a country club.  Most importantly, the S & C conference room was only used by the members of S & C, by special request, and rarely when no other meeting space was available.  Luckily, my office was in charge of reservations and has a key.

"Of course," Judy continued, "when R.I.P. found out that we were using *his* room, it pushed him off the deep end-- not that it takes much."  Judy pushed me toward the conference room, grabbing my briefcase from my hand as I went. In her haste, she failed to even notice the bloody gash on my face.

When I reached the room, the first thing I noticed was the silence. No morning banter about the previous night's dinners or movies. Nothing. This made me nervous. "Good morning everyone," I said grabbing a seat at the conference table. "What's going on?"

"We found another one," Sam responded flatly, not looking up from the table. "It's not good." She shook her head for emphasis.

"It's hooie!" interjected R.I.P.'s piercing voice, "You're all making a big deal out of nothing! Creating an issue that hasn't been a problem for over fifty years! And *you're* fueling the fire, Connors!"

"What did you find, Sam?" I asked, ignoring the professor.

"My guys found another skull."

"That's not exactly the situation, Dean," interrupted Quacky, whose pin-cushion-like coif was nearly sparkling under the fluorescent lights. "This one seems to be a prank or ritual of some sort. There were students at the scene." Everyone was giving me pieces of the story, all at the same time, and I was trying to hide my frustration. Jerry clearly echoed my sentiments, sitting quietly a few seats away from the group, shaking his head like a displeased Aunt.

"Someone please tell me the full story. From the beginning," I said. "Chief Braggish, why don't you start." Quacky shot a smirk at Sam as if she had just won an award, looked down at a pad that she had in front of her, and began.

"At approximately 0-three hundred hours," she huffed with the vigor of Barney Fife, "Nick Barrows from facilities management, uh, Chief electrical engineer I believe, found three perpetrators allegedly digging a hole near Watson Hall." She looked toward Sam for affirmation, but received only Sam's dissatisfied grimace in return.

"He called out to the three perps, who allegedly had digging instruments including a spade and a shovel, and subsequently they fled on foot. Mr. Barrows approached the scene where the perpetrators fled from, not that he should have mind you, and found what appeared to be a skull half-exposed in the ground. He called the security office immediately. Within the same hour, at approximately 0-three forty, we received a call from the Residence Life Administrator (RLA) on duty, indicating that three students in dark clothing were attempting to gain entry into Greenwich Hall, but were apparently having difficulty with a key. When confronted by the RLA, Jon Phillips, the students indicated that they were just out for a walk. However, RLA Phillips indicated that they are known to be part of the student organization Skull and Cross, and that they were dirty."

"*All* kids these days have foul mouths!" interjected R.I.P.

"No, Dr.," Chief Braggish corrected matter-of-factly. "Not foul, *dirty*. They had dirt on their persons." Obviously R.I.P. hadn't been paying attention and still sat un-phased by the correction.

"So, what's the resolution?" I asked a bit more impatiently than I intended.

"To leave us alone!" R.I.P. slammed his cane on the floor for emphasis, "and to stop harassing us!" The room fell silent, and all eyes looked to me, seemingly handing me a virtual baton that I was happy to accept.

"Who is 'us', Dr. Preston?" I asked, fishing. This ruffled R.I.P. even more, "You *know* who!" he shouted, leaning his lanky body over the table and pointing a boney finger at me. "And having this meeting in *our* conference room? No respect, Connors. No respect!"

"I didn't call this meeting, Dr. Preston, and are you suggesting that Skull and Cross has something to do with all of this?" I asked innocently.

"Traditions are traditions," R.I.P. barked back, "…and none of you have any right to question us!"

"Sir," Quacky jumped in without missing a beat, "as an officer of this College, I need to remind you that we cannot act above the law."

"What laws have been broken? Hiding a few worthless skulls around campus? That's breaking the law?" In his frustration, R.I.P. finally admitted something that I had suspected all along.

"So this *is* a Skull and Cross activity!" Sam practically shouted across the table. R.I.P. looked around wildly, "I didn't say that! I didn't say that! You're putting words in my mouth!"

"Let me tell you, I'm getting sick of this cloak and dagger secret shit," Sam responded with more irreverence than usual.

As the group began to bicker over who said what, and who was disrespecting whom, I began to look around the room. How fitting to be sitting in the Skull and Cross conference room. Whether a fan of the secret elitist society or not, you had to appreciate the history. The rich hunter green walls were covered with photos of the S & C members dating back from what looked to be the early 1900s. However old or new, the composition of the photos was all the same-- five men (until the eighties when women were allowed to join the ranks) standing in a semi-circle in black hooded robes, the middle person holding a skull. No smiles, no apologies for their manner of superiority. Tradition. Tradition, regardless of the appearance or cost to anyone outside of the group.

In my pensive haze, I could still hear piercing outbursts from R.I.P., and the occasional guffaw from Sam, but I continued to stare at the pictures and try to put the puzzle together. Three skulls. Two probably part of an S & C ritual-- one some sort of scavenger hunt, but another connected to a body. That needed to be the focus. I would let Quacky and Jerry deal with the current S & C members who were running around campus digging holes playing "hide the cranium." It occurred to me that if a scavenger hunt was part of a Skull and Cross ritual of some sort, then perhaps they scrambled to get another skull when their original one landed on my desk. That would explain all of the nighttime maneuvers, but not the full skeleton. I needed to work with Dr. Faust and Chief Morreale to find out who was buried at Asbury. I needed to avoid all of the extraneous static around me, to focus, and use the opportunity of all the distractions to my advantage. If everyone else was fired up over nonsense, perhaps I could focus on the real issues, such as who was buried in an on-campus grave? Was it an old member of Skull and Cross? At least initially, old black robe and all, it seemed likely.

　　　　"Admit it, Connors, you're just trying to put a dark cloud over our celebration!"
　　　　"And what celebration would that be?" asked Quacky, perking up with heightened intensity.
　　　　"It's our Annual Alumni Gala!"
　　　　"Whose?"
　　　　"*He* knows!" R.I.P. screamed in my direction.
　　　　"Well the rest of us don't, and this doesn't seem like much of a time to celebrate," responded Quacky with an uncharacteristic bitterness.
　　　　"It's our annual event for Skull and Cross, if you must know. In a few weeks, we'll be hosting our gala dinner right here on campus for all of our current members and alumni. It's a big deal, and *he's* trying to ruin it!" R.I.P. leaned over the table for emphasis again, glaring at me. "So, nothing to say, Connors?" R.I.P. shouted at me again, finally

breaking my concentration.  But given my new
resolve, I didn't respond. I was going to find out who
was buried on campus, and whether Skull and Cross
was involved.   Whether R.I.P. approved or not.
With my newly-found determination, I simply
looked at him and smiled.

~~~~~

Unlike many of my peers, I left the meeting
rejuvenated.  As we filed out of the S&C conference
room, residual bickering still alive and well, I headed
straight for my office.  As usual, I could hear
someone approaching me from behind, vying for my
attention, and was happy to find that it was Jerry.
"So, how're you feeling today, boss?" he said with
only a glimpse of a leer.

"Fine," I responded, "a little sore, but fine."
The smirk faded quickly, and Jerry now looked
troubled, "can we talk for a minute in your office?"

"Sure," I said, "You lead the way."

Jerry walked into my office and plopped
down on the sofa looking at me intently, "I'm
worried."

"What's wrong?" I asked.

"Well, after I stopped laughing about what
happened to you last night, I started to really think
about it.  Doug, what's going on?"

I paused and sat down at my desk.  "Your
guess is as good as mine," I said. "What's bothering
you in particular?"

"Well, it was the whole act. Those women really made a scene, took the time and trouble to write a note... and to get you kicked out of the joint. It was quite a production. Why?"

I sat silent, just listening to Jerry process the previous evening's events. He continued through my silence, "And that note. What do you think about that? Are you going to the motel?" Without waiting for a response, he continued, "If you do, I think I should go with you."

"But it said to come alone."

"No... it said not to involve the police. It didn't say anything about going alone. And after all, the note was given to me," Jerry said.

As I considered this, I realized that I had a lot to think about, and a lot of bodies. I had Darcy Green to think about, as well as the carcass of John Doe out in the azalea patch. Not to mention Ivory; I still had no idea who she was or what happened to her. I had to focus on all of these deaths simultaneously. Jerry interrupted my thoughts, "Doug, what are you thinking?"

I rested my head in my hands and said flatly, "I didn't go to school for murder."

Jerry paused. "Murder? Doug, what're you talking about? The woman from last night?" One of my worst characteristics is that I can never keep my mouth shut about my feelings. Go ahead, play poker with me, you'll win.

"I've got two bodies, Jerry. Three if you count Ivory," I said trying not to whine, "Darcy

Green is number one and our bag of bones downstairs is number two."

Jerry looked surprised, "So you think our friend downstairs was murdered?"

"Do you think he buried himself?"

"Could have been natural causes," Jerry spoke optimistically.

"And then fell into a pre-dug hole?"

"Oh," Jerry uttered, reality setting in.

"And I saw the crack on the skull. Even Dr. Faust commented on it. Someone whacked the guy on the head."

"How do you know it's a guy?"

"I don't… but I just assume. If the person was a member of Skull and Cross, and that seems likely, and the death occurred several years ago, which it appears so, then it must have been a man. Women weren't inducted until the eighties."

"How're you going to figure out who he was?"

"Maybe I'll leave that to Chief Morreale and the FBI."

"Yeah, right," Jerry chuckled. "After last month's 'case of the missing student,' I think this mystery stuff has seeped into your blood. I just don't want you to go it alone… especially after the last time. That's why when you go to the motel, I'm going with you." Jerry had always been protective of me, and I have always valued that in our relationship.

"Fine. Do you want to set a time?"

"No arguments?" Jerry responded, sitting up with interest.

"I'm too tired for arguments, and since I've never done any of this before, I kind of like the idea of having a sidekick. Like Batman… or the Lone Ranger."

"I'd much rather be Tonto than Robin, you ever seen a 6'5" man in tights?" he asked rhetorically, of which I was glad. He continued, "want to go tonight?"

"No," I said without even thinking, "not tonight." I hadn't even checked my calendar, but I felt as though I needed the night to prepare myself. "How about tomorrow? Maybe during the day, like 3 o'clock?" I glanced at my computer screen and consulted my calendar. Surprisingly, I was free after 2pm. Perfect. Jerry pulled out his smart phone and began tapping the buttons, "I can do 4. Does that work?"

"Fine. I'm putting you in." I said, typing "off-campus" in my calendar. Jerry pulled his lanky frame off the couch, "I'll see you later."

"Thanks, Jerry. I appreciate your help. I couldn't have done last night without you."

"No problem, it was fun." Jerry said with a grin and started out the door. As he went, Mr. Jordan popped into my mind. "Oh," I said, stopping him, "Mr. Jordan called. Jeffrey's awake. They think he's going to be fine."

"Really!" Jerry answered excitedly, "that's great news. Did they find out what did him in?"

"Apparently Oxycodone, a prescription drug."

"These days, you don't need a prescription to get the 'OC'."

"The 'OC'?"

"Yeah, that's what it's called... that or "Oxy"."

"How come you always know these things?"

"Because I'm hip." Jerry said, smiling. After a pause, he continued, "It helps to work with twenty RAs, they keep me up on the lingo."

"So what do you mean when you say that you don't need a prescription?"

"Oxycodone is like a street drug, the drug of choice for many, available to anyone who has the cash. Apparently, it's as popular as Ex-- that's ecstasy, big guy."

"You don't have to be hip to know that one."

"Is Jeffrey coming back to campus?"

"Well, I told his father that once he's out of the woods, we'd have to discuss the details on that. Have you gotten an incident report or Campus Security report yet?" Incident reports are completed by Residence Life staff, usually RAs, to document activities of concern. Many times, this means underage drinking, parties, drugs, fights, or similar shenanigans. In extreme cases like this one, resulting in a transport to the hospital, Campus Security would also be called in and would submit an additional report documenting the incident. Both of these reports are used for follow-up, which usually means disciplinary action.

"They are sitting on my desk."

"Well, let's wait to hear more, and then proceed with the conduct process."

"Will do.  See you later."  Jerry said as he walked out the door.  I sat at my desk for a minute, trying to figure out my next move.  Since I already had plans to visit Darcy's friend tomorrow, in the immediate future I would focus on the skeleton, when I wasn't trying to get my regular work done, of course.  I wanted to get a date on the bones, which meant another visit with Dr. Faust.  I also needed to call Chief Morreale to update him on Jeffrey Jordan, and maybe my impending visit to the Shore Thing motel, I hadn't decided yet.


I got up from my desk and bounded out of the office.  "Where are you headed to, fella?" Judy asked.  "You have an eleven o'clocker with Dr. Porter."  Ah yes, and I needed to update the president on all of the happenings as well.

"I'm going to see Dr. Faust, then I'll head straight over to Gwenyth's office," I said, not sounding at all as though I forgot my meeting with my boss, the president.

"Here," Judy said, handing over a stack of folders.  "Things you might need for your meeting.  I included a summary of the body.  Very sketchy."  Judy looked upward to the ceiling longingly.  I'm sure her summary would read like a trashy novel, and I couldn't wait to read it, even though I doubted that it would be something I would share with the president.

"Thank you, Judy.  Very helpful.  I'll see you around lunchtime."  I headed out of DOSO and down the stairs exiting through the back entrance of the Student Center.  There wasn't any activity around the shed, and students were passing without a second glance.  I approached and knocked on the plywood.  After a few seconds with no response, I knocked again.  Maybe Dr. Faust and his staff had left to get coffee?  I stepped my way around the boards until I could peer inside, not expecting what I saw.  In front of me was an empty hole.  The skeleton was gone.

-12-

"What's wrong?" was Judy's worried voice over the phone. I called her immediately to see if she could put me through to Dr. Faust's office. Since I didn't want to spread details, I played it low, "Nothing's wrong, the professor isn't here and I want to speak with him."

"Hold on, I'll look up his number and transfer you." A few clicks later, I got Dr. Faust's voicemail, just as quirky as he is. "Hello, this is Allen Faust, Associate Professor of Forensic Anthropology at Asbury College. I'm probably in the lab looking at body parts. Leave a message if you'd like and I'll try to call you back." Inviting; but I left a message nonetheless, "Hi, Professor, this is Doug Carter-Connors. I stopped by the site on campus to see you, but found that everything is gone. Please call me on my cell 732-555-3310. Appreciate it."

There was nothing to do but wait for a call back. The only person that might know something in the meantime was Quacky. Since she had been in charge of guarding the shed, she and her staff would know what happened. So, I dialed Campus Security, tapping my foot impatiently.

"Security- Sergeant Rockland speaking," came the deep voice on the other end.

"Hi, Sergeant," I said, "this is Dean Doug. Is Chief Braggish available?"

"Hello, Dean, one moment please." Quacky jumped on the other line quickly, in her ever-vigilant way. "Doug, what's wrong?"

"You tell me. Where's the skeleton?" No reason to beat around the bush.

"I'm not entirely sure. Dr. Faust told one of my guys that they were finished early this morning. I called first thing to check in, but had to leave a message. Is there something wrong?"

"No, not really, I was just surprised. Thanks, Tina, I'm running to a meeting with the president, thanks for your help." I wasn't in a chatty mood and wanted to get off the phone before Tina started with random banter.

"Anytime, Doug. Anytime. After that meeting today, I'm not surprised by much. Professor Preston is something." Although I'm usually up for a good dish, especially on R.I.P., I wasn't interested. "Sure is, Tina. Have a great day," I said, clicking the 'end' button on my cell. I stood for a second, in limbo, still having fifteen free minutes before my scheduled meeting with the President. I decided to call Chief Morreale to update him on Jeffrey Jordan and to get his advice on how to proceed.

I dialed, and struck out, having to tell him that Jeffrey was awake in a voicemail message. Might as well just head over to the President's office, which is just a couple of buildings away in Thompson Hall, a historic mansion in the heart of campus. As I walked, vacantly greeting students and faculty passers-by, Lacey popped into my head. How would she know I was planning on visiting her the next day?  I couldn't just show-up, that seemed rude, but how did I make an appointment with her?  Still clutching my cell phone, I looked down at it as if inspired.  I guess I could just call the motel?  Why not.

Not knowing the number for the Shore Thing Motel, I dialed 411.  "Directory assistance, what listing please?"

"Shore Thing Motel in Asbury Park, New Jersey," I said like I was ordering a pizza.  I could hear the operator tapping a keyboard on the other end before coming back to me, "Hold for the number, please."  Then, a digital female voice jumped in, "The number is 7-3-2-5-5-5-4-4-5-5."  The digital lady repeated the number again, and then asked if I wanted her to dial it for me.  Since I was still in the middle of campus, jotting down the number wasn't super convenient, so I decided to spring for the extra fee and have the number dialed.  I only had fifteen minutes, but I was being super-efficient.

A few clicks later, I was connected.  "Shore Thing, Mario."  The voice was stereotypical of what I would expect from a dive flop-house and probable house of ill-repute, gruff and short.  I pictured Mario with a half-eaten cigar hanging out of his mouth dripping onto his wife-beater undershirt.  Although I expected as much, I found myself stuttering, "Um, Hi Mario, this is Dean, oh wait, you don't care.  Um, I was told to call someone who is a guest at…" I was sounding ridiculous, and luckily, Mario felt the same, "Who do you need, buddy."

"Uh, Lacey."

"Hang-on." The phone crackled, and without the benefit of any campy elevator music on the other end, I wasn't sure whether I was still connected. I couldn't tell if I was on hold or in limbo. I waited, and then heard spurts of two short buzzes on the other end. Mario must have been dialing Lacey. After 6 rings, a woman picked up.

"Hello?" Her voice was raspy, as though coming from sleep.

"Ah, hi, Lacey?"

"Who wants to know?"

I hesitated, and then quickly stated, "Dean Doug Carter-Connors from Asbury College."

"Oh!" she sounded happily surprised. "You didn't tell the guy at the desk who you were, did you?"

"No, he didn't ask."

"You can't tell anyone... are you coming?" she asked urgently. There was an unexpected sense of familiarity, like I was making plans with a friend. Although she hadn't confirmed it, I assumed that I was speaking with Lacey. She sounded as though she was in her thirties and probably smoked.

"I'm planning on coming tomorrow afternoon... around 4?"

"Yeah, yeah, that's fine. I don't have to be at work until 7, so that will be okay. You're not bringing the police, right?" The last part was much more statement than question. "And you're coming alone, right?" she said, with more emphasis.  I hesitated, since I had already promised to bring Jerry with me, "Uh, sure.  I'm not bringing the police…" I responded, "and uh, and I'll be alone.  But why is that important?"

There was a pause, and suddenly, her demeanor changed.  Her voice changed in tone from hurried business, as if we were setting up a business deal, to sexy, "I want you all to myself.  Now don't be late… I'll see you tomorrow.  Room 104.  I'll be waiting." *Click.*  What was that all about?  One moment we were setting-up an appointment, and the next we were arranging a tryst?  If I wasn't uncomfortable before, and I was, I felt even more so. Maybe Lacey didn't want to tell me something-- maybe she wanted me?  No, that didn't make sense. Was someone listening to the call?  Mario, maybe? Is that why she changed her tone?  Why would it be copasetic to set up a "date" but not a business meeting?  I was feeling more and more uneasy.  I had no idea what I was getting involved in or why these women wanted me.  Instead of feeling flattered, like a normal man in his forties, I was starting to feel just a little bit nervous.

-13-

I walked into the President's Office suite on the second floor of Thompson Hall, trying to slough-off my discontent.  It is a dark suite of offices in an historic on-campus mansion, reminiscent more of a castle or palace, than a workplace.  It had dark, bold, flowery wallpaper in burgundy tones, and two or three chandeliers dripping in crystal and gold.  On the wall, just to the left of the entrance, is a five foot painting of a large castle overlooking a tiny, thatch-roofed kingdom.  Not exactly the kind of image you want to see hanging in your boss' office-- homage to the feudal system.

The president's assistant, Janet, in keeping with the tone of the space, greeted me as though she were at a royal tea, with just a touch of self-importance.  All that was missing was a double air kiss on each cheek.  "Doug," she said standing, "always a pleasure to see you.  May I get you anything?"  I thought it'd be rude to ask for Jack on the rocks, so I simply said, "No, Janet, thank you."

"Tea, perhaps?  I was just going to fix Gwenyth some tea."

"On second thought, tea would be great, thank you," I said, beginning to acknowledge my late night of carousing.  Janet jumped up and went to a little closet,  that looked like it was once a wet bar and began clinking cups and saucers.  "I'm just going to make a pot of decaffeinated Green tea, I hope that is alright with you, Doug," Janet called from the non-bar.

"It's fine, I need my antioxidants," I said, still wishing for something much stronger. Janet chuckled as Gwenyth walked out of her office, standing pristinely in a striking royal blue suit with white piping. Gwenyth Porter is the president of Asbury College, and the former provost. When the previous president died unexpectedly, just as the president before him, Gwenyth was named interim President. She did such a great job, she was named President of the College a year later.

Gwenyth is a petite, sixty-ish woman, with presumably gray hair that has been tinted a very nice shade of platinum. Although not exceedingly beautiful, Gwenyth has the familiar presence of your next door neighbor coupled with the mystique of a world traveler, which makes her extremely attractive. The ornate doorway to her office framed her diminutive figure like a first-lady as she called me in, "Well Doug, I expected to see you in a hazmat suit, that's about the only thing you haven't had to deal with yet." The other allure of Gwenyth is her dry sense of humor, not often expected in college presidential royalty.

"What do you think is first on my agenda?" I said, getting up and walking past her, "I think we should be proactive and invest in some hazmat suits." Janet moved in behind us, and sat the pot of tea and two cups down on a mahogany table in between two pink armchairs and left the room, closing the doors behind her. Gwenyth sat down in her usual chair on the left, I followed suit on the right. Since we met every other week or so, I was used to the routine.

"So, tell me what's going on. I understand you've dug up some trouble?" Gwenyth said, reaching for her tea and offering me my cup, "any one we know?"

"We've got to figure out the age first, I'm waiting for Dr. Faust to let me know what he finds."

"I *wondered* if Allen was working on it, he is one of the best forensic anthropologist and scholars in the country."

"Yes, I know that now."

"So, I don't really know the details, Doug. Please, fill me in."


I started from the beginning, which seemed like ages ago, with the first skull landing on my desk and ending with the skeleton disappearing just before my meeting with Gwenyth. The President listened intently, and drank her tea with fervor, as though she were listening to an old mystery serial on the radio. While I was at it, I also told her of our recent spate of drug transports. Of course, even though it was my duty to keep the President informed, I intentionally left out the parts about Ivory, Lacey, and Sissy the Nurse. When I finished, she took another sip, and took a long pause. When she finally responded, I was not expecting here comeback, "I'm worried about you, Doug."

I paused to take a drink of my tea, and think of a proper retort.  Always quick on my feet, I shot back, "oh?"  Brilliant.

"Yes.  Since school began this year you've had one thing after another, none of which any Dean of Students should be accustomed.  Missing students & skeletons, I'm just worried that you're getting involved in areas beyond the scope of your duties."  And there it was-- on the surface, a supportive response, yet an underlying tone that screamed, 'stop it, you're working beyond your job title.'

"I hear you, Gwenyth," I said, "and I appreciate your concern,  but I haven't gone seeking out any of these.  They have all fallen in my lap, some quite literally, right in my office.  And while I agree that they are unusual, I can't ignore them."  I stopped, trying my best not to be defensive.

"I'm not asking you to stop, Doug, just to remember your role," she responded, in an assertive, yet slightly more sympathetic tone, "Your title is Dean of Students, not Dean of Students and Detective.  I know you, you are a kind soul.  You won't stop, until you help the students,  no matter what it takes.  Of course, that's what makes you a great Dean of Students; but I think hanging off a Ferris wheel is above and beyond the call of duty."  There it was, the Ferris wheel biting me back again.  I wondered if I would ever live that down.

"Agreed," I conceded, sipping my tea again and repeated, "I hear you, Gwenyth.  Thank you for your concern.  I promise to watch myself, and to be more careful."  Gwenyth and I both chuckled, not knowing then that despite my best efforts, I wouldn't be successful in the task.

~~~~~

The first thing I did as I walked out of Thompson Hall was check my voicemail messages, finding that I had three waiting for me. The first was from Barbara, just calling to confirm that I would be home for dinner. The second was from Dr. Faust, saying that he would be in the lab through the evening and to "just stop by" anytime. Perhaps I wouldn't be home for dinner. The third was from Chief Morreale stating that he had received my message and that he was going over to see Jeffrey Jordan at Jersey Shore, he would contact me when he finished.

I headed directly to Dr. Faust's lab, calling two of the most important women in my life along the way-- Barbara and Judy. Judy was first, relaying a few phone messages that came in while I was away. Then I dialed Barbara.

"Hi, honey," she said, "so, what's the word? I just wanted to confirm that you were going to be home for dinner before I threw the roast in the oven." Mmmmmmm, roast beef, one of my favorites.

"Well," I responded, "I'm not sure. Dr. Faust called me and he's got some information to report on our friendly skeleton. I have no idea how long it

will take.  Go ahead and cook the roast, I'll eat when
I get home."

"Are you sure?  Ethan and I can have pasta,
and we can have the roast tomorrow night, if that's
better."  I mentally scanned my calendar, and
remembered my date with Lacey the next day at
4pm, which I had neglected to let Barbara in on as of
yet, "Um, tomorrow night's no good either, I'll fill
you in tonight.  Just go ahead, I'll eat when I get
home, should be in time to give Ethan a bath."

"Ok," Barbara said, sounding disappointed,
but sweet.  "Don't rush.  I'll see you when you get
home,  the roast beef will be waiting.  I love you."

"I love you, too." I said, and hit the "end"
button on my cell.  By the time I finished with all of
that phone business, I was standing outside of the
science building, home to the famous Dr. Faust.

~~~~~

I entered the large glass double doors and
emerged into a large glass lobby full of granite floors
and lots of potted plants.  Obviously, given its
pristine demeanor, the building was one of our newer
additions to campus.  Since I had never visited Dr.
Faust before, I gravitated to the large, illuminated
building directory situated directly in front of me
like a moth to a neon bug light.  I saw that Dr.
Faust's office was on the third floor, room 314, and
although I didn't know where the lab was in relation,
I figured that was a good place to start.

Since the elevator was right in front of me, and I was feeling tired, I pushed the button and hopped onto the lazy chariot up two floors, and jumped out looking for room 314. Although I found it quickly, just down the hall and to the left, it was empty. On his door was a note handwritten on a post-it in the shape of a shovel, "In the lab." Well, that didn't help me much. I looked around, as if to find another directory, but found myself alone.

I walked aimlessly down the hall like a new student on the first day of orientation, and finally found an open door, which appeared to be a lab. I stepped in gingerly, and knocked on the door. Two students, a young man and young woman, were sitting at a table with some sort of large machine in front of them and diligently writing. "Excuse me," I said tentatively, "I'm looking for Dr. Faust?"

The guy looked up, but the girl was so enthused, she didn't pay any attention. "I think he's next door," said the guy. "Try 320." And then he went immediately back to his writing. I thanked him, not that he noticed or cared, and then noticed the men's room directly across the hall-- too much green tea meant a pit stop. I pushed through the door and immediately saw Dr. Faust, standing at one of the urinals ahead of me. Even from behind I knew the silhouette of the disheveled man with his wacky gray hair sticking out all over.

Now the dilemma. Did I go to the urinal right beside the good Dr., or go into the stall and risk missing him altogether? I decided to break every rule of men's room etiquette, and saddled-up right next to Dr. Faust, who I must say, didn't even notice. Now the next question, did I say something to him in our delicate position? This one always perplexed me. Oftentimes, men who work with each other land themselves in the men's room together. Yet unlike women, from what I can tell, instead of taking this as an extemporaneous social outing, men mostly treat each other like strangers until they leave the room. Sometimes, and this is still iffy, a brief banter about the weather or other mundane topic might be appropriate at the sink, but the Cardinal rule is that no conversation should occur at the urinal-- whether there was a metal divider in between them or not.

Again, I threw caution to the wind, unzipped, and still looking straight ahead at white porcelain tiles, said, "Hello, Professor, I'm glad I found you." Maybe an awkward way to begin a conversation in the men's room, I'll admit. Luckily, given Dr. Faust's already strained social skills, he didn't seem to notice. He looked at me in his usual fashion, as though he had never laid eyes on me before, even though our last conversation was him opening up about his psyche. *Sure, purge and then move on,* I thought jokingly, *we counseling types are used to it.* "You called me earlier in my office and told me to stop by your lab today... I was on my way there, but uh, stopped here first."

A glimmer of recognition passed along the professor's face, and he said, "Oh, yeah, right, sorry, you're the Dean guy I was talking to before, right?"

"Yes!" I said, much too excited for my current location, "I'm the Dean guy!"

Dr. Faust finished his business and walked away from the urinal, and since he had a head start on me, I did the best to do the same. I twirled away from the urinal, still zipping up, and met the professor at the sink, "So, were you able to get a date on the bones?"

"You're just in time, we're about to work on that right now. In fact, I have a colleague who drove in from The College of New Jersey to help. He developed a process for dating just about anything," the professor paused. "Well, except himself." He then smirked and winked at me. I was slightly taken aback, since this was only the second time that Professor Faust had ever engaged in conversation, let alone make a joke. I guffawed appropriately and followed him out of the men's room and across the hall into a large lab. There were multiple stainless steel islands in rows toward the front of the room, which we passed through on the way to the back.

Standing next to a table, were the two students, Tommy and Jennifer, who I had seen several times at the dig site before, along with another man who I took to be the TCNJ prof. All of them were hovering over the table with great interest. It wasn't until I got closer, that I realized the focus of their fascination. On the table, was the assembled skeleton staring up at us.

-14-

The new professor was shorter than average, about my height and stocky, with a black beard touched with hints of gray. At the moment, he wore his eyeglasses on the top of his head and had his face inches from the skeleton's left hand. "Fascinating," he said in a breathy tone, "not complete by any means, but a beautiful specimen. Are you sure that you got them all?"

"The bones?" Tommy said.

"Yes, yes, the bones."

"We cleaned the site thoroughly, this is all of them."

"Were they in natural order, or in piles?"

"Uh," Tommy looked quizzically, "they were mostly in piles, but there was a couple of bone sections that were in some sort of order. Many of them weren't right, in the right order, I mean. I thought that was weird."

"He was probably moved."

"You mean all of the bones were moved from somewhere else?"

"If what you describe is true, then I would say 'yes', but the Mass Spec. will tell us." He moved around the table still examining the bones closely and continued, "The human skeleton is comprised of 206 bones. We are actually born with about 300, but many of them fuse together as the body grows. How many would you say we have here?"

"I don't know," Tommy answered cautiously, "maybe 150?"

"Or a little less," Dr. Allison responded, "probably more like 140.  Which leads me to the conclusion that the remains were moved at some point, leaving many of the bones at their original site."

We were now all standing around the table looking down at the skeleton, which was positioned on what looked like a large foam tablet. The TCNJ prof. suddenly stood up straight, repositioning his glasses in their proper place and acknowledged me immediately, "Oh, Hello.  Are you with the police? I'm John Allison."  I guess my suit and tie threw him off.

"No," I said, "I'm not with the police.  I'm the Dean of Students here at Asbury, Doug Carter-Connors.  You must be from The College of New Jersey?"

"Yes, I am," Dr. Allison said with a smile, "I see Allen's been talking about me."  It was nice to see that Dr. Faust wasn't much more engaged with his friend than he was with me as he moved straight past everyone toward a large machine on the back wall of the lab.

I knew The College of New Jersey well, and had even taught a couple of freshman seminar classes there a few years back.  It is about forty-five minutes from Asbury, a straight shot west on 195 to Ewing.  It's a beautiful campus right next to the city of Trenton, formerly named Trenton State Teacher's College.  Back in the nineties, the powers that be

decided to change the name, in part, to remove the
stigma of the troubled Capitol city of Trenton.
However to many, it will always be, Trenton State.  I
remember on the day that the college unveiled their
name change, all the newspapers had large photos of
the new sign at the main entrance, "The College of
New Jeresey."  Too bad the sign company spelled
the school's name wrong, and the folks who erected
it weren't proof readers.  Needless to say, the
problem was taken care of quickly.

      "So," asked Jennifer turning to Dr. Faust,
"how does the Laser Mass Spectrometer work?"
      "Allen," Dr. Allison interjected, "you haven't
showed them how the Mass Spec. works, yet?  The
prototype has been finished for months!"
      "We've only been in school a few months
and I've been making a few adjustments here and
there," Dr. Faust said, pushing buttons on a computer
screen.
      "This, Doug, is the Laser Mass Spectrometer
that Allen and I finally finished over the summer,"
Dr. Allison beamed proudly, raising his hands and
arms toward the machine like he was announcing a
prize.  The machine was about the size of a
Volkswagen attached to computer screens and
monitors. It looked like something out of a James
Bond movie.
      "We began working on it together a few
years ago, out of a grant that we received from the
National Science Foundation.  Allen and I were
undergrads together at Harvard, and when we ended

up teaching so close together in New Jersey, we got another chance to collaborate.  We wanted to create a device that would help us not only to determine the composition of materials, but to date them as well.  We can answer any chemical question with it," Dr. Allison continued, "thus far we've dated rock, paint chips, and pottery, but never human bones,  until today.  It's a forensic chemist's and forensic anthropologist's dream."

"But how does it work," Jennifer asked again, growing more impatient.  Dr. Allison moved to a dry-erase board next to the table and began writing.  "Okay, well, today we start with human bones, Calcium hydroxyapatite," he said, writing $Ca_{10}(PO_4)_6(OH)_2$ and drawing a stick figure of a person laying on its back.  "Now, how long does it take for flesh to decay from bones, Tommy?" He asked, clearly the quintessential teacher.

"About 18 months in humid soil?" Tommy responded.

"Excellent, now why did you pick humid soil?"

"Because we live near the beach, and the bones were found in the flower bed which would get watered regularly."

"Right on, Tommy boy," Dr. Allison replied, drawing a line and then flowers sticking up above the stick figure.  "Bones can last a very long time in the ground-- just consider Dinosaur fossils.  But bone is porous and water moves through bone, slowly mind you, but it moves carrying particles with it." With that, Dr. Allison drew a picture of a bone, with many dots around it, "The Laser Mass Spectrometer will tell us about the bones… everything about them… including the types of soil they were buried in."

"So you'll be able to tell whether or not the bones were moved," asked Tommy.

"In theory, yes," interjected Dr. Faust, "although as John said, we've never done it before. We do laser ablation for depth profiling."

"I don't understand," Jennifer said, and I was glad, because I didn't understand either. Next Dr. Faust took his turn at the board, "We use a laser to zap specimens, in this case, a piece of bone. The laser zaps the bone and vaporizes a tiny bit of it, not unlike dermabrasion, when the very top layer of skin is removed. One shot of the laser takes about a micron, a micrometer," he said, writing, "0.000001 meter" on the board. "Then, we hit it with another laser shot. Shot #2 vaporizes the freshly exposed material, the next micrometer's worth of material. Each shot goes deeper and deeper, like peeling away the layers of an onion." With this, Dr. Allison let out a "whoop!" and began clapping.

Dr. Faust continued, "For each little "poof" of vaporized bone, we send those vapors into the mass spectrometer to tell us, chemically, about its composition. So…" he persisted, moving away from the board and pointing to the Volkswagen machine. "This is the laser, and this," he said pointing to another much smaller device, "is a time-of-flight mass spectrometer. Light from the laser goes through this window into the Mass Spec. and hits whatever sample we choose to analyze. As I said, usually paint chips, or pieces of pottery, but today, our friend from the flower bed. We position the sample so that the laser shots hit the same location each time, and every laser shot digs deeper."

"Then, are we ready?" Dr. Allison asked eagerly.

"Why not," answered Dr. Faust. "The bone sample is in that plastic bag on the counter." Dr. Allison practically ran to a nearby counter to grab the bag. He grabbed some latex-like gloves, reached in and grabbed a gray object, about 3" long. Next, he moved toward the Mass Spec. and picked up a stainless steel cage, about nine-inches square and clipped the object inside.

"What is that?" asked Tommy.

"This is a fresh human bone, we'll use it as a control to determine what the spectrum looks like when zapped with the laser. Once we have that data, we'll zap a piece of our friend, and compare."

"A *fresh* human bone?" I asked. "I don't want to know where you got it," I continued jokingly.

"You're right, you don't," Dr. Allison smiled.

Dr. Faust moved toward the computer screens and controls. As Dr. Allison sat the cage down, it was quickly pulled into the Mass Spec. by a computer-controlled motion device. Almost immediately, they heard a "click!"

"That's the laser you hear," said Dr. Faust with a large grin on his face. He was becoming the most animated that I had ever seen him.

*Click!*

*Click!*

I could see on Dr. Faust's computer screen that a flat green line suddenly grew in tall peaks. "Jennifer, what do you think this peak could be?" he asked.

"Um, calcium?" she responded cautiously.

"Yes, and the atomic weight?"

"Um, 40?"

"Very good."

"And what about this peak, Tommy?"

"Phosphate," he said confidently.

"Correct. And now for you, Dean," Dr. Faust said, turning to me. "Your turn. What about this peak?"

"I got a 'D' in chemistry," I responded, fascinated nonetheless.

"Magnesium?" Jennifer chimed in, looking at the computer screen intently.

"Right on. You're witnessing history here, folks. Although we've never done this before, we're seeing that we can zap bone and get a spectrum. Fascinating."

After what must have been 50 or more clicks, and a lot of scientist-speak in the room, the cage was removed from the machine, with the piece of bone looking relatively unchanged; or at least is was to this Liberal Artist's eye.

"I think we're ready. Jennifer, do you want to do the honors?" asked Dr. Allison.

"Sure… uh, but what do I do."

"Put on a glove, and pick a bone from the table that will fit inside this cage," Dr. Allison responded, removing the *fresh* bone from the cage. Jennifer quickly took a latex-like glove from a box, put it on her right hand, and hovered over the skeleton as if at a buffet. Finally, she picked up a bone from the left hand, "Will this one work?" she asked.

"Perfect," Dr. Allison encouraged, opening the cage. "Now mount it with these clips so that it doesn't move." Jennifer complied and closed the cage. "Now what?" she asked. "I'll take it from there," Dr. Allison said, as he sat the cage down once again and it was mechanically swept into the device. More clicks.

*Click!*
*Click!*
*Click!*

"Look at that," Dr. Allison said, in something like an awed whisper. "Tommy, do you have the report on the soil samples we collected?"

"Sure, right here," Tommy replied, shuffling some papers in front of him.

"May I see them please?" Dr. Allison asked. Tommy handed him the papers, to which Dr. Allison responded, "Yes, yes, and do you have the soil samples handy?" Tommy reached next to him, and pulled two identical zip lock bags of dirt. "Okay, okay, Tommy, you just keep those handy."

*Click!*
*Click!*
*Click!*

"And we're out," stated Dr. Faust, tapping away at the computer screen and with a *whir*, the cage zipped out of the machine.  Dr. Allison moved next to Allen and both began looking intently at the computer monitor.  A couple of times, they both referred to the papers that Dr. Allison was holding and mumbled to each other.  Jennifer, Tommy, and I just looked at each other and shrugged.

Finally, after what seemed to be an hour, but was probably only five minutes, Dr. Allison and Dr. Faust turned to look at us, both grinning from ear to ear.

"What?" Tommy nearly shouted, "Do you know how old the skeleton is?"

Dr. Allison pointed to the bags of dirt, "First, Tommy, open the bags carefully.  Do you notice any difference in the samples?"  Tommy obeyed and stuck his head closer, "Not really, both look about the same."

"Okay," Dr. Allison said, "now use the top of your pen and poke around a little. See any difference now?"  Again, Tommy did as instructed, responding, "nope, still look the same."

"Hold them under the table lamp," Dr. Faust chimed in, pointing to a silver lamp that had been positioned over the skeleton.  "What do you see now?"

Tommy placed each bag under the lamp and poked around again, one at a time. "One has sparkling particles, one doesn't."

Dr. Faust turned to Dr. Allison and smiled. "Bingo," he said, "I think we've got our answers." Once again, Tommy, Jennifer, and I just looked at each other, perplexed. I felt like I was back in my high school chemistry lab, clueless about what was right in front of me.

"So you know how old the skeleton is?" I asked, jumping in whether I was clueless or not.

"Yes," responded Dr. Faust. "And a little bit more."

-15-

We all huddled around each other so closely that I could tell that someone had eaten onions earlier in the day.

"So how old!" asked Jennifer, just as eager as any of us.

"Not so fast," said Dr. Faust, "Let's look at the data. Come here and look at the monitor." I didn't care if someone had eaten a shit sandwich, as long as I found out how old the skeleton was so we could begin to identify its body of origin.

Next, it was Dr. Allison's turn to illuminate us. "Look at the spectra," he said, pointing to a bar graph on the screen. "As you can see, and heard, we zapped the bone sample 50 times, stripping off roughly 50 micrometers of bone. The first 44 all have iron present, which is consistent with the soil sample from the site that Tommy gave us."

We all moved in for a closer look, and sure enough, all of the spectra looked the same, numbers 10, 20, 30, 40, 41, 42, 42, and 44. But then, a change. The next two bars looked different, followed by four that were different again, but similar to each other. "What does this mean," I asked, pointing to the changing graph, barely able to contain my anticipation.

"Well," Dr. Allison continued, "we found iron from the surface of the bone up to the 44 micrometer point. Iron is consistent with the soil sample that Tommy collected. So, based on the diffusion coefficient we calculated, that would mean that the remains were in the flower bed for approximately 46 years."

"So that's the answer!" Tommy shouted.

"No, not exactly," Dr. Faust announced. "You can see from the spectra that numbers 45 and 46 are completely different, which I'll explain in a second, and spectra 47-50 represent basic components of bone. It's spectra 45 and 46 that are the most telling, beyond the age of the bones." Tommy, Jennifer and I were so eager for a resolution that we didn't even respond. We simply continued to listen.

"You can see," Dr. Allison went on, "the difference in spectra 45 and 46 and are consistent with Tommy's soil sample labeled, 'A.' Tommy, do you remember which sample that is?" Tommy thought a moment, "'A' is the one that I collected closest to the bones."

"And where did you collect the second bag labeled, 'B'?"

"I took that one after we removed the bones, about two feet below the resting place."

"Exactly," said Dr. Allison smiling. "In spectra 45 and 46 we can see elevated levels of sodium and potassium, as well as some silicates, which is consistent with the sparkles that Tommy said he saw in zip lock 'B'. Don't you love New Jersey, Doug?" He turned his attention to me, to which all I could respond was, "Yes?"

"Sand!" Jennifer interjected, "sodium, potassium and silicates. That's sand! Right?"

"Yes, yes, go on," cajoled Dr. Faust.

"The body was buried in sand first!"

"On the money!" shouted Dr. Faust, "excellent, Jennifer!" Jennifer jumped up and down as though she had just won Bingo, while I still looked awkward. "I'm sorry, can someone just spell this out for me in plain English?"

"John, why don't you do the honors," suggested Dr. Faust.

"Happy to. Here's our final answer. It looks as though the body was buried in the sand, the beach more specifically, and then moved to your flower garden here on campus." I nodded, and continued to listen intently as Dr. Allison continued, "The first 18 months or so, let's say 2 years even, the bones still had flesh on them, so, nothing interesting was happening. By the two year mark, however, the body was reduced to bone and sat in the sand for another two years. It was then moved to campus, and sat in the rich soil of the azalea bed for about 46 years. All told, our friend has been dead for 2 plus 2 plus 46 years, for a grand total of 50 years."

"Give or take a year or two," Dr. Faust chimed in.

"Fifty years ago," I said out loud, calculating. "So whomever this is, died around 1956?"

"Right," said Dr. Allison, "That's an accurate assessment based on the data."

Although I was happy to finally have an answer, my mind quickly raced with more questions. "So do we know how old the person was when they died, or the sex?" This time, Jennifer jumped in, "Oh, we've known that for a couple of days. Based on bone calibrations and other factors, it appears as though the skeleton is male and was approximately twenty years old at the time of death. Right, Dr. Faust?" Dr. Faust stood like a proud father and simply nodded and smiled.

"And what about the cross that was found with the skull?" I asked.

"We did tests on that earlier today, again, until now, we hadn't ever used the Mass Spec. on bones, only other objects," said Dr. Faust. "That appears to be about 47 years old. It may have been buried with the original body placement on the beach, or may have been left when the remains were transported, that we can't tell."

"So, let me make sure that I get this straight," I said, trying desperately to make sense of this whirlwind of information. "The body was buried in the sand, probably on a beach somewhere, then moved to campus. The bones were not buried here in order, but put in piles, right?" I remembered that from seeing the site myself.

"Yes," said Tommy, "there were several missing, as you can see from the table here."

"Anything else we can help you with today, Dean?" asked Dr. Faust, jokingly. I shook my head, "no, you've been a huge help."

"We cleaned up your cross," Dr. Faust said, pointing to a much more shiny piece of jewelry than I remembered. "I don't know if you noticed, but there's an inscription, ATTN."

"That's what I thought it said, but I wasn't sure.  Attention?" I asked, more to myself than the professors.

"I can't tell you what it *means*," Dr. Faust smiled.  "I'll leave that to the detectives."

"And the cause of death?"  I asked, was it trauma to the head?"

"Bingo," Dr. Allison jumped in.
"This is quite a machine you invented," I said. "And you have assembled quite a team.  Thank you."

"So, are you going to tell us who the bones belonged to?" asked Tommy excitedly.

"If I figure it out, yes, Tommy," I said.  "If I ever figure it out."

~~~~~

By the time I left the science building, it was six o'clock and with a five year old at home, I had surely missed my roast beef dinner.  After all, early bird specials aren't just meant for senior citizens, but for parents of small children, too.  I figured I would call Chief Morreale to tell him my news, and see how he made out with Jeffrey Jordan.

The evening had turned cool, and the breeze had picked up the briny ocean scent that made it feel chillier.  I pulled my sports coat around me, and dialed the Chief.  "Ocean Grove Police Department, Captain Montgomery speaking."

"Hi, Jack, this is Doug Carter-Connors, is the Chief available?"  Ever since last month's escapade,

I had been on a first name basis with all three of the Shore's PD.

"Oh, Dean Doug, sure, he just got back, I'll put you into his office." A few moments later, the Chief was on the phone, "Okay, so what'd you do now?" he joked.

"I found out how old our friendly resident skeleton is. How about you?"

"I did pretty well, too. I found out where our friend in the hospital got his stash and it's closer to home than you think. When do you want to get together to compare notes?" He was baiting me, and I couldn't resist. Since I had already missed hot roast beef, there was no reason to rush home (other than to see my loving family, of course). "I'm free right now," I said, "how about you?"

"I'm on my way home. Why don't I swing by the Student Center, pick you up, and we can talk privately. Then, I'll drive you home."

"Sounds like a plan. I'll be waiting," I said and headed back to my office to pick up my brief case before going to the parking lot to wait for the Chief.

~~~~~

Chief Morreale met me in the back circle of the Student Center around 6:20pm, and I jumped in, shot-gun. "Fancy meeting you here," I quipped, "who wants to share  first?"

"Please, you're the guest," the chief said, pulling away from the curb. I started telling him that the skeleton was been buried for approximately 50 years and then filled him in on the professors' hypotheses about moving the body.

"Interesting," the Chief said, frankly not sounding very interested. "I'll talk to the professors and we'll take it from here."

I sat for a minute. Just as my boss had done a few hours earlier, was the Chief discouraging my participation in this investigation? "Wait," I said, "are you saying I'm out of it now?"

"I didn't say that, although I probably should. I'm only saying that this needs to be a police investigation. I just don't want you getting in our way or hampering our progress. Capiche?"

"Got it… don't ask, don't tell."

"Sort of. Besides, you might have bigger fish to fry," the Chief said, heading his cruiser toward the beach.

"Bigger than a skeleton?" I asked.

"How about a drug ring?" he said flatly as though discussing the weather.

"What?" I asked, not expecting that response, "Jeffrey told you that?"

"Yes, and a whole lot more. Jeffrey was extremely cooperative, I think he's really afraid of what trouble he's in. He asked me about what will happen to him on campus, and I told him that was up to you to decide. I'll write it all up in a report and fax it to you in the morning."

"But you're going to give me the Reader's Digest version now, right?" I asked, as much on the edge of my seat as my seatbelt would allow.

"Sure," he said, pulling the cruiser up to the boardwalk and parking. The Chief then took off his hat, wiped his bald head with a white handkerchief and began, "Jeffrey says that the other night, actually the night before he was transported to the hospital, he went to a party. He said he couldn't remember the address, but that it was across the lake in Asbury Park." I assumed this to be true since other than the ones who live on-campus, very few Asbury College students live in town. The majority of our off-campus students live in Asbury Park, Bradley Beach, and Belmar.

The Chief continued, "At the party, Jeffrey says that there was a girl named Candy who was handing out caffeine pills-- she said that they would help the kids to study. Jeffrey says that she was giving them out for free, but saying that if he needed more, all he had to do was email her and then pay a fee for the next shipment."

"So, a free sample to get you hooked, and then a hefty price, huh?" I said.

"Yes, that seems to be the scheme. Jeffrey says that he put the pills in his pocket and forgot about them, until the next night when he and his roommate were studying in the library. He found the pills in his jacket, and decided to take them... 4 of them... to help him study. And, well, by the time he got back to his room, he was feeling pretty sick and passed out."

"Did he say anything more about this *Candy* person?"

"Not much, although he said that she is a junior at the College, and that he had never seen her before. I guess she told him that she lives off-campus. Jeffrey said that he knew about other students getting pills to help them study, or get high, and that before Candy he knew of someone called, 'Greenley', but she transferred to another school not long ago. Now, I'll need your help, Doug."

"So, you don't want my help with the skeleton, but I can help with the drug dealer?" I asked playfully, but the Chief didn't bite and started, "I'll need to know if there is a junior named…"

I cut him off, "Candy?"

"Well, I was thinking Candace, but yes."

"I'll have Judy look in the morning and let you know. No last name?"

"Well, Jeffrey thought that her last name was Kane, with a 'K', but he wasn't sure."

"Candy Kane? Do you really think so?"

"No, but we have to try. Have Judy check it out, and I'll touch base with you in the morning, okay?" And with that, the Chief pulled the cruiser out of park and headed toward my house a mere three blocks away. We were silent the rest of the way, until we pulled up in front of my white picket fence.

"Greenley, huh?" I asked, "So I have two dealers on my campus?"

"Had. Again, Jeffrey said that Greenley transferred."

I pondered that for a minute, only to be interrupted by the Chief, "Now do only what I ask, okay?  I know your track record-- you have a knack for getting in over your head."

"Me?" I asked mockingly, "I don't know what you're talking about.  I'll talk to you in the morning."  I shut the passenger door and he pulled away.  As I opened my front gate and walked down my walk, I remembered why I hesitated to tell the Chief about Lacey.  It was better to keep that one to myself-- or so I thought.

-16-

By the time I walked into my house it was just after 7:00pm and Barbara was giving Ethan a bath upstairs. I could still smell the remnants of roast beef taunting me as I walked up the stairs to meet them. Before I made it to the top, I could hear Ethan splashing around. "Anyone home?" I yelled playfully before I reached the bathroom.

"Daddy!" yelled Ethan, "we're up here!"

"You are?" I said, "but you're being so quiet…" Leave it to me to use sarcasm with a five-year-old. I leaned down and kissed Barbara, and leaned down further to get a wet, soapy one from Ethan.

"So, productive day?" Barbara asked, kneeling on the floor next to the tub.

"You could say that, I'll fill you in later. What about you?"

"You could say that. I'll tell you over a glass of wine."

"Daddy," interrupted Ethan, "Will you put me to bed?" It was the best offer I had all day, "You bet," I said, "I'll even finish your bath. Just let me change my clothes and I'll be yours until 8 o'clock." I went across the hall into our bedroom and began stripping my workday away. The tie went, and so did Gwenyth; off with the pants, and gone was the 50 year old skeleton; take away the shirt, and so went the drug dealers. I was becoming freer by the second. Standing in my skivvies I realized that maybe Nurse Sissy was on to something.

I threw on some sweatpants, grabbed a sweatshirt, and relieved Barbara from her bath duties. "I'll take it from here," I said.

"Ok, I'm going to work on my article until you come down."

"The one on secret societies?" I asked.

"Yes, I found some interesting material today. I'll tell you all about it."

"I thought everything was top secret?"

"Not for you, big boy," Barbara said with a wink and turned and went downstairs.

"Alright, buddy, where were we?" I asked, peering down at Ethan sitting in a shallow pool of suds.

"Mommy and I were playing submarine. Here!" he said, handing me a rubber dinosaur.

"This is the sub?"

"Yup, it's purple! Mommy is so silly."

I bent down gingerly, still being easy on my ankle, and started my best dive maneuvers. This continued until Ethan looked far too pruney to be having fun, and I scooped him out of the tub, under minimal protest. After drying off, a rousing game of teeth-brushing (who can find the plaque-bugs?) and a couple of books later, Ethan was down for the count and I joined Barbara downstairs.

The air was still thick with the savory richness of beef, and to my pleasure, I found a plate full of it covered in plastic wrap sitting next to a large glass of red wine on the kitchen island. Just more reasons to love my wife. I popped the plate into the microwave for a minute, decanted some of the wine directly into my mouth, and bellied-up to the island. Lured by the beeping of the microwave, Barbara wasted no time coming in so that we could share the sagas of our days.

"Sorry I missed the beef," I said, still feeling guilty.

"You didn't miss it, you're having it now. So, what happened today, more craziness?"

"Same old, same old," I said, cutting into my dinner. "Gwenyth chastised me for getting involved in things beyond what is normal for a Dean of Students, I got to see a big machine that shot pieces of the skeleton with a laser beam, and Chief Morreale told me that I have a drug ring alive and well on-campus. Just a typical day at Asbury."

"So many opportunities to choose from. Where do you want to start?" Barbara said sympathetically.

"How about with *you*. How was *your* day?"

"Well, not as exciting as yours, but I did do more research on my secret societies article. Did you know that there is an entire archive for Skull and Cross in the library?"

"The campus library?"

"Yes. Apparently it's not common knowledge, but I was in the town library and the reference librarian referred me to the College archives when I told her what I was looking for."

"And what were you looking for?"

"Anything.  Documents, pictures, anything on Skull and Cross that would help flesh out my article."

"So you were on-campus today?"

"Yup.  And I met your College Archivist, Myrna Waters.  Lovely lady."

"We have a librarian named, Myrna?  Does she wear a sweater and a bun in her hair?"

"I didn't notice, I was too distracted by the blinding gold chain that held her half-glasses," Barbara teased.  "I take it you don't know her?"

"Nope," I said, slurping my wine, amused by her sarcasm that far surpassed my own.

"Well as I said, she's lovely and apparently not concerned about the 'secret' nature of Skull and Cross.  She was eager to share all of the archival information she had on them."

"Probably because she hasn't had any human interaction in decades.  Where are the archives, in the basement of the library?"

"Exactly.  I don't think there's a lot of traffic down there, but there's an entire section on Skull and Cross... pretty extensive."

"But if it's so secret, how much could there be?"

"Well, although supposedly secret, like many of these college societies, there is a high level of prestige associated with the organization.  Many presidents and world leaders have been members of similar groups around the country.  And with prestige comes ego."

"And a desire to preserve their rightful place in history."

"Right.  Hence, a good deal of archival information kept for prosperity."

"So what'd you find?"

"Lots of governance documents, bylaws, things like that.  Many photos, several dozen hand written letters, journals, even some love letters and poems."

"Love letters to themselves?   Are they all narcissists?" I responded, feeling a bit more rancor that I expected.

"Doug," Barbara said in fake chastisement, "I don't know who they were to, but some were very sweet.  And they have group photos dating back from when the group started in the late 1800s. Anyway, I want to hear more about your skeleton. Did you find out how old it is?"

"Yes, it's about fifty years old."

"So, late 1950s?"

"You know me, math isn't my strong point."

"And are you sure that the body was a member of Skull and Cross?"

"Not 100%, but it seems likely," I said casually, even though I could see Barbara getting more excited.

"Then I bet there's a photo of the victim in the archives!"  Barbara blurted.

As she said it, I thought about the S & C conference room and all of the group photos in there, too.  "There are also photos in the Skull and Cross

Conference room in the Student Center," I offered, still chewing my beef.

"There are?  Why didn't you tell me?"

"I didn't know you were looking for them.  I would have thought that your new friend, Myrna, would have told you."

"They have their own conference room?"

"Yup, a rich alum donated the funds to redecorate and name it a few years ago.  It's right down the hall from my office."

"Can I check it out sometime?"

"Well, it's under lock and key, but luckily, we are a key-holder.  Judy is, anyway.  I'm sure we could sneak you in sometime."

"What kind of photos are in there?"

"Group photos, complete with dates posted on gold plates."

"I bet there are some from the 1950s."

She was right, and I was becoming more curious.  Was the victim's picture waiting for me right down the hall from my own office?  Did he look at me and laugh during that hellacious meeting earlier in the day?  I wondered, with growing anticipation, and just a hint of creepiness.  Who needs archives when I have them right down the hall?  I would have to find my way into the S & C conference room tomorrow.

"So, what about Gwenyth and a drug ring?" Barbara asked, pouring her own glass of wine.  But I was already tired of the day, and feeling warm with wine, beef, and my wife.  "How 'bout I tell you upstairs," I said with a wink.

"All this talk of archives doing something for you?" she said, smirking.

"Yes," I said, moving closer, "…and Myrna. Where are your half-spectacles?"  We laughed and made our way upstairs, wine glasses in hand.  Within seconds, we were wrapped in each other with a mix of urgency and trust and slowly, the chaotic day melted away into a pile of familiarity and comfort. Much needed comfort.

~~~~~

I woke up around 2am feeling something else-- the urge to go to the bathroom.  As usual, I didn't want to disturb Barbara by peeing in the commode in our master bedroom, so I went down the hall to use the main upstairs bathroom next to Ethan's room.  Before going to the toilet, I peeked in on Ethan, and found him breathing deeply and hugging a pile of books.  I went in, pried the books from his arms, and he rolled over contentedly.

Of course, I was conducting these common night time activities naked, since I hadn't bothered to grab my boxers or a robe; just call it a nocturnal omission.  I peed sitting down (a much quieter that way for men) and rested my head in my hands.  As I went, I decided that I could use a drink of water. Without flushing, or washing my hands, I tip-toed downstairs to grab a glass.

I got my drink and stood in the dim kitchen, lighted only by the overhead stove light, swallowing sleepily until…  I thought I saw something.  Out of

the corner of my eye, a shadow. Luckily, not in the
house, but outside at the side of the house. My heart
raced a little, as I left my glass and creeped toward
the dining room window, draping the curtain around
my waist as soon as I got close enough to it.
Without my glasses, which were still resting on my
nightstand upstairs, the dark night was even more
obscure. I strained to see through the shadows, cast
only by a few weak porch lights from neighboring
houses. But despite the darkness, I saw something
again. Something was moving outside... not an
animal, something tall. Something human that
seemed swaddled in the shadows.

It moved, now seeming shorter, toward the
back of the house. I followed, grabbing the morning
newspaper from the dining room table to shield my
privates; a move that was born more out of security
than modesty. As I moved toward the family room, I
ducked behind the couch and easy chair as I made
my way to one of the back windows. I cautiously
peeked through the cold panes again straining to see.
There it was again! I was following the shadow... or
was it following me now? I held the newspaper
closer and struggled to gain sight.

I could see my backyard, complete with patio
set and Ethan's swings resting idly, and suddenly
remembered the switch. I could turn on the patio
light. Maybe then I could see who was out there, or
at least scare them off. I moved to the sliding glass
doors, the threshold to the patio, and flicked the light
switch as though it was a scorpion's tail. The blast
of light illuminated the entire backyard, and I did see

something, or someone, dressed in something dark, fleeing from the light and heading to the other side of the house toward the front.

I moved straight through the house, running so quickly that I dropped my paper, until I reached the front door. Through the interior darkness, I fumbled for the porch light and brought it to life as quickly as I found it. I saw the figure more clearly then, running across the front yard and out the front gate of the white picket fence. It was indeed a person… in a dark cape or robe… running away from the house. I wished I hadn't dropped my newspaper or I would have gone out onto the front porch to catch a better look. My heart still raced as I watched the person race out of my sight, and past my neighbors' houses, using more shadows to cover his tracks.

A cape or robe. A robe! Was the intruder someone from Skull and Cross? What reason would they have for a middle-of-the-night visit to my house? Were they trying to scare me away from something? My feeling of urgency to go to the S & C conference room and investigate the skeleton's identity was not dissuaded, but suddenly heightened.

As I stood still straining to see, I felt vulnerable. Not because of my nakedness, but because of the violation. Someone had come to my home… while I was sleeping… while my family slept… to take advantage of the peacefulness the night brought. I felt angry and exposed and knew that my night's rest was over.

-17-

I dozed in my bed until I couldn't take it anymore- 4:45am and immediately jumped in the shower. Since I had been up at 2am, I had already planned my day. I was going to go to work early, well before the 8:30am opening, and go to look at the photographs in the S & C conference room. An early start would ensure that I could sneak the key out of the key box in DOSO, gather my information, and return it before anyone noticed; especially Judy.

I was toweled-off, shaved, gelled, and deodorized by 5am, snuck to my dresser to locate some underwear, and cursed the antique's creaky old drawers. But it was too late, Barbara was already awake, "You're up so early, honey," she said, sleepily.

"I want to go look at those photos in the conference room before anyone gets in," I responded.

"It didn't seem so urgent last night?" Barbara said lifting her head off the pillow.

"Well, that was before I found someone from Skull and Cross sneaking around our house in the middle of the night."

Barbara then sat up, "What?"

"I got up around 2 to go to the bathroom and saw someone sneaking around our yard."

"What were they doing?"

"I don't know, but they were on the side near the family room first, then ran to the back, and then left from the front, right out of the picket gate."

"And did you know them? How do you know that they were Skull and Cross?"

"I think that they were wearing a robe. It was dark and I'm not 100% certain, but I'm pretty sure."

"Did you call the police?"

"No. They ran away when I turned on the outside lights. I'll probably tell Chief Morreale later. I'm sure I'll be talking to him." I finished getting dressed and kissed Barbara, who was now wide awake and tossing, before going downstairs. I made a pot of coffee and stood next to the counter, anxiously watching each delicious drip flow into the carafe. I pulled it out before it was completely done, poured it into a tall travel mug and ran out the door. It was 6:15.

The October morning was chilly, but the sun was out giving the illusion of warmth. I walked briskly, my usual cadence, sipping my steaming coffee on the way. I was on a mission and focused on nothing more than getting to the Student Center. As I approached Main Avenue, I was disappointed to see Malificent standing on the corner. *Shit,* I thought, *I don't have time for you today.*

"Doug!" she shouted more loudly than anyone should at the hour of six in the morning, "No run for you today?"

"Nope, early meeting," I said, still moving and wishing that I could vaporize her. Not getting my sense of urgency, Malificent continued, "Well, I saw you and wanted to make sure that you're coming to Video Game Night this Thursday."

"It's on my calendar," I said, still inching forward.

"Great, we have another meeting with the Crisis Task Force tomorrow to finalize the details. It's going to be fantastic- the kids are going to love it. We've got interactive video games like bowling and baseball, where you actually have to move like you're playing. We're also having twenty *Dance, Dance Revolution* mats. Have you ever done that? It's wild!"

Although I was sorry to cut her off, well not that sorry, I responded, "Sounds great. I'll see you there. Sorry Malificent, I really have to run!" I sidled my way around her, back on my mission to campus. By the time I reached the Student Center, I was perspiring, and felt beads of sweat fall coolly down my back. The closer I got, the faster my pace.

I fumbled for my keys on the way up the stairs to DOSO, unlocked the main door, and quickly dropped my briefcase in my office. Without hesitating, I went directly to Judy's top desk drawer, opened an old paperclip box that contained one tiny key, and moved to the copy room to find the key box which housed copies of all our office keys, as well as many rooms within the Student Center-- including the S & C conference room. I studied the legend on the opened key box door and quickly found it, #18 marked, "S&C."

I grabbed the key, locked the key box back up, returned it to Judy's desk, and walked out the door of DOSO in a direct line to the conference room. As I approached the door, I wiped the sweat

from my hands and looked around.  No one.  I was
most likely the only person in the building, or at least
the second floor.  As I reached for the door handle I
thought quickly, *should I be wearing gloves?  But
wait, I'm only going to look at pictures, I'm not
going to steal anything.*  Nonetheless, I pulled my
white shirtsleeve down over my hand and opened the
newly unlocked door.

I moved inside and shut the door quickly
behind me with the same covered hand.  Whew.  I
made it.  The room was dark, made more so by the
cherry wood paneling.  I turned on the light and
didn't waste any time scanning the framed pictures
and gold date plates.  The photographs were
arranged chronologically in three even rows on three
walls and I quickly found the 1950s.  There they
were-- 1955, 1956, 1957, 1958, 1959.  All of the
photographs showed five young men staring
expressionless toward me.  Although I wasn't
exactly sure from which year my skeleton hailed, I
knew that I was looking directly at him and a shiver
went down my clammy back.

I stepped closer.  If the professor's machine
was completely accurate, the victim was in the 1956
or 1957 picture, but to be safe, I scanned a few years
before and after.  But I quickly realized that simply
seeing the pictures, given my easy access, wouldn't
give me the identity I was looking for.  There
weren't names listed on the gold plates.  Thinking
that maybe the names were listed on the backs of the

frames, I took 1956 down from the wall and turned it over-- nothing but cob webs and wire. Damn it. I would have to make a trip to the archives anyway. So did I even need the photos in front of me? I decided to take advantage of the opportunity nonetheless.

Having already calculated my every move, like a well-orchestrated bank heist, I removed my cell phone from my belt and pointed its camera viewfinder toward each of the five years I was interested in. Closer, closer, *click*! Got it. One by one, each of the photos were electronically stored in my phone, in the highest resolution I could muster. At that moment, I was glad that I sprung for the expensive phone smart phone and within a few seconds, I was finished. Mission accomplished. For a moment, I was surprised… at how easily I had accomplished the task. But then, my surprise turned in a different direction when I realized that someone was fumbling with the door handle. My secret mission was about to be exposed.

~~~~~~

I only had seconds and looked around like a panicked teenager with his pants down. I immediately saw that there was another door directly behind me. What was it? I didn't care, and lunged for the handle, wherever it went would be my salvation. I turned the handle to the new door just as the knob to the entrance was also turning, and found myself a closet. Perfect! I jumped inside, pushing aside boxes and hunks of dark, musty fabric, and shut the door behind me just as I heard the other door open.

"Who left the lights on?" came the crackly voice that would remove paint from the walls. It was R.I.P in all of his usual curmudgeonly grace. "Damn, kids," I could hear him say so loudly that it seemed as though he was inside the closet with me. I heard some fumbling and then a loud crack. He must have sat down at the conference table and slammed his cane on top. What was he doing so early?

I stood frozen in the closet as my eyes worked to adjust to the darkness. I couldn't see a thing and resorted to feeling my way around as quietly as possible. I tried to picture the layout of the space from the quick glimpse I had gathered before I rushed in. Cardboard boxes of various sizes piled on top of each other with rolled-up pieces of black fabric, maybe robes, laid on top of them. That was all I could remember, but it didn't matter. I was stuck for the time being.

I turned my ear to the door and strained to hear what was going on in the conference room. Whistling-- R.I.P. was either whistling "Hail, Hail the Gang's All Here" or "Wake Me Up, Before You Go Go," I couldn't tell which. Very quickly, his whistling was interrupted by someone else arriving to the early morning meeting. *'Who has a 7am meeting?'* I wondered.

"Good morning, Professor," I heard a young man's voice, "am I the first one here?"

"No, you're the second.  I'm here!" came R.I.P.'s snappy retort.  Even from the closet, I could hear them perfectly.

"I thought Jenny would be here, she's always early," said the young man.

"And what about Tim," said R.I.P., "He's coming too, right?"

"I think so... I talked to him last night."

I huddled in the closet and listened to them make small talk about the weather, midterms, even R.I.P.'s bursitis for what seemed like an hour (it was probably more like five minutes) until two more voices entered the room.  I couldn't help but wonder whether one of the morning's meeting participants was my late night visitor.

"Good morning!  I brought donuts!" came the distinctive voice of Jenny Robins.  Tim, who didn't sound familiar, jumped in with, "I call the glazed!"  I could hear the movement of chairs as everyone settled in for the meeting and then R.I.P. started.  "Well, you all know why we're here, and I hope that you came prepared.  Did everyone read the dossiers?"

*Dossiers?  What was this spy camp?*

"Wait, Professor," said Jenny, "we didn't say the sacred invocation."

I stood corrected.  It was *Gospel spy camp.*

"I'll do it," said young man number one.  "With the authority afforded us by the sacred cloaks and vestments shared by our brothers, I call this meeting to order."  Then, they all spoke in unison, "The skull is our symbol of power and strength, the cross, it stands for loyalty. Together they bond behind the cloak for now and all eternity."

I really stood corrected. It was *creepy Gospel spy camp*.

"Let's get started," said R.I.P. "I'll go over each of the candidates briefly and then we'll vote. We'll announce our choice at the general meeting next week."

"Well," stated Jenny, "The Sacred Skull is our biggest award given every year at the Alumni Gala. I think Arthur Thornton wins hands down for his work in the community."

"You're jumping ahead!" cackled R.I.P. "We will review all three candidates and *then* we'll vote! And we have to do them in order of graduation year. Now let's get on with it… the first candidate is Chet Livingston, class of '45. He served in the military for twenty five years, started Shores Savings and Loan and has provided over 200 scholarship opportunities for students over the years. *Next*, is Arthur Thornton, class of '63. Well-known philanthropist and has led the effort to revitalize Asbury Park. He has also funded scholarship opportunities to low-income and minority students for decades. Finally is Ira Davis, class of '70. Mr. Davis built an insurance business that now spans much of New Jersey. He has also created an endowed lectureship in the School of Business. There. Quite an impressive group… *now*… your thoughts?"

Jenny didn't waste any time. "Well, as I said, I think we should pick Mr. Thornton. His work in Asbury Park has really made an impact on that community… he's the one."

"I was thinking Mr. Livingston," came Tim's voice, "I have my bank account here in town and they're really nice."

"And that's why you think Mr. Livingston should be the Sacred Skull?" spoke the other student's voice, "I agree with Jenny.  Mr. Thornton is definitely the choice."

"Well, let the discussion begin!" R.I.P. blurted.  I could hear the joy in his voice that there was some conflict.  He continued,  "I have to say, although I know all of the nominees, I went to school with Arthur Thornton, and he is certainly an outstanding choice."  As I stood in the closet listening, I began to get itchy-- that sort of feeling when you know you can't scratch, so the urge gets more intense.  All I could do was wait it out and hope that they picked the Sacred Skull quickly.

Perhaps it was my location, but I was trying to resist passing judgment on the hokey rituals of Skull and Cross.  Opening meetings with poems… tres originale.  I bet they also had a secret handshake.

Distracted by my thoughts and my battle with myself over what itched, I was brought back to the meeting by the sound of the crack of R.I.P.'s cane on the conference table.  "Okay!  Thornton it is!" he shouted.  Well that was fast.  I could taste my freedom.

"Do we have any skulls left?" Tim questioned.

"I think so," student number one said, "didn't we order a bunch of them last year?"

"We have more," said Jenny. "We didn't use them all last week during the initiation. They're in the closet."

*Uh-oh.*

"Are you sure? They take a while to order," came the unknown voice.

Despite my sudden worry that I would be outed, I couldn't help but wonder from where one ordered a skull, or a case of them. Then Jenny spoke again, "No, I'm sure of it, you can see for yourself. They're right there in the closet."

I slinked backward as far as the cardboard boxes would allow-- boxes probably full of skulls. It was inevitable. I was going to be discovered and I had no idea how I would explain myself.

~~~~~

Just as I heard someone's chair scoot back away from the table, probably Jenny headed for the closet, I was startled by R.I.P., "What the hell is that?"

"It's the fire alarm," said Tim, "we better go."

Although it was barely audible from the recesses of my darkness, I could faintly hear the bell. I was saved, unless there was a fire, and I was cooked.

"This is ridiculous!" shouted R.I.P., "It's 7:00am!"

"Maybe there's a fire," said Jenny, "we better go." *Yes*, I thought, *go so that I don't die of smoke inhalation and the firefighters have to find my limp body draped over a box full of skulls.* I could hear movement outside the closet door, but how long did I wait? I decided to give it a couple of minutes and then make my escape. When the time came, I grabbed the doorknob and cautiously opened the door; the light hit my eyes like a laser. Slowly, I opened the door enough to peek out. The room was empty.

I shot out of the closet and headed directly around the conference table to finish my getaway. Again, I grabbed the door handle gingerly and peeked outside. It was clear. I ran out as though there really was a fire, yet hoped that there wasn't. But was I to do? Did I go to my office and return the key or exit the building? I was going to break the rules, the ones that I was responsible for enforcing, and go back to my office to return the conference room key and all evidence that I was sneaking around S & C affairs.

I walked to the DOSO entrance, still lurking like a common thief and shoved my key in the lock. Just as I turned the knob, a voice startled me from behind, "Shouldn't you be leaving the building?" I turned to look and found Miss Bettie standing behind

me with a wide grin on her face.  I realized
then that it wasn't God that I had to thank for saving
me, it was Miss Bettie.

-18-

"You could get into big trouble for pulling a fire alarm," I said to Miss Bettie.

"Oh I accidentally hit it with my broom, it was the darndest thing.  Hrumph… never  done that before," Miss Bettie said giving me a smirk.  It was the look that told me that she was on to me, "I'm not even going to ask what you were doing in there," she continued.

"Thank you," I said, not offering to explain, "shouldn't we be leaving the building?"

"It's okay… I already called security and told them that I hit the alarm by accident.  They're on their way to turn it off.   I bet if you go into your office, you won't hear it much and no one will ever know that you were here this early."

"Oh," I said, feeling a sense of guilt, "okay. Sounds like a plan."   As I opened DOSO, I turned to look over my shoulder, "thank you."

"When I realized that you were in there and then saw them go in behind you, I knew that you probably needed some help.  Whatever your reasons, they must have been good." Miss Bettie winked at me with the wisdom of a shaman and turned the corner still carrying her broom.

I smiled and shut the door behind me, breathing a much deserved sigh of relief.  I had my pictures, which included the owner of the skull.  I finally had him.  Now all I had to do was print the photos from my phone; of course, I had no idea how to do that.  I would have to hand the job over to

Ronnie, our resident technology expert. Ronnie was also a bit more discreet than Judy, which in this case, was important.

I returned the S&C conference room key without incident, and watched as R.I.P. and his students filed back in from their fire alarm interruption to finish their meeting. They had already picked the "Sacred Skull, " what was left? They probably had to recite another creepy poem to officially close the meeting. I went to my office and worked on paperwork until the campus officially came to life at 8:30am. Judy was shocked to find me in my office.

"What are you doing he-yuh?" she said, hand in its usual position on her hip.

"Uh, I just got here… I had a couple of things to take care of and I didn't want any distractions. Do you know if Ronnie is in yet?"

"We walked in together, why?" she said, in a protective tone. "What do you need?"

"Oh, just a technology question that I have to ask."

"Oh, okay… that's not my territory. But coffee is, it will be ready in five. Anything else?"

"Uh, yes… can you look on the student system and see if we have a student by the name of Candace Kane, with a 'K'?"

"Candy Kane?  Would you like me to look for Pepper Mint while I'm at it?"

"No, just Candace… and any variations thereof," I said with a smile.

"You got it."  With that, Judy turned, leaving behind the sweet scent of her freshly-applied perfume in my doorway.  As I walked through the mist, I was sure that I would be smelling like lilacs, lilies of the valley, or whatever the bloom du jour was for the rest of the day.  The *rest* of my day!  I was going to meet Lacey later, so it was going to be a banner day indeed.

I walked over to Ronnie's office, camera in hand.  "Good morning, Ronnie."

"Oh, Doug, good morning.  What can I do for you?"

"Could you print out the photos on my phone?"

"Of course.  I can download them now so that I don't keep your phone and then print them out.  Do you need them right away?"

"I have a jammed day, so by the time you leave would be great, thanks."

"You and Jimmy both.  He's booked solid until 4pm, but it looks like he's got something scheduled with you then?"  *Right,* I thought, *a date at the Shore Thing.*  Lacey was clear about not involving the police and I wanted to respect her.  Even though Jerry was far from a cop, I worried that bringing a friend might freak her out.  I made the spontaneous decision to cut Jerry loose-- I was going on the mission solo.

"You know what? I don't think I'll be able to make our 4 o'clock.  Tell Jerry that I'll talk to him later and not to worry about it."

"I'm sure he'll appreciate the time. I'll tell him and I'll have your photos for you by this afternoon."

"Thank you, Ronnie, I'll see you later," I said, and I went back to my office to occupy my day with meetings full of people vying for my attention. Hopefully, none of them would know that they weren't my first priorities of the day. Two people topped that list: the man in one of the photos that I had just taken, and Lacey.

~~~~~

I told Lacey that I would meet her at 4pm and since I had disinvited Jerry. That meant that I would have to walk to the Shore Thing Motel. That, or walk home and grab my car, which I was sure would raise Barbara's suspicions. I would have to leave my office by 3:40pm. I did my best to focus on my daily responsibilities but by 2 o'clock, I began to get antsy. By 3 o'clock, I was barely listening to anyone in my presence. I was eager to talk to Lacey and see what she had to say.

As I was eyeing the clock at 3:35pm, ready to give up and make my way to Asbury Park, Judy buzzed me. "Mary Mumford for you. I know you have an off-campus appointment, do you want me to take a message?"

"No, I have a couple of minutes," I said, welcoming the distraction, "I'll take Mary." A second later I heard Judy click Mary on, "Doug?" she said, sounding distressed.

"Hi, Mary. What's wrong?"

"I just got a call from the Ocean Grove Police Department. They want to talk to me."

"Oh?" I said, "what about?"

"I don't know, they wouldn't say. I thought maybe you knew?" Mary asked hopefully. I thought for a second. No, the Chief hadn't mentioned calling Health Services, perhaps he had a new lead? Although not as nervous, I was certainly as curious as Mary.

"No, Mary, I don't know anything about it. I'm sure it's just routine. My advice is to give the PD anything they ask for, you have no reason to be nervous."

"Oh, okay," she hesitated, obviously looking for more information than I had to share. "He asked me about Darcy Green. Do you know why?"

I realized that I wasn't sure if it was common knowledge that Darcy Green was found murdered, but I didn't have any clue why the Chief would be asking Mary about her. "No," I said truthfully, "I don't. Did you, uh, do you," I corrected myself, "know Darcy Green?"

She hesitated again, "Well, I'm not sure… I'd have to check."

"Okay, Mary, well like I said, just be honest and it will all be fine." Although I thought that the statement was proof that I wanted to disengage from the telephone, Mary continued, "Well, while I have you on the phone," she said, "are you coming to Video Game Night?"

"Yes, I plan to.  Malificent spoke to me about it this morning, sounds like a great event."

"Yes, I think it will be," Mary hesitated, "Uh, thank you, Doug.  I'll keep you posted about the Police."  We hung up but I could tell that Mary was still tense.  Why?  The thought crossed my mind to call the Chief, but I couldn't at that moment… since I was on my way to a meeting of which I was fairly sure he wouldn't approve.  I looked at my watch, 3:39pm.  It was time for my walk to Asbury Park and my date at the Shore Thing Motel.

~~~~~

As I walked off-campus, I began thinking about my recent life's events.  What I had once considered to be a normal existence had turned to be unusual of late, to say the least.  Why in just 24 hours, I had watched the bones of a dead man get dated, found a hooded stranger lurking in my backyard, shut myself in a closet while sneaking around where I didn't belong, discovered that the police were investigating Health Services, and was on my way to meet a stripper at a well-known house of ill-repute. It seemed as though mundane had left my life and I was slightly ashamed to admit that I was enjoying the fast pace. Perhaps it was because I had always been somewhat of a nerd, and now, I had a taste of what it felt like to be *involved* in the action, instead of being boring old Clark Kent.

Steel grey clouds darkened the afternoon sky and threatened rain without regard to the fact that I failed to bring an umbrella. I quickened my pace as I made my way over the footbridge across Asbury Lake, the slim body of water that separated Ocean Grove and Asbury Park. Once touted as one of the most polluted lakes in the country, Asbury Lake had been taken under the wing of a vocal citizens' organization who lobbied hard to gain State funding for its renewal. Within the last year, and several substantial grants, the swans that inhabited the lake, no longer swam in sludge. Some viewed this as another sign that Asbury Park was on the verge of a renaissance, others looked at it as just another good deed accomplished by the quirky do-gooders that lived in the Shores.

As I stepped off the footbridge, a mere 30 feet long, and into Asbury Park, I glanced to my left to take a look at my favorite restaurant, Moonstruck. Once nestled in a cozy little spot on Main Avenue, with a dining room seating 50, Moonstruck relocated to be part of the growing Asbury Park business life.

It now occupied a large three story building that looked more like a spacious Victorian hotel than a restaurant. Inside, Moonstruck had grown in an equally splendid way, with the first floor lounge reminiscent of something out of the classic movie, *Casablanca*. Complete with dark wood, potted palm, and a grand piano, Moonstruck had grown from a homey little bistro to a grand world-class eatery. Barbara and I made it a priority to walk there at least once a month for some rosemary chicken and a nice glass of wine. As I passed, I wished that my plans were different and that I was headed to the dining room instead of Lacey's motel room.

Other than Moonstruck and Smoke (which was just down the street closer to the ocean), I didn't know the streets of Asbury Park at all. I did know that since it used to be a premier tourist resort, there were a number of old hotels and motels sprinkled around the town, several situated around the perimeter of Smoke's parking lot. A quick internet search the day before showed that this was the resting ground for the Shore Thing Motel, which must have made a convenient commute for the ladies of Smoke.

I continued my quick pace, skirting around the famous grinning face, Tilly, painted on the dilapidated Palace Amusements building across the street from Smoke. Once a place where kids and adults alike could go inside for a ride on a tilt-o-whirl, merry-go-round, or even a dreaded (by me anyway) Ferris wheel, it was presently boarded up, trapping the laughter and excitement from long ago inside as mere shadows. I ignored Tilly's beseeching grin to come and play, and crossed the street entering Smoke's parking lot, which at that time of day was mostly vacant. Before me, on the west side of the crackled pavement, were two motels whose appearance gave new meaning to the term, "economy." Both were two story structures, one with the stairs to the second floor cordoned off with yellow tape.

Even from a couple hundred feet away, I could see draperies half-hanging like debris from dirt-tinted plate glass windows, and miscellaneous articles of clothing hanging off of plastic lawn chairs and railings. To the left was the Sea DeLite motel, the one with the yellow tape and condemned second floor. I wondered if the management boasted amenities such as, "Our custom SILENT ceiling! NEVER hear loud guests above your head again!" To the right, was a pink and lime green neon sign that screamed, "Shore Thing Motel." In a moment of procrastination, I looked to the sky, perhaps for some comfort, or maybe for a sign from God about my next move. All I received in return was a cold, galvanized stare. Whatever I was getting myself into, I was on my own.

-19-

I walked steadily toward the building and hesitated at room 104 on the ground floor of the Shore Thing Motel like a nervous prom date. I think I even primped my hair before I knocked. I tapped on the door quietly, fearing that Lacey would hear me and actually answer. What was I doing? Why didn't I let Jerry come with me? What would Barbara say? All those questions became moot as the door opened and I was standing face to face with Lacey.

~~~~~

In many ways, she was a contradiction of the image that my mind had created of Lacey "the exotic dancer" from Smoke. She was tall and reminded me of RuPaul as a brunette. She was a striking woman possessing both the carved features of a statue and

the softened subtleties of femininity.  In a word,
Lacey was beautiful.

"Doug?" came her familiar voice that I
remembered from our brief phone conversation.

"Yes.  Lacey?" I asked without any thought.
What other strange woman at the Shore Thing Motel
in Asbury Park would know my name?

"Come in," she said with a big smile, almost
seductively, as she put her perfectly manicured hand
on my shoulder and pulled me inside. *Oh, no!* was
my first thought. Did I misunderstand something?
Did she think this was a "date?"  Didn't she say that
she had something to tell *me*?  I reread her cryptic
note in my mind and replayed our phone
conversation.  She never actually *said* that she had
information about Darcy Green… or did she?  In my
desperation for information, did I make that up?
Was she more than a
stripper… was she also a call girl?  My stomach
knotted.

"Would you like a drink?" she asked, moving
toward a residence hall sized room refrigerator.  She
didn't walk, she floated, her gait accentuated by a
sheer black skirt with tiny white polka dots and fitted
black top.

"Uh, no, thank you.  Look, you may have this
wrong… I might have misunderstood…" I
stammered, reprising my role as the nervous prom
date.  She paused and turned toward me, "Don't
worry, darlin'.  I didn't misunderstand anything,"
she finished with a grin and a wink.  It wasn't good.

It wasn't good at all.  Lacey thought that I was her latest John.

~~~~~

"No," I said, "I think there was some miscommunication, here."  Lacey turned to me, having converted her congenial smile to pursed lips.  She said nothing, but shook her head and walked over to a small desk.  The furniture in the room looked like it had been purchased in the fifties and showed the wear that a half-century brings.  There was a double bed, a nightstand, a desk, and one dresser all situated against walnut paneling.  Clearly her abode, the room had a few futile touches that tried to make it homey-- a pink scarf draped over a chrome lamp, a lace accent pillow sitting pretty on the bed, and a few framed pictures on the top of the dresser.  Despite her best efforts, the motel room still felt suffocating, perhaps from years of wear and activities that the carpet couldn't forget.

She grabbed a piece of paper from a notepad and began scribbling.  I looked on in silence, as she held up her note to me:

> We can't talk here...
> SAY- "Let's do it on the beach"
> I'll explain.

This situation just kept getting more uncomfortable.  So, she didn't think that I was her latest customer, but did she really expect me to say that? I realized that I had no choice but to follow Lacey's lead, and continue to put my trust in this stranger.

"So, what's your pleasure?" she purred.

"Uh…" I hesitated, as she pierced me with an exaggerated stare.

"Let's go do it on the beach," I finally uttered, sounding like a bad actor in a porno movie, but it was the cue that Lacey needed, "Oh, well okay. You sure do know what you want, huh? Let's not waste any more time." She quickly walked past me and walked out the door. I gladly followed, shutting it behind me.

"Do you want to lock it?" I said, sounding more like a boy scout than a John.

"Won't matter if I do," Lacey continued walking, "nothing to take." She walked briskly through Smoke's parking lot and I realized how tall she was. My short legs were no match for her. She noticed me struggling to meet her pace, and slowed until we were side by side. I looked up at her and nodded a thank you, not knowing if it was safe to speak yet.

"It's safer this way," she said, "some of the girls think that their rooms are bugged… we know that the guy at the front desk listens to any call that comes through. Norman Bates piece of shit."

I chuckled at the humor, and ironic desperation, and took it as my cue, "So we can talk, now?"

"Let's chit chat until we get beyond the boardwalk. If anyone's paying attention, they'll get suspicious if we don't go to the beach. I mean, that is where you wanted to *do it.*" Lacey smiled, and I realized how much liked her. She was genuine and her personality was magnetic. I understood how she could excel at being an exotic dancer... or anything else she set her mind to.

"Have you been dancing long?" I asked, trying to make conversation and not get into counseling mode.

"Five years. First in Baltimore, now up here."

"Why the move?"

"My mother lives here in Asbury Park, I wanted to be closer to her." Lacey paused, then looked away from me, "she thinks I'm a nurse." Although I wanted to pursue it, it wasn't my place, so I said nothing.

We crossed Ocean Avenue in front of the boardwalk, barely looking for traffic. Except for a couple of parked cars and a few people loitering about, the street was deserted. Lacey led the way across the boards and directly down a set of aging wooden steps to the beach. I thought that she was going to walk straight down to the shore line, but she stopped half-way and turned to me.

"Thank you for doing this, I know it's a lot to ask."

"Well, after I got decked at the club, the note sparked my interest.  I assume you were there that night?  I don't remember seeing you."

"Yes, I was there, but you didn't see me. One of the other girls slipped my note into your friend's pocket."

"Well, you got my attention," I paused, not sure if I should ask specific questions or simply let Lacey talk.  I didn't have to wait long before she began.

"A few of us were worried that you were going to get into trouble… asking about Ivory and all."

"Ivory called *me*," I responded defensively, "she asked me to meet her there."

"But she didn't make it.  She lived in the motel room next to mine.  I'm the one who found her…the day before."

"What happened?" I couldn't help asking.

"They made it look like an overdose, but Ivory didn't get her name for nothing.  That girl was pure as snow.  *They* got her."

"Who's *they*?" I asked, curiosity pushing me to get the information faster.

"I don't really know, but a lot of the girls have gotten involved.  Drugs… dealing… it's bad news."  Lacey looked away, a move indicating that she was holding something back.

"But who is the leader?  Who's organizing the drug ring," I pressed, not believing that I just used the term "drug ring" in casual conversation.

"Uh… I don't really know… I mean, I think the big boss is out of New York City."

"So who organizes the women *here*?"

"I don't really want to say… I don't think it is something that you should know… not something that you *need* to know."

But I did need to know. If for no other reason than satiating my curiosity, I needed to know. So I continued, "Lacey, if someone was responsible for killing Darcy, who was one of my students, I *need* to know." That one got her, and she looked away from me again and said quietly, "Bruno. He works at the club. You met him, he's the one you talked to about meeting Ivory. That's why we had to get you away from him." She was right, I did know Bruno. He must have been the guy that I had referred to as Danny DeVito.

~~~~~

"So the women are getting involved in drugs?" I asked.

"Some are using, but more are finding it more worthwhile dealing. They're getting a 25% cut. That's what got Darcy."

"So she was your friend?" I asked. Just as I was getting comfortable, a seagull cried overhead causing both of us to jump and reminding us that a certain level of paranoia was warranted in the conversation.

"Yes, she was such a good kid. Although at first she liked the extra money, she wanted to get out from under *them*. She really liked your college. She was a good student, wasn't she?" I simply nodded, encouraging her to go on.

"She pushed for a while, mostly at the College, it was so easy. Young kids like candy. But she got tired of *them* pressuring her."

"The students?" I interrupted without thought.

"No, the bosses. Darcy wanted to be a normal kid. She even talked about living in the dorms… but they wouldn't let her stop. They warned her, they said that if she stopped working for them, she'd be dead. They didn't lie." She stopped and took a deep breath. Her gaze moved from the sand to me, "She liked you."

"I don't think I knew her," I said feeling guilty. The only time that I remembered seeing her was laid out on a stainless steel table at the funeral home.

"Well," Lacey consoled, "you can't know all of the students, right? Whether you knew her or not, she knew *you*. That's how we got your name. She would talk about the College and that good looking *Dean Doug guy*." I was sure that I blushed, and quickly looked down toward the sand.

Lacey continued, "She even had your picture posted in her locker at work… from the student newspaper, or something. You really made an impression on her." It was something that I said to my staff all the time, *you may never know what sort of an impact you make on a student, but you have to know that you do.* I believed it, but it was especially hard to consider when the student in question was dead.

"So what happened to Ivory?" I asked, changing the subject.

"When Darcy was killed, I hear that they shot her and threw her in the ocean, they didn't want to lose out on the market that she built at the college… you probably don't want to hear this, but it was big… still is. So, they tapped Ivory to take over Darcy's territory. Ivory was a little different. Her sister's in foster care down the shore somewhere, Ocean County I think. At first she was doing it to get some money together to get her sister out. You know, rent an apartment, make a better life."

"But then?"

"After she got enough money, Ivory wanted out, even found someone to take over her side of the business. She knew that she couldn't take care of her sister if she was dead. She was going to leave Smoke… go down to live near her little sister and find a way to be a family. When she decided to go, they got mad. Within the week, she was dead, too."

"So they're okay as long as they continue dealing?"

"Yes, as long as they continue dealing for *them*."

"What do you mean?"

"It's complicated. Darcy wanted out, it's true. But she was smart. She knew that if she worked for herself, she could make more profit."

"An entrepreneurial spirit, huh?"

"Yes, and like I said, she was smart. Darcy found a way to get the drugs herself. She even asked a couple of us if we wanted to work with her... for her. I think they got wind of it."

"So she found her own supplier in Asbury?" I asked. Then she hesitated, "No..." Lacey said, this time facing me intently, "On-campus."

-20-

I hadn't expected that.  There was a drug supplier on Asbury's campus?  "Who is it?" I blurted out, unintentionally.

"I don't know," Lacey responded, unfazed. "All I know is that Darcy knew someone on-campus who could help her get the goods she needed.  That's what I really wanted to tell you.  I thought that you should know."

"I appreciate that," I said, growing slightly suspicious.  "But why would you tell me this and endanger yourself?  You could have just written it down in the note?"

Lacey  faced the ocean again and then turned back around toward the boardwalk.  I sensed that I had offended her.

"It just seemed like the right thing to do," she said quietly, "but I suppose it has a different meaning, coming from a girl like me."  Yup, I had offended her.

"That's not what I meant," I said trying to back-pedal, but meaning it, "it just seems like such a risk for you."

"I've taken lots of risks in my life.  Everyday around this business is a risk.  I guess I'm used to it," she said, beginning to walk away.  There it was, an infinite difference between Lacey and me.  I was new to risk, yet for Lacey, it was a way of everyday life.

"I'm sorry that I offended you," I said.  "It wasn't my intent."

"Rarely is," she said, turning back and smiling sadly. It was that statement that made me realize how much prejudice Lacey endured on a daily basis in her line of work.

"We should probably get back," Lacey said, brushing off my offense with nonchalance typical of an abused human. "I'm sure you have other things to do." That bothered me, too. It seemed that another thing commonplace to Lacey was being abandoned after sharing intimate parts of herself.

There wasn't anything I could do but thank her. "Thank you for doing this," I uttered feebly. "I know you took a great risk."

"It's okay," she said. "I'm not sure that I did you any favors… now you've got even bigger problems."

We made our way up the beach steps and onto the boardwalk without any more conversation. As we looked to our left, the one-way stretch of Ocean in Asbury Park, I saw Lacey stiffen. Her head darted quickly to the left, and then she swung around and embraced me in a big bear hug. Both helpless and clueless, I stood like a rag doll waiting for Lacey's next move. "There's a black car down the street," she pressed in my ear. "I think he's been following us."

She held me so tight that I couldn't move. Then she continued, "I noticed it parked when we went to the beach and now it's closer," she said, pausing to kiss me on the cheek. Then she continued, "Take your wallet out."

"What?" I hoarsely whispered back.

"Take your wallet out. Just give me a dollar. We've got to make this look real."

"But what if it's the police-- undercover?" I asked.

"If they're an undercover cop, it won't matter. They can't prove what you gave me money for, especially if all's I have on me is a dollar. If it's not the cops, we'll be showing whoever it is that I provided a service-- and you paid me. Everyone's safer that way." Lacey released her tight hold on me, allowing me to reach into my back pocket. Instinctively, I began to look toward the car, but she stopped me.

"Don't do it," she said through gritted teeth and a smile. "Just look in your wallet."

I complied and picked out one of the only dollar bills I had. "Good thing you didn't ask for a twenty," I said, folding the bill so tightly that no one could see the denomination.

"Twenty?" Lacey said, hand on her hip. "Honey, if this were real, twenty wouldn't have gotten you the walk down here." She winked, took the bill, and put it in her bra. "Thank you, Dean Doug," she said with the stare of a cherished friend, "Now I know why Darcy had a crush on you." I didn't know it then, but I would never see Lacey again.

Lacey turned, looked toward the car one more time, and then crossed the street. I stood alone, watching her walk quickly through the Smoke parking lot and near the Shore Thing Motel. Suddenly, I felt vulnerable. Especially when the black car began slowly moving toward me.

~~~~~

I froze for a second. *What do I do? Run? Which way?* I needed to run right past the car in order to go back to Ocean Grove, but I didn't relish running *away* from the car and further from home. Maybe it was nothing. Maybe the car's occupants weren't watching Lacey and me at all. The thought made me glance toward the Shore Thing. I didn't see her. *Good.* She was safe.

I realized that I couldn't just stand there. I had to move. The beach. I could go back onto the beach and run toward home, then take a different set of boardwalk steps back up to the street level after I passed the car. That was the plan! I turned on my heels and moved quickly, but steadily, back down the rickety steps to the beach. Once there, I took off in a run south, toward the Grove, sand filling my wing-tips almost immediately.

I knew that I looked ridiculous-- a man in a sport coat and dress slacks and dress shoes struggling to run in the sand. If I hadn't looked like I was guilty of doing something wrong before, I certainly did now. Luckily for me, there wasn't another soul around. Also lucky for me, the next set of steps up was only about ten yards away.

Although I had my eyes on my target to freedom, a mere five yards away, I continued to struggle, wading like I was running through quick sand. Normally I ran on the boardwalk, and sometimes on the smooth, packed sand of the shoreline, but never in the thick of sand at the top of the beach. Suddenly, I heard something behind me, "Hey!" came the voice, and I lost my footing altogether. Whomever was following me in the car had joined me on the sand.

~~~~~

Although I had fallen on all fours, I immediately jumped back up, making a new break for the steps. "Hey!" came the man's voice again. I ignored him, not even bothering to turn around. If I was struggling in the sand, he would be too… unless of course, he was observing me from the boardwalk, looking down on my limited progress. *Shit!* I thought. If that was the case, I was merely a rat in a maze. I needed to take a second and turn to see my attacker… his position either behind me in the sand, or above me on the boards would tell me if I had a chance to get away safely-- or not.

~~~~~

I continued to move forward, while looking quickly and over my shoulder down the sand. I still couldn't see anyone. That meant that the person chasing me was on firm footing on the boardwalk.  I was sunk.  I stopped and looked six feet above me... again, nobody.  Did I imagine the voice?

But then I heard it again, this time, coming from my destination-- the steps I was struggling to reach.  "Hey, Doug.  What are you doing?"  That's when I looked up and saw Jerry, standing on the steps looking like a secret service agent in dark suit, white shirt, and sunglasses.

I stopped in the sand and began laughing.

"I thought you were after me," I said into the sand.

"I was," Jerry responded.  "I was trying to pick you up and give you a ride home... but you ran.  Who did you think I was?"

"A mob boss... drug lord... or pimp.  You know, no one special."  I started moving again and slumped down on the steps when I finally reached them.

"Didn't you recognize my car?" he asked.

"No.  The only time I was in your car was night, and Lacey put the idea in my head that you might be someone dangerous."

"You shouldn't have gone without me," Jerry said in a caring tone.  "I went back to the office to pick you up and Ronnie said that you had left for the day.  At first, I thought maybe you had decided to cancel your date, but then I realized that you probably just went alone."

"So, my knight in black armor, you came to save me?"

"I came to see if you needed me, and to give you a ride.  But as I saw it, it seemed as though you were doing pretty well.  That was Lacey, right?  I recognized her from the club.  She seemed, uh, friendly," Jerry smirked.

"You remembered her from Smoke?"

"I don't remember seeing her the night we were there,  but I've seen her there before."

"Oh, I forgot, you're a frequent flyer," I chuckled, reaching down to soothe my ankle which was throbbing.

"You okay, boss?"

"Running in the sand aggravated my ankle," I said.  "I'll be fine.  Let's go."  I got up and stretched my ankle on the stairs before going onto the boardwalk.  Jerry towered above me, watching.

"So, buddy, that was a pretty nice hug you got.  And was there a kiss, too?"

"There was no kiss," I said, more defensively than I needed to be, "and she hugged me because we didn't know who *you* were.  She thought that you might be someone watching us."

"I was," Jerry laughed.  We got to the car and he let me into the passenger side, bringing back memories of Smoke, which was coincidentally, only steps away.  As he got in the car, Jerry grabbed a large manila envelope and handed it to me, "Ronnie left these for you."

"Oh, great," I said, remembering the photos that I had asked her for.  "Thanks."

"So, boss, tell me what went on!"  Jerry blurted, putting the Caddie into drive.

"I'll fill you in," I said.  "Just get me out of here and home."

I was trying to decide just how much I would share with Jerry.  I knew that I couldn't tell him everything, which solidified the fact that I was once again involved in a very risky situation; one in which people were in danger—some even murdered.

~~~~~

Jerry pulled the Caddie up in front of my house at about 5:30pm.  I got out and walked straight inside with a fairly normal gait; my ankle felt better already.  Still feeling a little tense about my encounter with Lacey, I walked inside and pushed my back up against the door to close it.  I rested there momentarily, inhaling the comforting scent of home.

"Hi, honey!" Barbara's voice came from the kitchen, and again, I was comforted by her sound.  "I have an idea," she called as I made my way toward her.  I walked into the kitchen, and immediately gave her a kiss (which was normal), but then paused and embraced her (which was not).  "Oh," she said, almost startled, "to what do I owe this honor?"

"Just glad to be home," I said, smiling and looking over my glasses at her.

"What happened," she said, more like a statement than a question.

"I'll tell you," I began, looking toward the empty stove, "over dinner?"  Then I noticed that

Barbara was not wearing her customary jeans and polo shirt, but capris and sandals.

"That was my idea. Ethan's next door and is going to have dinner there. I thought that we could walk to Moonstruck!" It was the perfect plan, exactly what I needed. "Great idea," I said.

"And look what I found today," Barbara said, holding a folded taupe sheet of notepaper and handing it to me.

I scanned it quickly, "A poem?"

"Did you read it?"

I scanned it more closely:

"At last the Skull & Cross are joined, for all eternity. They don the hoods and hide their eyes so no one else can see.

The five revered, the chosen ones, will lead us not alone. They chart our course and set new heights, beyond the Wolf & Bones.

A kinship one, a Holy view, is guarded by the knife. For anyone, who dare cross skulls, will rue the day for life!"

"A threat?" I asked. "Where did you find it?

"Well, I found it this morning in our mailbox. I bet this is why we had a visitor last night... someone was dropping off a love letter. If it is meant as a threat, it's an old one. I went back to the archives today and found the same poem. Did you talk to Chief Morreale today?"

"I didn't get to it," I said. "I'll fill you in on our walk to the restaurant."

"Good," she said, "and I have a few more tidbits that I found for you, too."

~~~~~

I'm not sure that Barbara and I had held hands since BE (Before Ethan), but that night, we held hands the entire walk to Moonstruck. The threat of rain had passed, and it was just the right setting to relay to Barbara what transpired in my meeting with Lacey.

"Doug!" Barbara scolded, "what were you thinking going there alone? We talked about this! Why didn't you at least tell me? What if something happened? We never would have found you!" Her voice held an intensity that promoted worry.

"Jerry knew," I responded, "and in fact, he was there!"

"That's not the point. I don't want you running renegade. Wait, are you limping?" she asked, looking down. "Did you hurt your ankle again?"

"I guess running in the sand aggravated it. It feels better now," I said, remembering that even Superman had Lois Lane. "I'm sorry. I should have told you."

"Yes, you should have," Barbara responded, feigning anger, "so, what did Lacey say about Darcy Green?"

I hesitated, not sure how much I wanted to share, deciding that this time, I had better be up front. So I told her about Darcy, and Ivory, and the drug ring that seemed to have a hold on my campus.

"Doug! So there *is* a drug ring!" Barbara said, gripping my hand more tightly, "This is getting too dangerous. I don't want you involved anymore, it doesn't sound like you're dealing with amateurs."

"But Darcy *was* an amateur."

"Exactly, *was* is the operative term… she's not here anymore. Did you call Chief Morreale?"

"No. I was going to, but my beautiful wife whisked me away to go out to dinner. I didn't have time," I said, using my best skills at deflection.

"Well tomorrow, then, promise me?"

I considered her question, wanting to make sure that I could fulfill my promise to her, "I'll call him."

"Tomorrow," Barbara interjected, emphatically.

"I promise that I won't go running around Asbury again, or meeting anyone involved with the case until I tell the Chief," I said again, afraid to lock myself into a timeframe.

Barbara sighed, "Fair enough… I love you. I just don't want anything to happen to you." I squeezed her hand in acknowledgement, not knowing that the real danger was yet to come.

-21-

After two glasses of merlot, a plateful of rosemary chicken and garlic mashed potatoes, and sharing Moonstruck's famous crème Brule (with a thin layer of chocolate on the bottom), I was relaxed. I was also intrigued by what Barbara had found on her latest venture to the library's archives.

"So, you found the same poem in the archives?" I asked.

"Yup," she said, savoring a mouthful of Crème Brule. "The one I found was dated 1875. The one we received, however, was obviously transcribed on a computer."

"What other *tidbits* did you find?"

"More photos. There is literally a box full of photos that doesn't look like anyone has touched it for decades. Luckily, many of the photos have dates and even identifying information on the back. I pulled as many as I could find and placed them in a pile. Myrna knows where they are… when do you think you'll go down there?"

"Maybe tomorrow, I'll have to see what my day looks like."

"Just tell Myrna. She'll point you in the right direction."

I scraped a little more of the crème and chocolate goodness from the dish and then savoring the mouthful, asked, "So what kind of photos?"

"A lot of events… activities… even some candids. I thought that once you identified your person, the photos might help you get a better sense of who they were… help tell their story." Spoken like a true journalist.

"Now," Barbara continued, "have you identified your person, yet?"

"No, but I have all of the group photos."

"From that secret conference room?"

"Yes, I took them this morning." Of course, I couldn't simply say it, without telling the details. Not with Barbara Carter-Connors.

"Wow!" she said, with a hint of sarcasm, "you've had quite a day!"

"Yes," I emphasized, "I have.  We can look at the photos later.  Ronnie printed them out for me and I have them back at the house."

"Sounds like fun," she said seriously.  "And wait until you read some of these love letters… I transcribed a few… I'll read them to you at home. They are just beautiful… poignant.  They might have been an elitist bunch of guys, but they were far from unfeeling."

I looked at my watch, noticing that it was almost 8pm, Ethan's bedtime.  We finished the last couple of bites of Crème Brule, paid the check, and walked directly to our neighbor's house to get Ethan; in total about twenty minutes.  Ethan and I caught up on our days (I left out a lot of details) and I read him a few stories before putting him to bed.  When I went back downstairs, Barbara was sitting in the family room holding a legal pad on her lap and reading intently.

I walked over to her and gave her a peck on the cheek, "What do you have there that's so interesting?"

"These poems. I mean, they really give this group heart… read for yourself." Barbara handed me the pad where she had jotted notes and I read the first one:

"Each day I love you… ever more.

Your heart I need beside me.
If we can't meet, clandestinely-
Your love is there to guide me."

"Well," I said, "I don't think Emily Dickinson has anything to be worried about, seems pretty elementary to me. I didn't think you were this sappy?"

"Oh, so now you're a poetry critic? All I'm saying is that all we ever see of Skull and Cross are dark robes, elitism, and righteousness. This adds an entirely different dimension. Read on…"

I looked down again, and read another one:

"my soul is with you, from
Afar...
you're with me no maTTer
where you are.
If life were new, a place
refreshed, we'd be together...
and both be blessed.
I love you MORE, each
passing day, yet still we
seem alone.
I wonder- a new time, a new
place, a new decade still...
Will our love be truly
shown?"

"Same old, same old," I said, mockingly. "I
love you, I can't have you... it's what soap operas
are made of. At least it's not as dark as the one left
in our mailbox."

"But don't you see it?" Barbara stated, sitting
straighter in her chair. "He's hopeful that it will
work out." She grabbed the pad from my hands, "I
thought you'd appreciate the poetry, aren't you a

*renaissance man*?" Looking over my glasses, I could see a hint of mockery in her eyes.

"Maybe I'm just not a poetry connoisseur. I'll trust your judgment. Now, you've shown me yours, do you want to see mine?"

"I saw it last night," Barbara said with a smile.

"Not that," I winked. "The photos I took. I haven't even looked at them yet." I led Barbara into the kitchen where I had set the envelope on the island. I eagerly pulled out the half-dozen photographs and arranged them in a line. Ronnie had printed them out in 5x7 format. Barbara leaned over my shoulder and examined them, "Yes, these are just like the ones in the archives… with less resolution."

"I know," I said. "I took them with the camera on my phone. The quality isn't the best, but it's something."

"No, they're not bad," Barbara reassured. "It's just that the photos in the archives are originals. So, are these photos in any order?"

"No, but I took them in order of date from 1955 to 1960. Even though I think the victim's in the 1956 or '57 picture, I took the others just to be safe. But now that they're out of order, I have no way of knowing what year is what," I said, dejectedly.

"Not so fast," Barbara said excitedly. "Look in your phone. If you took them in order, all we have to do is match the order on your phone to the photos here on the counter." Barbara was brilliant, one of the many reasons I married her.

I pulled my phone from my pocket and began scrolling through, rearranging the photographs on the counter as best I could tell from the tiny pixilated photographs. The end result didn't look much different than before. I stood, realizing that I didn't have much at all. Although I suspected that the murder victim was staring back at me, without names, it didn't mean much at all. I was beginning to feel deflated, when Barbara chimed in, "That's interesting."

"What's interesting?" I said, looking at her.

"This one," she pointed to the picture I believed to be 1957. "This one is different."

I examined the photo: Five white guys standing in a row in black robes... just like all the others.

"This guy," she said, pointing to the young man on the end. "I don't remember seeing him in the photos in the archives."

"And you remember them in that detail?"

"He stands out, he's the only one with a beard," Barbara said, still pointing. I scanned the photos. She was right. He was the one who was clearly not like the others. "So you don't think this guy is in the supposedly same photo in the archives?" I asked, growing hopeful.

"No," she said shaking her head and flashing a smile. "I don't think so... trust my investigative mind. Now you have more reasons to visit the archives, not only to read more poetry, but to see if I'm right."

~~~~~

I woke up the next morning and once again decided to forgo my run.  Since aggravating my ankle in the sand the day before, I didn't want to push it.  I chose, however, to get up, put on my sweats and walk the boards just so I didn't break the habit that I had spent years developing.

The air wasn't chilly, it was cold, and my breath wafted around my head like pipe smoke.  I ran back inside, traded my baseball cap for a knitted hat, and got on my way.  Despite the chill, it felt good to be out and moving at 5:45am, and in many ways, it felt good to bring some normalcy back to my life.  I marveled that regardless of my preoccupation with skulls, murder, and drugs, the Grove remained largely unchanged.

Mrs. Crosier's porch swing still served as a bed for neighborhood cats, the sign touting fresh donuts at the bakery still encouraged visitors to the "AKERY" (the B fell off during the recently passed hurricane season), and Cruzer was up and making his rounds.  It was the beauty about living in a small town-- so many comforting constants that some people found claustrophobic, but I found comforting.

I hit the boards and immediately turned right toward Bradley Beach, perhaps choosing not to go in the other direction toward Asbury Park subconsciously.  I walked at a brisk pace, even further than my normal running route, going through Bradley Beach and into Avon-by-the-Sea before turning around.  Probably only a mile, but I felt like I had run a marathon, in a good way, refreshed by the experience.  I was ready to start the day, not knowing that during its course, I would solve one mystery and uncover a new one.

~~~~~

It wasn't until I was primped and pressed and ready for the start of my day at the office that I remembered that I had to pick-up my glasses at the Optical Shoppe.  It was 9:15am by my watch and I decided to make a quick diversion on Main Avenue before proceeding to campus.  The bodiless faces greeted my return through bespectacled eyes in the storefront window, as I pushed my way through the front door, jingling as I passed through.  Dr. Farrow's portly frame hovered over one of the display cases and greeted me warmly.

"Dean Doug!" he said as though I was an old friend.  "Wonderful to see you.  I have your new glasses right here, they came in late yesterday afternoon."  He pushed himself off the stool on which he was sitting and walked my refurbished glasses, complete with new faux black leather case, to the cash register.  "The total," he extolled, "Is $63.07, including the tax.  A high density lens is typically more expensive, but I gave you an educator's discount." He grinned widely through his bushy grey mustache, either about cutting me a break or about the fact that he had a customer with expensive needs, I couldn't tell which.

As I reached for my wallet and pulled out my credit card, I noticed a hand-written sign that was posted on the register:

"No $100 bills accepted.  No foreign currency.
Thank you for your understanding-
The Management"

"Glad I rarely have a $100 bill," I quipped, handing him my plastic.

"It's a wolf's shame," he said, reminding me of his quirky response from my last visit, "counterfeit bills.  Have you heard?"

"No," I said casually.

"They started filtering in a few weeks ago, it hasn't affected some businesses like the coffee shop or the bakery who don't often get bigger bills, but for places like mine who have higher ticket items, we've been hit harder."

"So you've received counterfeit bills?"

"Yes-- about $500 worth.  Of course the Savings and Loan got hit the hardest since we all make our daily deposits there.  Apparently the loss is in the thousands.  They're the ones who alerted all of the local businesses."

"Wow, that's something," was all I could manage to say. "And what about foreign currency?"

"Although it's rare, since we're a town that gets lots of tourists, we occasionally receive foreign currency, Canadian really. I have always accepted Canadian currency, making the appropriate exchange, of course. But according to the S & L, there has been a rash of counterfeit Canadian bills floating around town, too. Luckily, I didn't get any of them."

"Well, good luck," I said, barely interested. Little did I know that my interest would be piqued as the months progressed. Dr. Farrow prepared the credit card slip for me to sign and ushered me to sit down to be fitted. "Let me see," he said, "just a minor adjustment... there. How do they feel?"

"Great," I said. "Thank you."

"My pleasure. Now you're already for the Alumni Gala? You will be going, right?" I had no idea what he was talking about.

"I'm not sure," I responded, trying to mask my ignorance.

"Well, I hope so," he said, then leaned closer to me and whispered, "I'll see you there." *What was he talking about?* I wondered about the secrecy, which made me realize that he was referring to the upcoming Skull and Cross alumni event; the one that R.I.P. had been talking about and the purpose of the early morning meeting the day before.

"I hope so," I said vaguely, not knowing how else to respond, and then headed out of the shop toward my office.

On my walk I thought about Dr. Farrow's cryptic conversation. I knew he was an Asbury College alum, but of course had no idea that he was a member of Skull and Cross. Did he think I knew? More importantly, why did he make it a point to make it known, if even in an obscure way? I wasn't sure, but couldn't take the time to think about it. I had more pressing things on my mind, like clearing part of my morning's calendar to go visit the archives.

~~~~~

I walked into the office around 9:50am greeted by Judy who was busily typing at her computer. "Good morning, sir. Did Jerry find you yesterday?" she said, fishing for the scoop. "He came looking for you at the end of the day saying that you had an appointment. I told him that you were scheduled for something off-campus, but I didn't know what. He said he'd catch up with you, did he?" Her tone was at the same time beseeching and scolding, and I knew that she was annoyed that there might be a secret of which she was not privy.

"He found me, yes," I said matter-of-factly, and quickly diverting her attention I asked. "Any messages?"

"Nothing from yesterday, but Mary Mumford called first thing this morning. I booked her for 10am, sounded important."

"And what else do I have this morning? I need to go to the library."

"I haven't heard you say that since your dissertation days... what's the occasion?"

"Oh, just need to help some students find something in the archives," I lied. "Can you look at my calendar and call over there to see when I can stop down? I think the archivist's name is Myrna."

"It's a do. Her name is Myrna Waters. Very nice... a little mousey... but very nice." I could always count on Judy for descriptive commentary.

"Thank you," I said heading toward my office, "let me know when Mary arrives." I had barely turned on my computer and sat down before Judy was in my doorway, "Mary's he-uh," she said, hand on hip and sounding annoyed. "Do you want me to have her wait? She's early and you haven't even had your coffee."

"I had coffee at home so I'm fine," I said appreciatively, "this must be important, have her come in."

"You got it," she said, "I'll bring you more coffee, too." Within seconds, Judy returned with coffee and Mary in hand.

"Hi, Mary," I said, "did you want coffee?"

"No, thank you, Judy already asked me." Of course she did, I looked at Judy who was glaring at me over her half-glasses, but smiling, "Did you underestimate me?"

"Never," I replied, "just a brief lapse in judgment. Thank you, Judy. Mary, please, sit down." Judy closed the door behind us and we sat on the upholstered furniture in front of my desk. Mary, wearing her usual cream sweater and floral skirt, seemed nervous, not making much eye contact. She sat down, straightened her skirt, and folded her hands quietly. I'm not sure if she would have initiated conversation if I hadn't started.

"So, Mary, this must be important," I began, sipping my coffee, "what's up?" She looked at me briefly, and then back down at her hands, "I wasn't totally truthful with you yesterday."

"Oh?" I said, "what about?"

"About Darcy Green." Well that grabbed my attention. I waited for follow-up information and realized that Mary wasn't going to offer it without being asked.

"What about Darcy?" I asked in a measured tone. Again, Mary looked down but then turned her head upward and met my eye, "I do know her… I mean I did," she began beginning to cry, "I knew her very well."

-22-

Well, that got my attention.  I crossed my legs and sipped my coffee, trying not to fidget in anticipation of what Mary was about to reveal.  Mary sat up in her chair, seemingly empowered by the truth and continued without provocation.  "Darcy worked in my office… not for long, really only for a week until she disappeared, but certainly I knew her.  I was quite fond of her, in fact."  Since she was using past tense, did she know that Darcy was murdered?  I didn't have to wait long for the answer as she continued, "I can't believe that she's gone."

"When did you find out?" I asked.

"Yesterday.  Chief Morreale told me.  So sad, she was such a good kid.  Troubled, but good.  I'm sorry I didn't tell you on the phone yesterday," Mary continued, "I don't know why I didn't.  I guess I felt protective of Darcy.  The second I didn't tell you I felt awful."

"Well, thank you for telling me now," I said, not sure how I felt about her transgression.

"There's more," Mary began again, still sniffling but more resolute.  "Apparently Darcy was involved in some wrongdoing."  I breathed a sigh of relief, thinking that Mary was going to tell me about Darcy's other job as an exotic dancer, but was surprised by the information that she shared instead.

"The Chief thinks that Darcy stole blank scripts, prescriptions, from Health Services. I never would have thought that Darcy would do anything like that, until Chief Morreale's meeting yesterday."

"He thinks that Darcy took scripts from your office?" I said, proudly showing that I was in on the medical vernacular.

"Well not from *my* office," Mary protested, "from one of the examining rooms, I guess. He didn't come right out and say it yesterday, but he implied that it was a possibility that she took an entire prescription pad." Mary looked down at her hands again.

"Did you notice whether any scripts were missing, Mary?"

"No," she cried again, glancing up at me. "The docs keep them locked in the office at the end of each day. If I had found missing prescriptions, then of course I would have told you. Like now... I came here right away!" For the first time, Mary sounded fearful. Perhaps for her job, but there seemed to be something more. "I'm so sorry, Doug. So very sorry."

"For what?" I asked, not sure of the genesis of her guilt.

"For getting Health Services involved in this mess... for not being able to help Darcy."

I grabbed a box of tissues from the side table and handed it to her, "We'll figure this out, Mary," I said, being careful not to make any promises until I knew more about the situation, "Thank you for coming to see me."

"I came as soon as I knew... I'm so sorry, Doug." Of course she really hadn't come as soon as she knew, it was the following day, but I wasn't about to quibble.

"Mary, thank you." I said, not exactly sure what else to say. Mary stood up, "The Chief said that he'd be in touch. I promise to alert you the moment he does."

"Okay," I said, "That would be great." As she opened the door she turned and it looked like she was going to say one thing, but decided on another, "I'll see you at Video Game night tomorrow?"

"Yes, I plan to be there. Nine o'clock?"

"We decided that seven would be best, try to get them after dinner before they start partying," she said, smiling. "Get there early, especially if you want to play."

I walked Mary out, pausing at Judy's desk afterward, "any word on my date with Myrna?" I asked.

"Boy, I have nevah seen a fella so eagah to spend time with dusty books," Judy said, again, pulling out her Brooklyn accent for the second time that morning. "But yes," she continued, "I have freed your calendar between 1:30 and 3pm. You have a 3pm conference call that you can't miss. I hope that will be enough time."

"That will be just fine," I said, patting her shoulder, "you're the best."

"Tell me something I don't know," Judy quipped, heaving her bosom forward and turning toward her computer. I took that as my cue to return to my office and get some work done before I went to the library.

~~~~~

I finished everything in my inbox, both email and the physical one that rested on my desk by 1:15pm, quickly grabbed lunch and was standing in front of Myrna's desk by 1:35pm. Judy was right, Myrna Waters was a little mousey, but very nice. She wore a dark brown frock that might have been made out of burlap and a stereotypical bun kept in her hair by something that looked like an oak knitting needle. Upon my approach, she lowered her reading glasses from her nose and allowed them to hang from the gold chain that fastened them. Even without showing any teeth, her smile was uncharacteristically bright. "You must be Dr. Carter-Connors," she said, in a huskier voice than I expected.

"Please, call me Doug."

"I'm not sure that I can do that," she said demurely. Was Myrna flirting with me? "But maybe," she continued, "we can compromise on Dean Doug."

"Whatever makes you comfortable, Myrna. Nice to meet you. My wife has told me a great deal about you." I thought that Myrna was going to fall out of her seat in elation, "Oh, what a doll! Here, let me take you into the file room, that's where Mrs. Carter-Connors left some items that she tagged. How wonderful that you and she are collaborating on a story for Time magazine? It must be so nice to collaborate with your spouse." So that's what Barbara told her, she had neglected to tell me that she told Myrna an untruth.

"Yes," I fibbed, surprised that Barbara had lied, but more that she hadn't clued me in on the story, "I'd love to see everything."

I followed Myrna into a tiny room behind her desk. As I expected, the College Archives office was dark, without any windows in the Library basement, and smelled of musty paper. There were metal shelves lining every wall, all filled with labeled black boxes. As we passed, I noticed one that read, "Athletics 1967-68."

"I've never been down here before," I said feeling the need to make small talk. "Not many have," Myrna said, directing me to an old wooden desk and seat combination, "But you are welcome anytime." I was afraid to look at her, fearing that I might catch her winking, instead, focusing on getting into my seat.

The "file room" as Myrna called it was about the size of a closet and held only the desk and four black four-drawer file cabinets. "If you don't mind," Myrna said, pawing through something that looked like a thin tissue box, "Please wear these when handling the materials." She handed me a pair of latex-like gloves and quickly put a pair on herself, "...and of course I don't have to tell you, be delicate." She handed me a stack of photographs and papers, which I realized were probably more inane poems. "Thank you," I said, "I'll be gentle." That time, I was sure that Myrna winked, and she left the room saying, "I'm sure you are. If you need *anything*, please call me." I hoped that I wouldn't have to.

I turned immediately to the stack of material set before me.  On top, were copies of the S&C conference room group photographs, which I leafed through as quickly as my fingers would allow. Barbara was right, even my cursory review didn't reveal anyone with a beard.  I pulled out the envelope that I brought with me containing the photos that I had taken, and rested them on my lap. Turning back to the archive photos, I examined the back of each one and saw that they had been labeled with the year and names of each of the subjects.

I started with 1955 and held up the archival photo and my copy side by side.  Identical.  The same was true for 1956.  However, 1957 showed a problem, just as Barbara suspected.  That was the year where *my* photo included a man with a beard, but the 1957 copy in the archives showed all five men clean shaven.  My heart began to thump as I turned the archival picture over and saw the names clearly printed:  Jackson Rittling, Robert Meisner, Arthur Thornton, Tom Reilly, and Thomas Moore.  I compared both photos again and confirmed that in my copy, Thomas had been replaced by the bearded man.  But then I noticed another difference-- Arthur Thornton.

Arthur Thornton was missing from my copy, and replaced by someone a good six inches shorter. Why the switch?  Why would there be two stand-ins in the conference room copy of the photo?  I looked closer at the original and examined the men. Turning more attention to the one on the end, my heart jumped when I realized whom I was looking at.  As I hoped, I was pretty sure that I was staring at the fleshed-out face of my skeleton, and his name was Thomas Moore.

~~~~~

I sat and studied his face for at least ten minutes realizing that even though I knew his name, I still didn't know anything about him.  He was a handsome young man, who looked younger than his twenty or so years.  He stood, resolute, staring at the camera with bright eyes and tussled brown hair that hung on his forehead.  The others had similar looks, clean-cut and clean-shaven, and all made me wonder what had happened with these all-American boys.

Anyone of them could have been a 1950s teen movie star, a la Ricky Nelson or Frankie Avalon, especially the one in the middle.  Who was he?  I turned the picture over to re-check the name… Arthur Thornton.  His was the only name I recognized.  Wasn't he the one voted to get the Sacred Skull award?  But I didn't remember that he was in the class of 1957, wouldn't I have remembered that from my previous day's eavesdropping?  As I stared at the photo, I realized that I wasn't sure of the significance.  Who were the five men who stood for a group shot each year?  I would ask Myrna on my way out.

I reviewed the rest of the photos, just to be thorough and then checked my watch for time.  I still had almost 45 minutes, which I spent sifting through all of the materials that Barbara had left for me. More bad poetry, and lots of group shots, many of them candids. Actually, it was the snapshots, not the poems, that gave me more insight into the spirit (and heart as Barbara put it) of Skull and Cross.

Many of the pictures were playful, and other than the fashions, could have been taken at any college at any time. There were even pictures of people playing on the beach-- throwing Frisbees, burying each other in the sand, jumping in the water. Guys, and some women, who were forging lifelong friendships. There were even a few photos of the 1957 crew that I noticed. Arthur Thornton standing on the beach, blond hair tossed in his face by the wind, standing in his bathing suit revealing chiseled features. Tom Reilly mugging for the camera. Even a shot of Thomas Moore, playfully giving one of the guys a noogie. Silly, fun college times. What had happened that one of them ended up dead?

I was almost finished looking through all of the writings and photos when one piece of handwritten paper caught my eye. At the top of the paper, written in capital letters, was "Wolf's Shame." The text underneath it read,

Our group is one, solid to the core, our ties cannot be broken.
We carry on, despite all else, even when no truth is spoken.

Our goal is sound, our path is forged, our actions cannot be blamed.
For right or wrong, heaven or hell, we have only the wolf to shame!
-H.F. 1955

*H.F.,* I wondered. Could that be Harold Farrow, our town optometrist? If I was right, not only did he still *speak* about the "wolf's shame", he *wrote* about it. He was part of Skull and Cross, alright, and for some reason, he wanted me to know it.

~~~~~

On my way out, I found Myrna sitting at her desk applying lip gloss.

"Thank you, Myrna," I said, trying not to startle her. Unfazed, she put her cosmetic bag back in her purse and turned toward me. Rather than glossy, her lips now looked as though she had just been sucking on a cherry popsicle. "You are welcome, Dean Doug," Myrna responded. "If I can do anything for you, or that wife of yours, please ask." Then I was pretty sure that she licked her lips. Although I wanted to run screaming, I did have one question. "Myrna," I asked, "do you know the significance of the five men in the Skull and Cross group photos?"

"Oh sure!" she responded, as though I had asked for her phone number. "Each year since 1875, the graduating seniors pose for a commemorative photograph. It's their tradition to honor the graduates."

"Thank you," I responded, already beginning to exit. I thought about asking Myrna about the different photos in the S&C conference room, but then decided not to bring it up with her. If it was a secret, I wasn't sure who knew about it, or why. I walked back to my office developing my game plan, jotting things down on my mental list:

> *1.  Call Chief Morreale*
> > *a.  tell him about Thomas Moore*
> > *b.  ask for Mary and Darcy Green update*
>
> *2.  Call alumni office to find out about Arthur Thornton graduation date*
> *3.  Go to see Dr. Farrow, find out what's going on with him*
> *4.  Avoid creepy Myrna at all costs*

I arrived back in my office just in time for my 3 o'clock conference call with two of my former mentors and now cherished friends, coincidentally both with names beginning with Mary. Mary Alice Notting was the Vice President for Student Services at a private New Jersey college a little farther down the shore, and Mary-Grace Cooper was Vice

President for Student Affairs at a large private university in upstate New York. While we chatted over the conference call, brainstorming ideas for a collaborative presentation at an upcoming national student affairs conference, I grazed through my mail folder that was sitting on my desk.

The office's phone log was in there, which I quickly turned over and ignored, a few memos that I had already seen via email, and then something that Judy had tagged with a red sticky note indicating that it was urgent. I saw that it was the result of Judy's search for "Candace Kane." There were five names listed, complete with address, contact information, and photo ID picture. I didn't have to go very far before recognizing one of them, Candace King from Asbury Park-- dance major. But I didn't know her as Candace, or even Candy, I recognized her immediately as Nurse Sissy, exotic dancer at Smoke.

-23-

Although I loved talking with Mary Alice and Mary-Grace (or the Marys, as I often called them), I couldn't wait to get off the phone with them so I could call Chief Morreale. In fact, I barely said goodbye before dialing the Ocean Grove PD. The dispatcher, one I didn't know, answered on the second ring, "Shores PD, dispatcher Billings."

"Hi, officer, this is Doug Carter-Connors from Asbury College. May I speak with Chief Morreale, please?"

"Is this an emergency, sir?"

"No, but I need to speak with him, he's a friend." I had never thought about it before, but the Chief and I had become friends over the past few months. Working through challenging circumstances can do that to people.

"One moment," the dispatcher said flatly, then a few seconds later, "he's on another call, but said that he would call you right back. Can I have your number?"

"He has it. Just tell him that I'm in my office." And the dispatcher clicked off. I took the opportunity to run down the hall to use the restroom, and within seconds, I heard a loud knock and then Judy's voice, "Doug, are you in he-ah?"

"Yes," I said, standing at the urinal.

"So sorry, but the Chief is on the line for you," she called through the door, "he said to interrupt you... well, so I am."

"I consider myself interrupted," I said, flushing. "I'll be right there." I was glad that I was the only man in the restroom. I washed my hands, jogged back to my office and hit the flashing red hold button on my telephone, "Chief?"

"Hi, Doug," he said, "hope I didn't interrupt anything important."

"No, not at all," I chuckled, "hey, I was wondering if I could stop by."

"Funny, I was going to ask the same thing."

"Well, I think I'd rather talk in your office, might be a little more private."

"Okay," the Chief responded. "When would you like to come over? I'm free now."

"Now's perfect," I said, already shutting down my computer and grabbing the ID pictures Judy had given me. "I'll be right over."

Never ignoring an opportunity to multitask, on my way out I asked Judy for Tish Vogt's phone number. Tish is the Director of Development and Alumni Relations, and I figured that I could give her a call on my walk to the Police station which was just off Main Avenue on Pilgrim Pathway. Hopefully, she would give me some information about Arthur Thornton and Thomas Moore, and I could cross something off of my mental checklist. Number in hand, I left the office energized. Although I had many more questions, I had finally discovered some answers and I was careful to acknowledge small victories.

~~~~~

As I walked off-campus, I was struck by the beauty of October. Fall had officially arrived. Sunlight dappled the grass through Technicolor leaves that struggled to cling to tired branches. The wind was growing chillier by the day, and I knew that tomorrow would be the day when I pulled my overcoat from the closet. I would try, however, to keep the warm liner for my overcoat idle until November.

Rarely one to get distracted, I continued soaking in the scenes of Fall by the seashore, and grabbed my phone to call Tish. Although her given name is Elizabeth, she goes by Tish-- don't bother with the "Tish the Dish" jokes, she's heard them all before. An attractive woman with a slight build, Tish has the energy and enthusiasm of a marathon runner, or, talented fundraiser. She and I had worked together at several fundraising functions, and I found her to be a skilled schmoozer. Whether on the golf-course, or the ballroom, Tish had a way of asking for money that was genuine, straightforward, but subtle. One minute she was asking donors to pass the sugar, the next she was asking them for five million dollars, and rarely did they notice the difference. Although it was just about 5 o'clock, I hoped that I would catch her in her office.

"Tish Vogt," she answered on the first ring.

"Hi, Tish, this is Doug. I expected to get your assistant?"

"She left for the day, but I'm waiting for a few phone calls so I picked up  What can I do for you, my friend?"  Her tone was businesslike, but warm, and I continued without hesitation.  "What can you tell me about Arthur Thornton and Thomas Moore?"

"Thornton's a great guy.  Wonderful to us and throughout the community.  Funny you should ask, he just called me last week about giving us another substantial gift."

"What year did he graduate?" I asked.

"Early sixties, I think.  Why?"

"Can you check that?"

"Sure, hold on," Tish said as I heard her clicking away at her keyboard.  "Yup, 1963.  I thought so."

"Interesting.  Are you sure?"

"1963.  What's wrong, Doug?"

"Nothing… what about Moore?"

"That one's not ringing a bell, but let me look." Tish typed again, and then replied, "is he an alum?  I don't have anything on him."

"You're sure?"

"Yes, there isn't anyone by that name."

"Thanks, Tish, you've been a big help," I said, closing my phone.  I didn't want to tell her that actually, she hadn't helped me at all.  How come everyone thought that Arthur Thornton graduated in 1963, when in fact, he was a1957 alum? And why wasn't Thomas Moore in the alumni database? I wondered about that until I reached the Grove PD and walked up the steps to see Chief Morreale.

~~~~~

The Ocean Grove Police Department resides in a tiny cottage that resembles a doll house. Painted light blue with white and navy trim and two overflowing flower boxes on the front porch, the PD offers an inviting presence to crime fighters and foes alike. On the front porch sat two painted white rockers, and I pictured criminals shackled to them rocking sublimely while they awaited transport to jail. Simple pleasures associated with being in a small seaside town.

I opened the door and was immediately faced with a four foot counter that blocked my entrance to the two offices in the back. "Can I help you?" said the uninspired man sitting behind the counter. I recognized his voice as the dispatcher. "Hi, I have an appointment with the Chief."

"Your name?"

"Doug."

"Your *last* name?" he responded, annoyed.

"Carter-Connors."

"Connors, got it," he said, and then walked three steps to the Chief's office. Who was I to correct him and tell him that he didn't get it at all. I heard the Chief's voice, "Yes, bring him right back!"

"You can go in," the dispatcher said, walking toward me and lifting a section of the counter like a draw bridge so I could pass.

"Thanks for your help," I replied, walking into the Chief's cramped, but very tidy office.

"Long time, no see," I said, taking a seat in front of the Chief's desk.

"My thought exactly," the Chief replied. "I'm not sure I want to know what you've been up to." The Chief was a wise man, indeed.

~~~~~

"You could have been picked up for soliciting," the Chief scolded after I told him about my meeting with Lacey.

"But I didn't do anything, or give her money, well, other than the decoy dollar," I responded, innocently.

"Maybe not, but that wouldn't stop one of the Asbury boys from picking you up. How would that have looked?"

"It didn't happen."

"Doug," the Chief said, rubbing his bald head and looking concerned, "you should have told me." He paused, and I could tell that he was choosing his words very carefully. Finally, he said, "You need to stop." He had never given me a directive like this before, and I wasn't quite sure how to respond. After a brief staring contest, I decided to say something so that he didn't take my silence as defiance, "What's going on with the case? Mary Mumford was pretty shaken up by your visit."

Chief Morreale looked at me and leaned back in his oak desk chair. For the first time ever, I thought he looked tired. Worn. He rested his hands behind his head, settling in as if he was going to tell a long story, "Mary just might be the key to this thing. We think that Darcy Green stole blank scripts from her office and used them to fill a couple of prescriptions for Oxycodone. We don't have any leads that tell us she actually started pushing her own drugs. They probably got wind and stopped her before she could start."

"So Lacey was right, she had her own supplier on-campus-- Mary."

"Looks like that might be a possibility."

"Do you think Mary is in on it?" I blurted, shocked at the prospect.

"I don't know, yet," the Chief said, as I repositioned myself in my chair to get more comfortable. He took a sip from a stained coffee mug on his desk and continued, "They definitely had a relationship."

"Yes, Mary told me. I mean not at first, but she came to see me this morning to tell me that she knew Darcy."

The Chief paused, continuing to look pensive, "What'd she tell you?"

"All she said was that she knew Darcy, originally she said that she didn't know her, but she said that she knew Darcy and that you thought Darcy took some blank prescriptions."

"Interesting," the Chief smiled for the first time in our conversation, "because I never said anything of the sort."

~~~~~

I sat in my chair trying to replay Mary's conversation with me earlier that day. *Yes*, I thought, *she definitely talked about prescriptions*. "You didn't say that Darcy took prescriptions?" I asked.

"Nope," the Chief responded, still smiling, "I asked her where they kept their prescription pads, but I never implicated Darcy in any way."

"Maybe she just assumed," I tried, not sure why I was making excuses for Mary.

"Maybe she did," responded the Chief, "but I never said anything of the sort."

"But that's what you think happened?"

"Yes. Apparently Darcy visited the Health Center during the first week of school," he reached for a notepad that was sitting in front of him. "She actually visited the Center five times between August 31 and September 15. According to her chart, she was complaining of stomach pain."

"Who'd she see?"

"Uh," the Chief looked down at his notes, "Dr. Carty. He saw her again three days later on September 2nd and wrote her a prescription for Xanax which she filled at the pharmacy on Bangs Avenue in Asbury. Two weeks later, she filled another prescription there for Oxycodone."

"So I assume that Dr. Carty didn't write that one."

"According to the Pharmacy, that one was written by a Dr. Perlman on September 15th." For some reason, that didn't sit right with me. Dr. Carty and Dr. Geddes, our town's medical examiner, had offices in town but held office hours on-campus a few days each week. Dr. Perlman was an intern working with them, and I remembered authorizing him to see students on-campus during the first week of school when there is typically a rush. I remembered, even without looking at the paperwork, that he worked on-campus through September 6th, only.

"But that can't be right," I explained, "Dr. Perlman's last day with us was September 6th."

"That's what he said."

"You spoke with him?"

"This afternoon. He also said that during that week he wrote seven prescriptions. Let me see..." he muttered checking the pad, "two for prescription-strength ibuprofen, three for amoxicillin, one for an antihistamine, and one for vaginal cream." With that, he looked up and smirked, but I wasn't in a playful mood.

"But no oxycodone."

"Did you hear the vaginal cream?" he asked, sounding much more disappointed than a grown man should.

"I heard you," I replied curtly. "None for oxycodone?"

"No... we checked his signature on the script... someone forged it."

"Did he notice if any blank prescriptions were missing?"

"No, and neither did Drs. Carty or Geddes. But there are some scripts that are unaccounted for."

"From where?"

"From the pad that Dr. Perlman left with Mary Mumford on his last day."

-24-

Was Mary involved in this mess?  She certainly had been acting strange lately.  Was she involved with dealing drugs on-campus?  "But when I spoke with Mary," I started, "she didn't mention that prescriptions were missing from her office?"

"I'm not convinced that she knows, " the Chief confided.  "Before Dr. Perlman left, he gave the pad that he was using to Mary for safekeeping. I'd like to keep an eye on her to see if she is keeping it safe, or handing them out to wayward girls."

"You're making a sting?"

"We're just keeping an eye on her, and not just her.  We're looking for frequent flyers at the Health Center."

"You might want to keep your eye out for this one," I said, handing the Chief the picture and information for Candace King.

"So this is Candy Kane."

"Yes, and I know that she works at Smoke."

"You saw her when you were there?"

"She was on stage, and it would be appropriate for her to spend time in Health Services. The night I saw her she was dressed as a nurse, she went by the name Nurse Sissy."

"But now she's Candy Kane."

"Looks that way," I said, "and the Greenley that Jeffery Jordan talked about before-- Darcy Green?"

"I think so, yes."

"I'm not a detective, but if Candy took over where Darcy or Ivory left off, I bet you'll find her visiting Health Services… I wonder if Mary knows her already."

The Chief smiled at me, "We'll keep you posted.  Those are questions for me to answer, remember?  Now, what else do you have for me?"

"Oh not too much," I said smugly.  "Just the name of the skeleton."

~~~~~

"You have been a busy boy," the Chief said, folding his hands.  I couldn't tell if he was unhappy with me, or not, so I decided to give him the name and leave it at that.  "Well," I hedged, "it's only a guess.  I think his name is Thomas Moore, class of '57, even though the Alumni office doesn't have a record of him."

"And how did you come to that conclusion?" the Chief deadpanned.  I explained about the photos in the S & C conference room, Barbara's insight from the archives, and my conversation with Tish.  I chose to leave out anything about Arthur Thornton, since at that point, I had no idea where it was going.

The Chief seemed thankful, but a little awkward about receiving the information, "Just remember," he said thoughtfully, "there's information gathering, and then there's police work.  Don't cross the line."

"I'm here, aren't I?" I said trying to establish some distance, "what I know, you know."  The Chief

looked at me suspiciously and with good reason.
Although I hadn't lied to him, I hadn't told him
everything.  I had gone down this road before and
clearly hadn't learned my lesson- yet.

~~~~~

      I walked into the Student Center the
following morning, forgetting all about the much
hyped, often teased Video Game Night.  Admittedly,
my first reaction was not common, or expected, at
least for a Dean of Students, '*Shit!*'  I thought, ' *An
evening with Malificent and her committee
distracting students from drinking and drugging with
video games.  Did she realize that they would
probably come wasted?  I have to call Barbara to
tell her that I'll be late.* '  I wasn't normally that
cynical, but I was certainly distracted, or maybe
preoccupied was a better descriptor.

      I was trying to figure out my next move,
being careful not to cross the line, of course.  I had
interrogated Lacey and the Chief was on the trail in
Health Services.  Although it may not have seemed
like it, I wasn't interested in getting involved with
the drug world, whatever that meant.  It sounded
dangerous, and people had already been killed.  I
was happy to stand aside and let the Chief pursue the
death of Darcy Green-- any answers that I felt I
could provide were already found.
      I was increasingly intrigued by Thomas
Moore.  To be exact, I was more curious about

Arthur Thornton's connection to him.  The thought had crossed my mind that Thornton had been excommunicated by Skull & Cross, but then I remembered that he was getting their coveted alumni award.  Now that I thought I knew the name of our skeleton, Arthur Thornton was at the bull's eye of my radar.  But there wasn't any reason to tell the Chief, right?  I couldn't bother him with every vague hunch that I fabricated.  I decided to continue my course of thinking, and promised myself to tell the Chief if I found something.

After a morning of meetings that occurred all over campus discussing hot topics like early registration, trademark policies for AC, and planning a campus-wide party to celebrate our accomplishments under Gwenyth's leadership for *next* fall, I was happy to return to my office.  The air outside had grown colder still, and I was happy that I remembered to wear my overcoat before returning to the warm, canned air of the zip-locked Student Center.

When I arrived upstairs to my office, I noticed two students sitting in the comfy chairs in our waiting area.  One was Jenny Robins, I didn't know the other.  *Oh no*, I thought, *did Jenny know that I had crashed her early morning meeting?*  I did my best to swallow my paranoia and said hello, "Hi, Jenny," I said, reaching for my messages on Judy's desk, "how are you?"

"Great, Dean Doug!" she replied, standing up in her ever-peppy manner, "We came to see you!"

She seemed extremely excited, and not accusatory at all, so I breathed a little easier. "Well, alright," I said, removing my coat. "I think I have a few minutes, come on back." Judy nodded in affirmation, not breaking her gaze from her computer once, and I led the way down the hall to my office.

I invited my young guests to sit and said, "Jenny, I don't think I know your friend?"

"Oh, yeah, this is Tim," she leaned in and whispered, "we're in *the Secret* together." Tim didn't seem to mind that Jenny had outed him as a member of Skull and Cross, or *the Secret*, and sat down.

"I see," I said, then remembered seeing Tim file back into the conference room after the fire alarm. "So, what can I do for you?"

"We're here to invite you to our Annual Alumni Awards Gala, do you have the invitation?" she asked, turning to Tim, who reached into his backpack and pulled out an oversized ivory envelope. "Since you do so much for us," Jenny continued to babble, "we wanted to invite you." With that, Tim handed me the invitation.

"I've never been invited before," I said. "I thought it was only for Skull and Cross members?" Tim shot Jenny a quick look that I couldn't translate, and Jenny continued, "Well, it's for members and special guests. This year we thought you should be a special guest, with everything you've had to deal with and all."

"What do you mean," I asked with my best poker face.

"Well," Jenny replied, shifting in her seat, "with all the skulls buried around and all, we just…" Tim shot her another look and the meaning was clear, *stop talking*, but when Jenny continued, he entered the conversation for the first time, "We're inviting the President, too. Administrators who help us throughout the year. We'd really like you to come-- bring your wife, too!" *Ah*, I thought, *bribing me with a fancy dinner so that I wouldn't scrutinize their creepy rituals.*

"I'll check my calendar and try my best to make it," I said.

"Great!" Jenny said. "It's a really cool event." Did she know how many times, most of them inaccurate, I had heard that phrase? "It's the night that we give out our Sacred Skull award," she persisted. "This year the recipient is Mr. Arthur Thornton." This time, Tim stood up and glared at her, "But that won't officially be announced until the dinner."

"He's a great guy," Jenny continued, naive to Tim's message to be quiet, "He helps so many people…" I remembered that Tish had used similar words, *"a great guy."*

"I'm sure he's a great choice," I said, standing as well. "And don't worry, I won't tell anyone. Thank you for the invitation. I appreciate that you thought of me."

"You will need a tuxedo," Jenny interjected, "it's really classy."

"I'll dust off my cummerbund," I responded and showed them the way out. I wondered if R.I.P. knew that the students invited me? I also wondered if they had other motives for bringing me closer to their incestuous circle? It didn't matter. Although they didn't know it, I was already interested.

~~~~~

The day moved quickly and it was after 5 o'clock when I thought of Arthur Thornton again. I was sitting at my desk when Judy buzzed me, "Tish for you." I picked up and said, "Hi Tish, how are you?'

"I'm fine," she said eagerly, "but I just discovered something that I thought you would be interested in."

"A new prospect?"

"No a current one. Arthur Thornton."

"What about him?" I asked, sitting up straighter in my chair.

"Well, remember you asked about the year he graduated? I told you that I've been working with him recently on a major gift, so I've been speaking with him quite a bit. He just told me today that he got his Masters in 1963-- he got his Bachelors in 1957." *Bingo*, I thought, not exactly sure why I felt that I had won something.

"Yeah," Tish continued, seeming a little defensive. "I was talking about what we wrote for the alumni magazine, and when I said something about the class of 1963, he said that he preferred to be listed as BA '57, MBA '63. He even joked about his age when I said that my records had him as class of '63 only, saying that he wasn't surprised, computers hadn't been invented yet." Tish paused, "How did you know?"

"Oh, I don't know," I said fibbing. "I probably read something in the paper some time and it just jogged my memory."

"Well good memory, thanks for catching that. I also checked a bit more into the other one, Thomas Moore?"

"Yes," I said eagerly.

"Well, we don't have him on the alumni database because apparently we don't have a record of him graduating, but evidently he was a student. According to credits, he should have been class of 1957 also. But I don't have anything else on him. No current address or job history."

"Thank you so much, Tish. You've been a big help," I said, growing impatient to disengage from the conversation. The mysterious persona of Arthur Thornton was eating at me. For some reason, he had become a hang nail that I knew I should leave alone, but couldn't fight the urge to pick. I couldn't resist the urge to find out more on this "great guy," and there was only one place to go-- back to the archives.

~~~~~

Since it was closing time, I asked Judy to call Myrna before I went over, "You owe me big," she said, applying a scarlet shade of lipstick while packing up for the day. "Myrna is only there until 6:00, but I used the Dean card and asked if you could stay later. She said that if you can get there before 6'oclock, she'll let you in, as long as you give her a little peck on the cheek."

"What!"

"Just kidding," Judy said, examining her artistic lip work in a pocket mirror. "I made that last part up. I think she has a little crush on you, fella."

"Whatever works," I said, coat and briefcase in hand and moving toward the door.

"What is so interesting down in those dusty archives?" Judy called behind me.

"I don't know yet," I replied truthfully. "I'm still trying to figure that out."

~~~~~

I called Barbara on my way and told her that I wasn't sure how long I'd be. Although I couldn't imagine that I would need to stay in the archives for too long, I did have to stop-by Video Game Night at 7:00pm. I wouldn't have time to walk home and back again before then. I would much rather make an appearance early, and then head home for good.

I walked briskly into the main library entrance and immediately down the stairs to the archives, passing the circulation desk, reference section, and reading room. The library sat on the far perimeter of our campus and I often blamed its remote location for its limited use by our undergraduates. Housed in a historic mansion, the summer home of an oil tycoon who liked to vacation at the shore, the library was another one of our hidden campus gems.

I was sorry that more of our students didn't visit to appreciate the library's beauty, or utility, but understood that it wasn't the most user-friendly building. In fact, the first time I went I couldn't find the front entrance. Since it was formerly a mansion for the rich, the ornate front doors didn't invite visitors, and in fact, dissuaded them by a series of wrought-iron gates. The entrance to the library was actually around back, in an addition built in the early sixties. An architectural oddity, the new wing was brick chicken coop meets stucco neo-classical, and given its odd juxtaposition, it made sense that it was hidden behind the main mansion.

I found my way back to the archives through a labyrinth of dark corridors and narrow hallways, one of the downsides of converting an historic residence into a building fit for a different purpose. Despite the new flooring and walls, the mansion's basement still seemed like a glorified cellar, trying to pass as space for collections of books. As I entered Myrna's office, I found her standing impatiently, inspecting her watch.

"Hi, Myrna," I said knocking on her door. "Thank you for waiting for me." Myrna looked up like a star-struck school girl, and her face turned from annoyed to sultry, in a mousey sort of way.

"Oh, Dean Doug," she purred, "my pleasure. Your secretary said that you had more important business, and that it was urgent." She slinked around her desk in a red gingham dress, black mary-janes, and pony tail, looking like a modern day Dorothy Gale. Normally I don't find gingham sexy and discovered that still to be true.

"I have an appointment off-campus," Myrna said, grabbing her purse and coat, "or normally I'd be happy to stay." *Wizard of Oz tryouts?* I thought, but said instead, "I didn't think you'd let anyone stay in the archives without staff?"

"Well," she blinked, "sometimes we make exceptions for friends. And besides, you won't be alone. There is a student working in our curriculum library just across the hall. She'll be checking on you periodically. When you're finished, just tell her and she'll lock up behind you. We close at eleven." She made her way past me, and I swore that she made kissy-face noises, but I perhaps I was mistaken.

I moved to the back room that I had visited before and found the stacks of pictures and poems unmoved. I pulled out the 1957 group photo and studied it again, hoping the faces in black and white would talk this time around. I also took another look at the snapshots. There was Arthur Thornton still standing at the beach-- handsome and self-assured. It wasn't until I looked more closely that I noticed something I hadn't before-- a cross hanging around his neck. I grabbed for more beach photos, looking for other bits of information that I hadn't seen. Were other guys wearing crosses? I assumed so, but upon closer inspection, didn't find any. There was only one other guy who appeared to be wearing a necklace, and I squinted to identify his face. Although I wasn't sure, I thought he was Thomas Moore.

~~~~~

It was the poems that I had made fun of that confirmed, at least in my own mind, my newest hypothesis. While sifting through the piles that I had inspected before, I found the poems that Barbara had shown me. Perhaps I had been thrown off by Barbara's handwritten transcription the night before, but seeing the words in the writer's handwriting on aged, ivory parchment provided me with new depth, a more personal message. The pages looked as though they had been ripped out of a journal or notebook, and they were exactly the same as Barbara had transcribed-- with one telling exception that further confirmed the growing feeling in my gut.

-25-

I read and re-read the two poems that Barbara had shown me, now written in their original form on weathered pages:

> Each day I love you... ever more.
> Your heart I need beside me.
> If we can't meet, clandestinely—
> Your love is there to guide me.

And:

> my soul is with you, from Afar...
> you're with me no maTTer where you
> are.
> If life were new, a place refreshed, we'd
> be together... and both be blessed.
> I love you MORE, each passing day,
> yet still we seem alone.
> I wonder— a new time, a new place, a
> new decade still...
> Will our love be truly shown?

Then, I turned each page over and saw something else written on the back of the aged pages, "ATTM." ATTM. All this time we were wrong, even the scientists.  It wasn't an abbreviation for "attention" or "ATTN" inscribed on the cross that was with the skull, it was "ATTM"-- the initials for Arthur Thornton and Thomas Moore.

~~~~~

I stared at the passages again growing more confident that the love letters that I was reading were between Arthur Thornton and Thomas Moore.  All of the capital letters and highlighted pieces were either the initials, AT or TM, or, variations of their names- ART and MORE.  Was Arthur Thornton gay?  I had never heard that, but I didn't know him.  If Arthur Thornton and Thomas Moore were lovers, the thing that struck me first was how difficult that must have been.  In the present day gay people struggled for acceptance by mainstream society, but back in the fifties?  Especially among college men?  I assumed that it must have been far worse.  It must have been very difficult for them.  Did others know?  I wondered.

As I sat and looked at the rest of the photographs and poems one last time, I looked at my watch, 7:03pm.  Despite my consternation about time, I had been there much longer than I anticipated.  I was late for Video Game Night.  I placed all of the materials back where I found them, still unsatisfied.  Even with my new revelation, I had no idea what happened to Thomas Moore, and wasn't any closer to figuring out how he was killed.

Figuring out that Arthur Thornton was having a relationship with another man might have been juicy, but the idea still didn't provide me the satisfaction I was hoping for.

I walked through Myrna's office and briefly thought about leaving her a note of thanks, but then thought better of it. I didn't want to encourage her infatuation with me. I stepped out and went across the hall to the curriculum library to tell the student employee that she could lock up, but didn't find her.

"Hello?" I called to an empty desk, "Hello?" But no one responded. Maybe she was in the bathroom?

I went back across the hall and examined the outside door to Myrna's office; I could just lock it myself and close it behind me. It wasn't until I turned the knob, switched off the lights, and started to shut the door when I first felt a breeze on the back of my neck. Distracted, I paused, in the doorway when I felt it again, this time, it felt as though a bumble bee had whisked by my right ear. Had the glass window in Myrna's office door not shattered in front of my eyes, spraying tiny shards into her dark office, I might never have realized what was happening.

Someone was shooting at me.

-26-

My first instinct was to run, but since I was crouching in Myrna's threshold, I didn't know which way to go. I wanted to look behind me to see who was shooting, but I didn't dare. Where were the shots coming from? Was someone in the hallway? Standing across the way in the curriculum library? I didn't know what to do. If I ran out into the hallway, I might be running into the person with the gun; but if I ran back into Myrna's office, I would be trapped.

I only had a second to make a decision and chose the sanctity of Myrna's office. Down on the floor, fighting the sting of miniscule pieces of glass imbedding themselves into my palms and knees, I slammed the door shut and moved like an unarmed soldier in combat toward the archive room where I had spent the last hour. That room had a door too, right?

I pushed past Myrna's desk, keeping my hands on the floor, but lifting my knees up off the floor and running on all fours toward the archive room. I could feel the warmth of blood from my palms as I smeared it across the surface. Even in the darkness, illuminated only by the fluorescent light from the hallway that wasn't filtered anymore by glass, I could see streaks of blood. *Oh no*, I thought, *was I shot?* I didn't have time to check, especially, when the limited light was eclipsed by a shadow, whose owner I assumed to be the shooter.

Although originally Mryna's office seemed tiny, it now felt vast, as I tried my hardest to reach the back room. Once there, I moved in quickly and shut the door behind me, fumbling for the lock. I realized that a locked door wasn't much protection from a gun, but it was the only defense I had. I momentarily rested my back against the door, but then realized that if the shooter opened fire again, I'd be shot in the back. Thinking that a back wound wouldn't be attractive, I felt panic bubbling up inside me. With the door shut, and the fact that I was in the basement with no windows, the room was jet black. Barely a glimmer of light pushed under the door.

I tried to picture the layout of the room in my mind's eye. Wasn't that always the way-- no matter how many hours we spent in a place, we often didn't notice the details. I pictured the desk chair combination, feeling it beneath my burning hands and then tried to think about the rest of the room. As I pored over the photos, what was around me? What was in front of me? What was behind me? File cabinets. Metal file cabinets. Could I move them to form a shield?

I stood and lunged blindly toward the back of the room, protecting my hands, and hitting one of the filing cabinets with my shoulder. It didn't budge. I reached to my left and felt another one, the metal feeling good against my pitted and bloody palms. I pushed and it moved- only slightly, but it moved. *Slam!* What was that?

It was someone in Myrna's office.  I had actually expected to hear something sooner.  *What had taken my attacker so long?*  I knew that I didn't have much time before they shot their way in.

I fiddled with the handle and opened the top drawer of the file cabinet, using it for leverage to push it to the left and away from the wall.  It was then that I heard the door knob jiggle from the other side.  I didn't have much time.

~~~~~

I pushed the file cabinet a little more and inched my way behind it.  Yes, being five foot six has its advantages, especially in tight situations.  I crouched down, folding my still tingling knees to my chest and resting my forehead on them.  Hidden behind the metal casing, it was even darker than before.  As I rested, I strained to listen for the shooter.  I didn't have to listen intently, because a moment later, I heard the pinging of metal on metal.  Then, I heard the splintering of wood.  The shooter was gunning his way through the door, and closer to his target-- me.

~~~~~

I heard another shot, but the splintering wood made much more noise.  Although I didn't know anything about guns, the shot sounded more like a fart than a blast so I assumed that he was using a silencer.  *Ping!*  More breaking metal and then wood creaking; either the shooter was a bad shot, or the door was really strong.  I wished for both.

But then I heard more than the shots and breaking pieces of door, I heard yelling.  Yet through my barricade, I couldn't really hear what was happening.  I thought I heard, "Hey!" then another shot, then a woman's scream, then another "Hey!" followed by silence.

Almost immediately after the hush, I heard a man yell, "Doug? Doug are you in here?"

Was it safe?  Was it someone I knew?

"Doug!" came the voice again urgently, "Are you in here?"  Was that the Chief?  Then I heard a familiar woman's voice, "Dean? Dean, are you okay?"  Quacky?  Had the Chief and Quacky saved me?

I stood up slowly and peeked over the top of the file cabinet.  The light from Myrna's office filtered through the door, with a curtain of splintered wood hanging in strands in the middle; the rest of the door, however, remained intact.  One long circle of light beamed like a flashlight, coming from the hole where the door knob used to be.  I was thankful to whomever was out there, because I could see that the shooter had successfully opened the door.

"Hello?" I called cautiously.

"Doug!" came Quacky's voice, and all at once, she plowed through the door like a Sumo wrestler.  I was never so happy to see Tina "Quacky" Braggish.  As I stood up straight, Quacky turned on the light switch, causing me to shield my eyes.  I emerged from behind the file cabinet, and was met with Quacky's scream, "Chief, we need the paramedics! Stat! He's wounded!"

I was?

I looked down and saw what I expected, my pants were torn on both knees and blood spattered. I then turned my palms to face me and again, saw both of them speckled with tiny cuts veiled in blood. I held out my arms and looked down at my torso, I didn't *see* a gunshot? I felt my chest. I didn't *feel* a shot.

"He's got a head wound!" Quacky yelled again, and body checked me to the ground. "You're going to be just fine, Doug. Just relax."

Quacky's girth on top of my chest made it difficult to respond, or even breathe for that matter. After I was still for a moment, she rolled off me, finally allowing me to gasp, "Tina, I'm fine."

"No you're not," she said, putting her face so close that I could tell that she had eaten a tuna on rye not long ago, "You've got a head injury."

I did?

"No," I said, "I hurt my knees and hands, but not my head."

"Why is your forehead all bloody then?" she asked, a question for which I didn't have a response.

"It is?" I asked, trying to sit up, and being slapped down immediately.

"Yes, but you're going to be just fine." I truly hoped so. As I lay still, I could hear groans coming from Myrna's office, and then a man yelling,

"That bitch! It's that whore's fault!" I recognized that voice, but who was it?

"That whore!" he moaned, "this is her fault." Then I recognized who it was. It was Bruno, a.k.a. Danny DeVito.

~~~~~

What was Bruno doing? Was he my shooter? I heard him yell again, "She was going to work that party tonight, I was stopping by to make sure I got my cut, but then I saw *him* and got distracted."

What was he talking about? I raised my head enough to see him, laying in front of Myrna's desk on his side, holding his left leg. Was he shot? The Chief was hovering over him. Beyond Chief Morreale, I could see Al Towers, from Quacky's security force, standing in the hallway ushering in two paramedics wearing blue uniforms. A tall African-American man immediately paused and hunched over Bruno, while a tall blonde woman rushed over to me and began inspecting my head, "Sir, you're going to be okay."

"Thank you," I said, and met her shocked gaze.

"He's responsive!" she yelled in my face, although I suspected that she wasn't actually talking to me.

"Can I sit up, please?" I asked.

"Not until I check you out first. I'm trying to evaluate your head injury."

"I don't think I have one," I said, and then I realized, "if there is blood on my head, I think it probably got there when I rested my forehead on my knees while I was hiding from the shooter." The blonde paramedic paused, and came in closer to inspect my forehead. She then touched it lightly with a gloved finger and finally responded, "You may be right, you can sit up now… slowly."

~~~~~

I was sitting in Myrna's desk chair recovering from the experience, including the carrying out of Bruno who shouted every known expletive, and some unknown, that I had ever heard. "He thinks *he's* mad," I quipped, looking around the office that looked like a war zone, "wait until Myrna comes to work tomorrow." Quacky and Al had just left, saying something to the Chief about meeting him "over there." I then looked at him, "You got here awfully fast, who called you?"

"I was already on-campus dealing with the party. In fact, I need to get there. I got *this* call and never made it."

"What party?" I asked, "a campus party?"

"Yes, right next to your office in the Student Center."

"You mean Video Game Night? Is that what Bruno was talking about, too?"

"Apparently, and I need to get over there. From what I gather, Candy Kane is actively recruiting customers on site."

"But it's supposed to be an anti-drug and alcohol event?"

"Apparently no one told her… look, I've got to go.  The paramedics are going to take you to Jersey Shore to get checked out.  If you see Bruno, tell him that I said hello."

"But I'm fine, just some scraped knees," I protested.  "I don't need to go to the hospital."

"Yes, you do.  College policy.  When someone is shot at and has to crawl around on the floor to save their life, a trip to the hospital is mandatory," the Chief winked.  I'll have one of my boys meet you and take your statement tonight, I'll catch up with you either later tonight or tomorrow morning."

"So you're going to Video Game Night without me?"

"You've got other plans.  I'm going to run over there and hopefully pick-up Candy and wrap this up tonight.  Too many people have been hurt… including you.  And from what I hear, there may be some more drug transports tonight.  Whatever the event is, there are a lot of wasted students there."

"You can't drop a bomb like that and run," I objected again as the blonde wheeled-in a folded-up gurney.  "Maybe I've got something to tell you, too!"

"I figured as much, since I didn't know why else you'd be down here," the Chief responded on his way out the door, "But I'll wait…"

"What if I told you that I know who killed Thomas Moore?" I yelled to him, causing the blonde to raise her eyebrows.

The Chief immediately popped his head back inside the doorway, "Even for that, I'll wait.  Even for that."

And then he was gone.

-27-

By the time I got home, it was 1:00am, and as the Chief alluded, I wasn't the only person who had a rough night. While I was sitting in the Emergency Room of Jersey Shore Medical Center, two of my students joined me in order to have their stomachs pumped. Given the events of the night, it also didn't take long for Jerry to find me.

"Hey, boss," he said, peering around the curtain of the examining area where I had been sitting in for over an hour, "are you okay?"

"I'll be fine, just some scraped knees and hands, toddler stuff. Are you here to see me or check on our students?"

"Both. How'd you know about the students?"

"One of the techs told me. How are they doing?"

"Looks like we dodged another bullet," Jerry responded, and then winced. "Sorry, I didn't mean to say that. They're going to be fine. I'd rather hear about what happened to you." He moved closer to the examining table and folded his arms, "Did someone really try to murder you?" Funny, I hadn't thought of it that way before, and I was glad. For some reason, "shot at" didn't sound nearly as bad as "murder."

"Well, if you put it that way," I responded, adjusting the hospital gown that they had given me for the examination, "I suppose so. It was Bruno."

"The guy from Smoke?"

"You knew his name?"

"The short guy, right?"

"Right.  I haven't gotten all of the details, though.  I'm not sure what I did to grab his attention."

"Word on the street is that you were trying to stop his drug business, so he went after you."

"Word on the street, huh?"

"Well, everyone's talking… about you, about Bruno, and about Candy."

"Yes," I said, trying to pull the gown around my backside to stop the draft.  "What happened with her?  Was she at Video Game Night?"

"You mean the rave?"

"Rave?"

"That's what it amounted to.  Students came wasted, students were getting wasted, they had to call Security and the Police to shut it down.  All complements of Candy Kane, apparently she had been pushing the event all week, and even offered some *in house* specials for participants.  It was total chaos, man.  Total chaos.  Loud music, students dancing, stumbling, tripping over themselves trying to play Dance Dance Revolution and falling all over themselves.  A total debacle."

"How did Mary and Malificent react?"

"Malificent was like a deer in headlights, she wasn't even in the room.  I ran into her outside, chain-smoking, as I walked in."

"What about Mary," I wondered, still not sure if she was involved with the drugs or not.

"I'm not really sure. I didn't see her when I walked in. The Chief was there mopping everything up, I'm sure he'll fill you in tomorrow morning."

"Later today, you mean?" I said, looking down at my watch.

"You're right. So, are they discharging you? I'll give you a ride. I heard that you were taken here by ambulance."

"Yes, it was a perfect addition to a perfect evening. Now, to address your question about me leaving, I don't know. Maybe you can find someone and ask them?"

Jerry walked out of the examination area, and I sat on the table and examined my wounds for the hundredth time. My knees had been cleaned, but they still looked raw, covered with hundreds of miniscule cuts, some still bleeding slightly. Although they had removed most of the pieces of glass, the nurse said that I might still find some tiny specs as the days went on. The same was true for the palms of my hands.

A few minutes later, Jerry returned with one of the nurses that had been in and out all night. "Tall, dark, and handsome here says that you're ready to go home," she said, with just the hint of a Spanish accent. "You're ready to go. You know how to take care of those cuts, right? Jeez, you've got a lot of them."

"Yes, they told me," I said.

"Okay, then... the only problem with getting you out of here is your clothes-- your pants are ruined," she said, pointing to my tattered, bloody, slacks resting on a plastic chair next to her, "and those gowns are a little breezy, if you know what I mean. Let me see if I can find you some scrubs."

I shrugged, thinking that at least if my butt had to swing in the breeze, I was wearing sensible underwear; unlike last month when I was transported to the hospital in a thong. That, however, was another story.

The nurse quickly returned with royal blue scrubs which consisted of pants and a top, "Here you go, honey. Your friend said that he would meet you outside, he's pulling up the car." I took the scrubs from her, "Thanks," I said, "I've always wanted these." She looked at me and laughed, "You can buy them in K-mart, you didn't have to go through this to get them." It was a simple statement, but for some reason it resonated with me. I never took the easy way. Maybe I liked a challenge-- maybe I was too independent for my own good. Maybe I just over-thought everything. I'd think about that later; I was tired and ready for the nurse to wheel me out and for Jerry to take me home.

~~~~~

Chief Morreale called around 9:00am and said that he'd like to come over to my house, finish taking my statement and fill me in on the night before. Still feeling sore and tired, I had already called Judy and told her that I wouldn't be in. She said that DOSO had been a flurry of activity with calls questioning what actually took place at Video Game Night. "So I heard that someone fired a gun at you at Video Game Night, is that true?" she asked, practically panting with anticipation.

"Nothing of the sort," I kidded her. "I was shot at down in Myrna's office-- at Video Game Night there were just lots of drugs and students in danger. What's the big deal?" I just pictured Judy hanging on my every word, taking notes on one of her steno pads. I reassured her that everyone, including me, were accounted for and fine, and that she could call me at home if she needed to. I was confident that within seconds, she was setting the phone lines and internet on fire spreading the word.

With Ethan in school, it was easy for me to fill Barbara in on the details of what happened. Although I had called her with updates throughout the night, I was too tired to discuss the details by the time Jerry brought me home. We sat over coffee, still in our robes, chatting like it was Sunday morning; except that the content of the conversation was much more sensational than our usual Sunday morning fare.

"I just can't believe it, honey," Barbara exclaimed. "You were almost killed!"

"Yeah, it's funny," I responded. "Jerry said the same thing to me and I hadn't thought of it like that. In the heat of the moment, I was just trying to stay out of the line of fire."

"And you didn't see who was shooting at you?"

"Not at the time, no, I didn't want to take the time. I didn't see him until he was laying on the floor complaining. I think he was shot, but I never got the details. Hopefully, the Chief will fill me in." We continued to talk about various details, when the doorbell rang. Barbara got up and ushered the Chief into the family room where we had been sitting, and then left to get him a cup of coffee.

"You look tired," I said, noticing the dark circles under his eyes.

"I could say the same thing about you," the Chief said, sitting down on the couch, "How are *you* feeling?

"A little sore, but I'll be fine.  So, care to fill me in on what happened?"

"Sure," he said, pulling out his pad from his back pocket. "You tell me what you know to complete your statement, and I'll share what I know along the way."

I told him about going to the archives, Myrna letting me stay after hours, going across the hall to find the missing Curriculum Library worker, then the first gunshot as I attempted to leave. Chief Morreale didn't ask why I was there, something for which I was glad; one case at a time. I then gave him details about how I attempted to barricade myself behind the filing cabinets. That was all I knew and I waited for him to fill in the missing details.

"Well, you need to thank that student worker from the Curriculum Library, she's the one who called 911. She was in the bathroom when she heard glass shatter, when she looked out from the women's room, she saw Bruno with a gun.  She knew that you must be in there because the Archivist, he consulted his notes, "Myra,"

"Myrna," I interjected.

"Thanks… Myrna," he scribbled, "told her to lock up when you left."

"But how did Bruno know that I was there?"

"Well, did you hear him complaining when the paramedics took him out?  He went to campus to confront Candy, apparently he received word that she was going to do some major pushing last night and he didn't know anything about it.  He was worried that he wouldn't get his cut.  But, he saw you, and got distracted.  His goal was to get rid of you, Doug.  You're lucky."

"But why?"

"He said that he saw you with Lacey."

"That day at the motel?"

"Yes, walking to the beach with her.  Didn't you walk right by Smoke?"

I nodded, and he continued, "Bruno didn't take you for a 'John' and worried about what she told you." The Chief paused, "he killed her, Doug."

A wave of panic washed over me and sagged in my stomach.

"Because of me," I said.

The Chief's tired eyes squinted with congeniality.  "We don't know that," he said.

But I was pretty sure that we did.

~~~~~~

The Chief drank greedily from the coffee mug that Barbara had given him and continued with his story. "It was Video Game Night that apparently pushed Bruno to his breaking point. After he was finished with Lacey, he went straight to the campus to find Candy. As I said, you were an afterthought, a product of his rage." I sat quietly and thought about Lacey, and Ivory, trying to suppress my guilt.

"So my being there might have saved Candy?" I rationalized.

"Most likely," the Chief responded. *Great,* I thought, *one out of three.*

"What happened with her? She was our drug dealer?"

"Yes, after Darcy and Ivory. She was trying to get out from under Bruno and start her own business. She followed in their footsteps, right down to taking blank prescriptions from the Health Center."

"She admitted to it?"

"Yes."

"Where'd she get them?"

"She took them from Mary Mumford's desk... she was talking with Mary one day and saw it. So she befriended Mary, although I know that Mary feels that it's the other way around. Candy played the troubled teen so that she could gain easy access to the tools she needed to build her business."

"Prescriptions."

"Right."

"So Mary wasn't involved in any other way?"

"No.  In fact, she's the one who called the PD when she saw all of the students out of control.  She also made sure that she kept an eye on Candy until we arrived.  Once Mary figured it out, she did the right thing to try and stop it… despite her fondness for Candy."

"So was Candy put under arrest?"

"Yes… and she admitted to everything.  But, if she helps us get Bruno, that may help her in court a little bit."

"So it's over?"  I asked, hopefully.

The Chief scratched his head and sighed, "Yes," he said emphatically.  "It's done."  At that point, Barbara poked her head back in the room and offered more coffee, and I welcomed the interruption.  We all moved to the kitchen and the change in scenery lightened the mood.  After more coffee and some bagels with cream cheese, we were laughing again; until the Chief turned our attention back to business.  "Now I'm ready to hear *your* story," he said.

"I just told you."

"Not about the drugs, about the skeleton. You said you knew who killed Thomas Moore?"

"You just move from one murder to another," I joked, but the Chief turned serious.  "It was murder?" he asked.

"I think so," I confirmed for the first time out loud. "I'm just not sure why."

-28-

Still sitting at the kitchen island in my robe, I shared with the Chief all that I knew about Thomas Moore and Arthur Thornton. It was helpful to have Barbara there, too, to bring out details on Skull and Cross that she had found for her article. The Chief looked pensive, "Sounds like you've got it all figured out," he shared, "how did Thornton do it? Allegedly, of course."

"That's your department," I said, suddenly worried that the Chief was mad that I had stuck my nose in his case. "From the beginning the examiners said blunt force trauma to the head. I could see that when the skull was in my office."

"I don't know, Doug. Sounds like a pretty big leap. A couple of photos and some poems leads you to think that Thornton killed Moore? You haven't found anything that explicitly links the two men together. Besides, no one has even officially determined whether or not the skeleton belonged to Moore. No one's even confirmed that Moore's dead. That will have to be confirmed, first."

"That's why I didn't tell you. It's only a hunch-- I don't really have anything to go on."

"Not even circumstantial evidence."

"But what about the inscription on the cross?"

"If that's all we've got- a faint inscription that even the folks in the lab can't read correctly, it's pretty weak."

"Okay," I conceded. "You're right. So where do we go from here?"

"*We* don't go anywhere. I might look into it a little more, but you're getting into a criminal investigation."

"But you said that there isn't anything to link Thornton. That doesn't make a criminal investigation, it's the whacky hypothesis created by a humble Dean of Students."

"Doug," the Chief scolded, "let me handle all murder suspects."

"So you agree that Thornton could be a suspect?"

"Anyone could be a suspect, but it's not your place to find that out. Barbara, help me out, here."

"*Right*," she said rolling her eyes. "You know as well as I do that once he gets something in his mind, it's there until he removes it."

"I remember," the Chief smirked. "Then I'm going to just have to say it again-- leave this investigation to me."

"Okay," I said making an attempt to smile. "Thornton is yours. I won't even accuse him of murder when I see him at the Skull and Cross gala next week." I was joking at the time, trying to lighten the mood, but who knew that that was exactly what I would end up doing.

~~~~~

I spent much of the day reflecting-- about the ladies of Smoke and about my actions. I also thought about my latest brush with death and considered the juxtaposition between me leading an ordinary life and the uncommon events that had infiltrated it. Again, I rationalized that it wasn't my fault, the skull had literally fallen into my lap, and the women of Smoke had called *me*.

Also, I couldn't get Lacey out of my head. How had Bruno killed her? Where did she die? Would there be a funeral for her? I was sure that her mother would have a service and wondered whether or not it would be appropriate for me to go. What would I say to Lacey's mother? *Hi, I'm responsible for your daughter's death. I'm so sorry for your loss.* None of it felt right.

I also thought about Arthur Thornton and Thomas Moore. If they were lovers, what would cause Arthur to kill Thomas? Why did I even think such a thing? It was the poems. They were so in love. Something must have happened to change that.

I took a shower and then laid down for a nap, one of the guilty pleasures that I enjoy almost as much as wine. As I went to sleep, I ran through the mental checklist that I had created. Dr. Farrow-- did he have something that he wanted to tell me? He wasn't a suspect, according to the Chief's guidelines, certainly it would be okay for me to talk to him. Right? The next day, on my walk to work, I would stop by the Optical Shoppe and find out.

~~~~~

I slept in until 6:00am, then bounded out of bed and threw on my sweats. My ankle felt fine, and my knees were only a little sore, so I decided to go for a quick walk. On my way to the sidewalk, I picked up the *Asbury Park Press* lying on my walk and winced at the headline:

# SHOTS FIRED AT AC: DRUG RING UNCOVERED AT CAMPUS RAVE

Below the headline was a picture of Quacky, arms folded standing outside of the Student Center like an over-stuffed toy soldier. If parents hadn't called the College yesterday, they certainly would now. I threw the paper back on the porch and walked out my gate toward the beach. As I did, I remembered that I should have called Gwenyth to discuss all of the latest developments. Damn, I hated it when I forgot a step-- especially an important one like keeping the President in the loop. She would be my first call of the morning, after my stop to see Dr. Farrow.

~~~~~

A couple of hours later, I was announced by the jingling bells on the doorway as I entered the Optical Shoppe. Dr. Farrow greeted me promptly, as if waiting for me. "Dean Doug!" he said, putting down the glass cleaner and rag that he was holding, "everything alright with your glasses?  Do you need an adjustment?"

"No, my glasses are fine," I said, moving up to the counter.

"It's a wolf's shame about what happened at the College the other night, huh?"

"A wolf's shame for sure," I said, looking at him directly in the eye.  It was too easy a segue, he was dying to tell me something.

"Wolf's shame," I said, "that's an interesting statement.  I've never heard anyone use it, other than you.  The only other time I've seen it written was in a Skull and Cross poem that I found in the College archives."

Dr. Farrow smiled at me, "Well," he said, "I *was* right!  It's about time."

~~~~~

Dr. Farrow's response confused me.  It seemed that my acknowledgement of "Wolf's shame" had confirmed something for *him*.  "So you have been trying to tell me something," I said.

"I figured that *Wolf's shame* was a subtle reference and that if you discovered its origin, it would mean that you were investigating Skull and Cross.  Isn't that what happened?"  His kind demeanor had shifted to something that resembled smugness.  I couldn't believe it, *I* was busted?

"So you were setting some kind of verbal trap for me?" I asked, trying to get it right.

"Well," he said sitting on his stool behind the counter. "If you must say it that way. So, you've been investigating us, I see?" I stood there, trying hard to find my poker face and figuring out what to say. "So you are explicitly letting me know that you are a member of Skull and Cross?" I said, biding time to find something to say.

"Well, no member actually discusses allegiance with non-members, but I figured that you knew when I mentioned the Alumni Gala the other day. So, you haven't told me, why were you looking at Skull and Cross archival information?" Dr. Farrow asked, growing more superior by the second.

"My wife's working on an article about secret societies. She found some poems and showed them to me," I couldn't believe that I thought of that one so quickly. "When I saw the one that said 'wolf's shame', I thought of you." This removed the shit-eaten grin from Dr. Farrow's face, and it made me happy. He sat up straight and tried to recoup himself. "Oh, well, I apologize, Dean… I just thought I could help you."

"Really?" I responded sardonically, "help me with what?"

"With whatever information you were looking for!"

"I'm not looking for any information… in fact," I said growing angry at the haughty nature of S & C, "I think I've got it all figured out." Although I had successfully derailed his suspicion, no matter if it was true or not, I was dangerously close to tipping my hand again.

"Figured what out?" he said, smiling. If it wasn't rude to hit a man with glasses, I swear I would have smacked him.

"I'm not looking for anything," I responded, composing myself, "and don't worry, I wouldn't dream of outing anyone in Skull and Cross." That sparked a flash of anger and his face suddenly swelled with rage, "What did you mean by *that*, sir?" But I tried to reflect on what I said that caused his reaction. I said that I *wouldn't* tell that a person was a member of the organization, right? Wait. *Out*. I said that I wouldn't *out* a member. And although I was talking about outing someone as an affiliate of Skull and Cross, did he think I meant sexual orientation?

"Whatever lifestyle a man chooses should not reflect in any way on the organization. It was true then... it's true today. Now if you will excuse me."

*I was right*, I thought, *he thought he had caught me, but he actually confirmed my own suspicion...someone in Skull and Cross* was *gay, and they were desperate to hide it...then and now. Is that why Arthur had killed his own lover?* I remained silent, turned, and headed toward the door. Although the visit hadn't gone the way I expected, it had been useful. As I opened the door, I turned back to face Dr. Farrow, "See you at the Gala," I said, not intending to zing him, but as I saw the redness return to his face, I realized that I had.

~~~~~

It felt like my day was fraught with confrontation from the moment I woke up. First I was confronted by the newspaper headlines, next by Dr. Farrow, and as soon as I got to my office, the onslaught persisted. As I walked into DOSO early, it was barely 8:30am, Judy was already busy at her desk looking like she hadn't left the previous day.

"Good morning," I said as I walked through the front door.

"Doug," she said getting up from her command center and rushing over to me, "how are you feeling?" As she said it, she grabbed me in a bear hug and held me tight. "I'm so glad you're okay!" she said, face planted on my shoulder.

"I'm fine," I said, "none the worse for wear. I'm ready to be back in the office." Although in reality, I wasn't sure if that was true.

"Well good," Judy said, disengaging from my shoulder, "because things have been crackin'. Did you see the papuh this morning?" *Uh-oh,* I thought, *she's pullin' out the Brooklyn… this can't be good.* I told her that I had and braced for her retort. "Well," she said, placing her hand on her left hip, and using her right as though she was directing traffic, "it's a clustah fuck, if you'll excuse my French. Since I'm a lady, I don't normuhlly speak like that, but in this case, it's appropriate."

"What's happening," was all I could find in response.

"The phones have been non-stop since yesterday, some people hearing that you were

murdered in the library, most upset staff and parents
worried about safety. Chief Braggish has been
*wonduhful*, fielding those concerns. The President's
office," she continued without taking a breath,
"…oh! What a pain in the you know what. Janet
called five times yesterday for updates, *like I knew
what happened*, and the President herself called once
looking for you. I told huh that you were resting at
home and she should call you they-uh… did she?"
All I did was shake my head, since she was on a roll.
"Good, she can wait. You've been shot at for God's
sake, and she wants to bothah you? Hrumphh!
R.I.P. also hobbled in he-uh, too. P.S.- I told him
that he could hobble his wrinkly ass right out the do-
uh, *if you get my drift*." I cringed, at the same time
hoping that she did and did not actually say that.
"Don't worry," she continued after seeing my face,
"all I really said was that he should leave and I
would call him when you came back."

　　　"Thank you, Judy," was all I could respond,
since there wasn't really more that I could say, "I
really appreciate you managing all this." She batted
her lashes, heavy with mascara, and I knew that what
I said was all she needed. Just another thing about
Judy, a "thank you" for her hard work and effort was
almost always all that she needed. I grabbed my
stack of telephone messages from her desk, and she
noticed my right hand, which I had covered in gauze.
"Poor baby," Judy said, "are you in much pain?"

　　　"No, not too much, just a little tender."

　　　"Well you've been through a lot. Like I said,
I don't know why you wanted to go down to those

archives anyway. I hear that there was a lot of damage to Myrna's office, they've had to relocate her to the second floor of the library." *Note to self*, I thought, *send Myrna flowers*. Even though she might take the gift as a come-on, she deserved it.

I walked to my office and barely got comfortable in my chair before Judy buzzed me, "Sam for you."

I picked up, eager to chat with my buddy, "Hey."

"Holy shit!" were her first words. "Are you okay?"

"I'm fine."

"What the fuck! Someone shot at you?" Leave it to Sam; always the lady.

"Yes… but it's fine."

"What happened?" She pressed, and I filled her in on the details. Before we hung-up, she said, "Anything new with the bones?" I paused, not wanting to get into another conversation, and then responded, "I'll keep you posted." I put the receiver back on its cradle, and within seconds Judy buzzed me again. "It's the President's office."

"Hi, Janet," I said in the most friendly voice I could muster.

"Doug," came a voice that didn't belong to Janet, "this is Gwenyth." It was the President, herself, and she didn't sound happy.

I shifted myself in my desk chair and responded, "Oh, hi, Gwenyth, I didn't expect you." That was an understatement.

"I'm glad to see that you're back. Are you okay?" she asked curtly.

"I'm fine," I said, realizing that she hadn't called to check in on my health.

"Good.  Doug, I'm on my way out of the state or I would have asked you to come to my office.  I think you know from working with me for a while now that I don't like surprises.  The phones in my office have been incessant, and I have been inundated with email."  Although I conceded that I should have called her, I had been in the hospital and was injured, why was she so upset?  Gwenyth continued, "I have been barraged with questions about my ability to lead this College and manage my staff, most recently by one of our major prospects, Arthur Thornton."

So, Arthur Thornton had fired up my boss.  One more reason not to like him, aside from the fact that I suspected him to be a killer.

~~~~~

She continued in one of the most business like manners I had ever experienced.  Although I would never have called Gwenyth warm, she was a caring person.  I found her unsympathetic manner to be disarming.  "Arthur and I have been personal and professional acquaintances for years.  We sit on several community boards together, and I have been working on him to give us a major gift.  He called me just a few minutes ago on my cell phone asking about what happened… he even mentioned your name."  Well, that didn't take long.  Dr. Farrow must have called him.

"I don't know Mr. Thornton." I said, coolly.

"That's what he said. But he used you as an example of me not managing my team appropriately. I assuaged him, I think, and told him that you are the best Dean of Students in the region, maybe the State of New Jersey; but Doug, I have to question your involvement here. We've talked about this before, your apparent inability to keep out of situations that are not in your purview." Well, that was clear.

"Gwenyth," I began, trying to maintain my dignity, "I don't have any excuse for not calling you after the other night. I was wrong, preoccupied by the experience, but wrong. I'm sorry. And I'm sorry that you've been challenged, your leadership should not be in question." I should have stopped there, but I couldn't. "However," I continued, "we have had a number of unusual circumstances this semester that have caused many of us at the College, including me, to move beyond the normal parameters of our jobs. We have had a student found murdered on the beach and dug up a skeleton on our campus. We've all been pushed into new territory and we're charting new ground. I see it as my responsibility to assist in any way necessary to find resolutions to these situations. If you disagree, please tell me. If Mr. Thornton disagrees, I would be happy to speak with him personally." *Just let me at him*, I thought, *he caused this mess*.

For the first time since the conversation began, Gwenyth seemed slightly conciliatory. "I don't think that will be necessary, Doug, and I know that this has been a difficult couple of months. I just need you to communicate with me so that I'm not caught off-guard," she said, but then followed-up with, "I like to be able to prepare my responses." Which I found odd. Although certainly a college President should be prepared, shouldn't they also be accustomed to being asked for statements at will, without advanced notice?

"I'll apologize to Mr. Thornton when I meet him at that gala next week," I said. "I don't think that will be necessary," Gwenyth responded quickly, but then she hesitated, "Doug, how did you know that Mr. Thornton was receiving an award at the gala?" *Well*, I thought about saying, *I heard Skull and Cross select him while hiding in the closet during their meeting.* But luckily, I didn't have to.

"The students told me when they invited me to the event."

"So you knew that he is a member of Skull and Cross?"

"They said that he was getting the Sacred Skull award, so I didn't think his membership was a secret," I said hastily, "after all, his picture is on the wall in their conference room in the Student Center." But the moment that it was out of my mouth, I realized what I had done. Arthur Thornton's picture was not on the wall, it was in the archives. I had just tipped my hand at the fact that I had been scrutinizing him and Skull and Cross. If Gwenyth went back and told Thornton that, they would all know that I was up to something. All I could hope was that Gwenyth wouldn't find my response suspect enough to inform Thornton.

"Oh," Gwenyth replied, seeming appeased. "Of course. Are you going to the gala?"

"I think so, the students seemed as though they wanted me there."

"Oh…" she paused, and I waited for her to ask me not to attend, but she didn't. "Well," she continued, "like I said, I am going out of town this morning. I have to be in Atlanta for an alumni event; I'll be back in a few days. If anything else happens, Doug, please call Janet. I'll be checking in with her regularly. And of course, in the case of an emergency, you can always call me on my cell phone." I promised, and we ended the call.

I was slightly unnerved by Gwenyth's reaction, but even more so about the fact that Arthur Thornton had called my boss. It was evident that the Skull and Cross network was alive and well and trying to get me off their backs. What they had unknowingly succeeded in doing, however, was pique my interest even more. Even worse, they were getting me angry-- they were hiding something, had been hiding something for years, apparently without any accountability. Thomas Moore hadn't simply disappeared. He was murdered, I was sure of it. I was determined more than ever to figure out why. Despite the Chief's and Gwenyth's cautions against it, I was resolved to find out what Skull and Cross, especially Arthur Thornton, were trying to hide.

As I pondered my next move, I heard an all too familiar bellow from the outer office, "Is he here, yet!" came the shriek.  Dr. Reginald Ichabod Preston had come to see me.  Perhaps Arthur Thornton had called him, too?  If R.I.P. had come for a fight, he picked the right day.  I was growing more irritated with each and every confrontation.  My only hesitation in blasting him was that I might accidentally let something slip about Thomas Moore. I would have to try and resist the urge to tell the truth-- at least for a little longer.

-29-

That day his ascot was scarlet and as he clutched his cane, he resembled an ancient soldier ready for battle.  Although I had misplaced *my* ascot that morning, I was ready and willing to face him.

"I'm here," I called, stepping out of my office like a wounded gladiator ready for battle, "come in."  As he ambled his way toward me, two or three heads, one of them Judy's, peeked out behind him.

"You're not going!" he said, even before he stepped into my office.  "You can consider yourself officially *uninvited*.  I don't know why those kids invited you in the first place.  Had I known, I would have put a stop to it!"  We stood in the doorway glaring at each other, before I pushed back my resentment and walked inside.

"What are we talking about, Reginald?" I asked sarcastically.  "Your birthday party?"

"The Alumni Gala!" he screamed, sounding like an angry rooster.  "You know that we've been planning it for months and I'm not going to have you come and ruin it!"  He stood in the middle of my office, braced up against his cane, and I worried that I would knock him over as I moved around him. Well, I didn't worry that much.

"Why wouldn't you want me there, professor?" I mused.  "I've already pressed my tuxedo.  I'm going with the red cummerbund, in fact, could I borrow your ascot?  I think it would complete the look perfectly." As I had hoped, this enraged him.

"You're not going!" he screeched. "And If you show up, I'll have you thrown out of there!"

"Reginald," I condescended, "you're hurting my feelings. Why wouldn't you want me there?"

"Because you're a trouble maker, that's why. And a nosey trouble maker at that! I hear that you almost got yourself killed digging around the archives trying to find dirt on our organization, our very *powerful* organization, I might add!"

"Funny use of language, professor" I replied, trying my best to hold my tongue and not say anything more. He turned to meet my eye so quickly that he stumbled before regaining his balance. This time his response was less of an outburst, and more measured and low, "Mind your business, Connors," he growled.

"I haven't done anything, professor. I was invited to the gala by my students and I'm going. Do they know that you are discrediting their invitation?"

"It's not about them! We have alumni coming from all over the country. Arthur Thornton is worried sick!" And there it was, perhaps the most telling piece of information of the day. Arthur Thornton *had* called R.I.P., because *he* was worried. *Worried sick*, in fact. Everyone, including Gwenyth, was rallying around Thornton. But did they know why? What had he told them, 'I killed Thomas Moore so you have to protect me'? Obviously not.

"I wasn't invited by Arthur Thornton, in fact, I've never met him.  I was invited by my students."

"Stay away," R.I.P. snarled, "or…"

"Don't!" I interrupted, coming very close to yelling before composing myself.  "Do not threaten me."

R.I.P. looked me in the eye briefly, but my stare must have suggested that I wasn't amused.  He quickly turned to leave.  As he walked away, he muttered, "For anyone, who dare cross skulls, will rue the day for life."

"What did you say?" I questioned, remembering the passage.

"You heard me Connors.  This time, follow it."  And he hobbled out my office door.  He recited the poem that was left in our mailbox by the hooded stranger.  Had he left it?  No, the intruder was much too nimble.  But he clearly knew about it and had considered it a warning; one that I had not heeded.  If I wasn't angry before, I certainly had become so.  How dare they threaten me, and my family.  How dare Arthur Thornton call my boss.  I was ready to end this and had begun to craft a plan to do just that.  I had to go to the gala, because that's where it would all unravel, or so I hoped.

-30-

I was glad that I had several days before the gala, it gave me time to solidify my plan. It wasn't really splashy, in fact, it was fairly passive. Just a way for me to communicate to Arthur Thornton that his secret, if I had it right, was out. Of course, during the course of the preceding week, I had fancied a whole host of ideas.

First, I considered standing up in the middle of Arthur Thornton's acceptance speech for the Sacred Skull Award and accusing him of murdering his lover. Then, I thought about sending him a dozen roses to his office with the note, "Love always, Thomas." Finally, I thought about confronting him in the parking lot after the event, showing him all of the pictures and poems as evidence. What I ended up doing, was somewhere in between.

The gala was held at the AC Club on-campus with a reception at 7pm and dinner beginning at 8 o'clock. The AC is the faculty/staff dining room that was once a Victorian home sitting on the perimeter of campus. When the owners died in 1970, the College scooped it up and made it a restaurant with multiple dining rooms. Downstairs, there is a bar and lounge, an adjoining small dining room for twenty, and an adjacent room for parties. Upstairs, is a fairly expansive banquet room, that easily seats two hundred diners. It is intimate, yet not cramped,

and the perfect place on-campus for fancy
gatherings.

My plan was to arrive by 7:30pm in order to
have a little mingle time, but not too much. Since
Barbara's name was also on my invitation, I was
happy that she would be with me- in case I needed
help making a fast exit after executing my plan. In
fact, I had incorporated her as my accomplice.

That night, our babysitter arrived at 7:00
o'clock, we kissed Ethan good night, and made the
quick drive to campus (walking seemed odd in
formalwear). Contrary to my threat, I chose a black
tie, sans cummerbund, and Barbara wore one of her
staple black evening dresses. She looked beautiful
with her shapely figure and crimson lipstick
complementing the elegant dress perfectly.

On the way, Barbara put her hand on my
shoulder as I drove, "Are you sure you want to do
this?"

"Yes," was all I said, keeping my eyes on the
road and navigating our way through the thick, misty
air. "Did you bring it?" she asked.

"Right here," I said, pulling a piece of paper
from my jacket pocket and handing it to her. "The
better question is, are you okay about helping me
with this?"

"Sure," she grinned, "If you are right, this
will be a major scoop."

"And if I'm not right, no one will be any the
wiser."

Barbara folded the letter-sized piece of paper,
along with a silver paperclip that I had attached to it

purposefully, and placed it in her black handbag. Her part of the plan was a bit tricky, but fairly straight-forward. During our time at the reception, she would sneak up to the podium where the evening's speeches would ultimately rest, and clip the piece of paper to Arthur Thornton's acceptance speech. That was plan "A." If for some reason that didn't work out, plan "B" would be simply to hand him the note at the end of the evening and watch for his reaction. Either way, Thornton would be responsible for the outcome. The note would simply be the catalyst.

We walked into the AC by 7:30 as planned, and since it was an "invitation only" party, I made sure that I had mine in hand upon arrival. A student, who I assumed to be Skull and Cross, stood at a table shrouded in black, greeting guests, asking for invitations, and handing out name tags. Barbara and I made it through to the party without a hitch, and walked directly to the lounge and reception. I smiled politely at a few faces, but was surprised to see so many people that I didn't know. Most of the participants were middle to senior middle age and beyond, most holding cocktails and guffawing like the old days. I moved straight to the bar and ordered a glass of merlot and a vodka and cranberry with lime for Barbara. She proceeded straight up the stairs, looking like she knew what she was doing, to accomplish her task and follow through on our plan.

As I turned from the bar and scanned the crowd for a familiar face, any familiar face, I saw R.I.P. talking to a bunch of people I didn't know. I must admit that he looked more dashing than usual, complete with slicked-back grey hair that cast a silvery hue, and a tux complete with tails. He didn't notice me, and I didn't care. I wasn't at the gala to mingle, but with a very specific goal in mind. I was happy to be a wallflower.

I turned back toward the bar and took a drink of my wine. I held it lovingly in my mouth until I had depleted all of the flavor, and then reluctantly swallowed. From behind me, came a voice, "Hi, Dean Doug!" I knew that voice from anywhere- perky Jenny Robins. I turned to face her with a large pasted grin, "Hi, Jenny," I said, "Beautiful party."

"Thanks!" she said, practically jumping. She was wearing a royal blue gown that looked as though she bought it for a prom. Her hair was done in ringlets that hung around her face like ribbons. "Was that your wife I saw?" she asked, and a wave of fear coursed through me. "Yes," I responded, "She's here with me somewhere."

"Upstairs, I think," she said innocently enough. "I was up there making sure that all the tables were ready and I bumped into her. She's so nice. She said that she was writing an article for the newspaper and needed the correct spelling and titles of all the speakers. Luckily, all of that was already on the podium with all of tonight's speeches. I showed her where to go… isn't that great?" she said, swishing her curls away from her mouth. "We're going to be in the paper!"

"I'm sure that you were a big help, Jenny, thank you," I said, considering her understatement.

At that point, a young man in a suit, not a tuxedo tapped Jenny on the shoulder and whisked her off, "Oh, sorry Dean Doug, I have to take care of something. I'll see you at dinner!" This gave me another opportunity to take another swig and then turn and face the crowd. R.I.P. caught my gaze only once, and grimaced as though he had just been afflicted with gallstones, I raised my glass to him, causing him to move toward me through the crowd like a barracuda.

Contrary to his usual approach, he waited until he was within earshot to speak to me, and when he got close enough, he spoke in a measured voice. "I don't know what you're up to Connors, but you better not ruin this."

"I'm up to the bar right now," I said irreverently, "can I get you a drink?"

"You can leave."

"I'm all dressed up, professor, I need someplace to go."

"Where's your wife?" he asked, just as I was beginning to wonder the same thing, "Even *she* can't be seen with you?"

"Oh she's around here somewhere... powdering her nose or something." I said... but it had been awhile and I was just starting to get concerned. How long did it take to clip a piece of paper to a speech? Had Barbara gotten caught?

-31-

At ten of eight, Barbara still hadn't come back downstairs, and I was becoming extremely nervous. Not being able to wait any longer, I grabbed both of our drinks, and made my way to the stairs going up to the main dining room to find her. On my way, I was stopped only once, at the entrance to the dining room, by Gwenyth, dripping with silver sequins. "Doug," she said, fake kissing me on the cheek, "So good to see you. How are you feeling?" It seemed to me that she had befriended the bartender.

"I'm fine," I said, distracted and scanning the room for my wife. "Feeling better every day. How was Atlanta?" I said, feigning concern and becoming more concerned by the absence of my wife.

"Oh you know," she sang, "sweet tea and mansions… it gets old after a while."

"I'm sure," I lied, "Well, if you'll excuse me Gwenyth, I'm going to find my seat and find my wife."

"I'm right here," came Barbara's voice from the stairs behind me, "Gwenyth, it's wonderful to see you again." Barbara reached out for Gwenyth's hand. "Likewise," the President said, seeming genuine, "… now please take care of your husband here. He's been working too much."

"I'll try," Barbara responded, "But it's a losing battle." Everyone chuckled, except for me, and we excused ourselves to our table. "Where were you," I whispered, handing Barbara her drink, "I was getting nervous."

"Mission accomplished," she said, taking a sip and then stirring her now watered down drink. "Your student showed me to the podium, I gave her some line about writing a story, and then I got right down to business. The podium is all set... Mr. Thornton's speech is lovely. I hope it doesn't get ruined. Anyway, that took two seconds and then I walked down the back stairs to use the restroom. I'm sorry, I ran into a few people I know and chatted for a few minutes. I didn't mean to worry you."

"It's okay," I said, "I'm just nervous. What if this doesn't work? What if I'm wrong?"

"Are you having second thoughts?"

"No... but it's a long shot. I know that. I just want this over..."

"All we can do now, is wait." Barbara said, kissing my cheek, and sitting down to table number 25, full of strangers, and all the way in the back corner near the plating area. "Wow," she said to me quietly, "you really are a V.I.P. with this group!" It was true, and if I was unpopular then, I would be downright hated by the end of the evening.

~~~~~

During dinner, I made simple conversation with the other guests at the table, and searched the head table for Arthur Thornton. Although I had only seen a snapshot of him in the Archives, as a handsome and physically fit young man, I recognized him by his smile. He had aged gracefully, but had given up his wispy blonde hair for a cut very close to his scalp, exposing a bald crown and grey sides.  He appeared to be much more frail than his pictures showed, perhaps a result of age and the ravages that carrying a secret will bring.

On one side of him sat R.I.P., to the left of him, Dr. Farrow, and they laughed like college buddies half their age.  I watched them, acting as though they didn't have a care in the world all through dinner, and by the time dessert arrived, I had lost my appetite.  "You're turning down cheesecake?" Barbara leaned into me.  "I can't eat anymore," I whispered, "I just need this over.  I need this night to be over.  I don't know what I was thinking... this past couple of weeks has been too much."

"Well, I think you're going to get your wish," Barbara responded, nodding toward the podium, "It's time to rip the Band-Aid off;  looks like the show's starting."

~~~~~

Dr. Farrow stood at the podium, cleared his throat, and began, "Good evening Skulls and honored guests!" he said, eliciting an explosion of cheers and applause.  "Let's start, with our customary opening, please join me," and the majority of the crowd chimed in, *"The skull is our symbol of power and strength, the cross, it stands for loyalty.  Together they bond behind the cloak for now and all eternity."*  Again more cheers, and then Dr. Farrow carried on, "Never has a statement been so true.  We are the skulls, and we are bound by the loyalty of our organization. For over a century, Skull and Cross has prevailed... not only at Asbury College, but all over the world. We are second to none, not even our rivals, The Wolf's Call." And there I had it, the derivation of "wolf's shame"- a rival secret society.

"Tonight," Farrow continued, "We are here to celebrate the best... the best members of our organization who are some of the top leaders globally. Tonight, we honor one of our best, who happens to live right in our own back yard. I will now turn the podium over to Dr. Gwenyth Porter, President of Asbury College, who will introduce the recipient of this year's coveted, Sacred Skull award. Gwenyth?"

Applause rippled throughout the room, and Barbara had to nudge me to begin clapping. Although I knew that Gwenyth was in attendance, I didn't realize that she would be so high-profile. What would she say if she realized what I had done? She gracefully sashayed toward the mic, and began her comments. "Skulls and honored guests, as the President of Asbury College, the institution of higher learning where Skull and Cross began, it is my distinct pleasure to be here tonight, and to introduce tonight's recipient of the Sacred Skull award."

"For the past 25 years, the Sacred Skull has been presented to a member of the Skull and Cross alumni to honor excellence. Excellence in leadership. Excellence in service to the community; and an overall excellence in character. Tonight, I can't think of a more fitting recipient. Tonight's honoree is a member of the class of '63." *Bullshit*, I whispered under my breath. "Well-known philanthropist who has led the effort to revitalize Asbury Park. He has also funded scholarship opportunities to low-income and minority students for decades. On a more recent note," Gwenyth smiled, looking toward Thornton, "he has just made one of our longtime goals at Asbury College, possible. Tonight, for the first time, I am pleased to announce the creation of the Langston Hughes Center at Asbury College.

"Thanks to his generous gift, the Langston Hughes Center will forge new territory at Asbury, allowing funding, support, and services to our growing Gay, Lesbian, Bisexual, Transgender and Questioning community. This Center will keep Asbury College on the cutting edge of serving the unique and important needs of our community by providing direct contact with our LGBTQ students, faculty, and staff, as well as progressive leadership and resources for us all." *Well I'll be a son-of-a-bitch*, I thought, *What's Thornton trying to do, appease his guilty conscience after all of these years?*

"So, without further ado, I am honored to introduce to you, this year's Sacred Skull, Mr. Arthur Thornton." A standing ovation ensued, and I was so shocked, Barbara had to pull me up. As I stood, and as Thornton walked to the podium, my stomach flipped. *He's going to see it,* I thought. *He's going to turn to his speech and see it...*

Arthur Thornton stood in front of the podium with a wide grin and waved to his admirers, present company excluded.  As he pulled out reading glasses from his tuxedo, he said, "If I would have known that I'd get treatment like this, I'd have given the money a long time ago."  Everyone rolled with thunderous laughter and applause, while all I wanted to do was sit down before my nervous energy prompted me to fall down.  As everyone began to reclaim their seats, Thornton turned to his speech on the podium.  As he looked down, my heart jumped again, and I unconsciously put my hand over my mouth as if to stifle my own yell.  He was about to come in contact with his past, and I couldn't wait to see his reaction.

~~~~~

Anticlimactic is the word that first comes to mind as he began reading his speech without a blink. *Shit,* I thought looking at Barbara, *didn't he see it? Nothing? No reaction?*  How would we ever figure out if my hypothesis was right, then?  But Barbara looked at me calmly and made a subtle motion with her hand telling me to calm down. *Why was she so calm?  It was her work, wasn't she disappointed, too?*

I didn't understand as Thornton droned on. "I spent some of my best years at Asbury College, but I felt that I hadn't fulfilled my obligation to the school that allowed me to fulfill my dreams... and that is what we all should do.  It is all of our responsibilities to make the dreams come true for our young people." *Right,* I thought, *like Thomas Moore's dreams. What did you do to them?* And he continued, "It is time for a renaissance within our community, one where we accept each and every member for who they are, and never, *never*, make anyone feel badly about themselves for being unlike the norm." *What a hypocrite*, I said to myself, and again looked to Barbara for reassurance. She put her hand on my knee and squeezed softly, then leaned in to my ear and whispered, "Here we go…"

Had she not said anything, I might not have noticed. There was a subtle pause in his speech, a blip really, one so infinitesimal that it was barely audible. But it wasn't his words that struck me, it was the look on his face. He blinked once, then twice, adjusted his glasses, and then unclipped the piece of paper from page two of his speech and placed it in his jacket pocket. "Sorry," he said attempting to chuckle, "My shopping list… and I need some new reading glasses… talk about celebrating all kinds of difference!" The crowd cheered and laughed again, allowing him to mask his pained expression and finish his talk.

"Bingo," Barbara whispered again, "I said that it was a good speech… but the poem just seemed to fit better on page two." That's what I had printed, and Barbara had clipped to Thornton's speech, one of his love poems. The one that read:

my soul is with you, from Afar…
you're with me no maTTer where you are.
If life were new, a place refreshed, we'd be
together… and both be blessed.

> I love you MORE, each passing day, yet still
> we seem alone.
> I wonder- a new time, a new place, a new
> decade still...
> Will our love be truly shown?
> -ATTM (forever)

I added the "forever" part... who ever said that I wasn't poetic?  I didn't know what to expect, but hoped that the poem would show him that someone knew his secret.  In a way, I had hoped that he would confess right there at the podium, although I knew that was only a slight possibility.  Now I would have to follow him for the rest of the evening to see the full effect of his reaction.  He finished his speech and thanked everyone, then waved profusely as Dr. Farrow and Jenny Robins handed him his Sacred Skull award.  It was perfect timing; because holding the award, a skull mounted to glass, in his hands seemed to be the final straw.  I could see his hands begin to shake, even from the back of the room.

Thornton waved a final time, but instead of reclaiming his seat at the head table, walked directly off the tiny stage and out a door at the back of the room.  I had to seek him out immediately, and find him while he was raw... it was the only way to get the answers I grew desperate to find.  As I got up, I leaned into Barbara and said , "I'm going after him."  Once I got him, my goal was to introduce myself, and tell him what I had discovered.  In his vulnerable state, one that I wasn't sure would ever develop if my hypothesis wasn't true, I hoped that he would tell me the truth.

~~~~~

I had been to enough dinners at the AC to know my way around the entire building. The kitchen, preparation rooms, even the coat rooms were all familiar to me. The back staircase led to a small reception room, often used as a preparation or "green" room for speakers, behind the main dining room. That's where Thornton went, and I knew that if I ran down the main stairs then returned up the back stairs, I would have to run into him.

As I bounded up the narrow back staircase, normally used for staff, I was surprised that I didn't run into him on his way out. *He must still be in the green room*, I thought, breathing a little heavier as I got to the top of the stairs. I paused outside of the door on a small landing and listened. At first I didn't hear anything, but then, I heard voices.

I pushed my ear to the door, but couldn't make out what was being said. Looking down, and being grateful that it was an old building, I saw light emanating from the crack between the door and the bottom door frame. I didn't even hesitate, and as quietly as I could, maneuvered myself onto the floor, and rested my ear next to the opening; classy as always. Although uncomfortable in the way that I had to contort my body onto the floor in the tiny entryway, I could hear everything perfectly. Thornton was yelling at R.I.P.

~~~~~

"Why would you do this to me?" Came Thornton's voice, brimming with anger, "How could you let this happen?"

"What did he do?" cackled the memorable voice of R.I.P.

"He… or someone… put this on my speech. It was *paper clipped* to my speech. Here!" I could hear the notepaper hitting the floor, then the crack of R.I.P.'s cane hitting the hardwoods in search of it. There was a silence, and I assumed that R.I.P. was reading the note. Finally he said, "I don't understand?"

"That was a note that I wrote to Thomas… back when we were in college."

"You wrote it for Thomas? *You?* Thomas Moore?" R.I.P. seemed confused, "Why?"

"Because I loved him… and it was mutual." I could hear the exhaustion in Thornton's voice, apparently after years of pent-up anguish. I could also hear that R.I.P. was taken totally by surprise. For a while I had been unsure whether R.I.P. was involved in the death of Thomas Moore, or implicated in covering it up for Skull and Cross; but his reaction told me that he wasn't. Despite my usual rancor for the Professor, I was happy about that.

-32-

"Why would he do this to me?" Thornton seemed to ask through clenched teeth, "I thought you were going to stop that Dean from coming tonight?"

*Was Thornton referring to me?* R.I.P. responded again with another, "I still don't understand?"

"I told you! That was a note that I wrote to Thomas. Where did *he* find it? Was it in those archives? How did it ever get there!"

"You wrote it for Thomas? *You?* Thomas Moore? Why?" R.I.P. still wasn't getting it, and I could hear him struggle to understand.

"Because I loved him!" Thornton exclaimed, yet through his excitement, I could hear the exhaustion in his voice, apparently metastasized after years of torment.     "Artie," R.I.P. responded tentatively, "You've had a long day… why don't you just…"

"Stop it, Reggie!" Thornton yelled, using a nickname for Reginald Ichabod Preston that I had never heard, "There is no excuse… Thomas and I were in love… and even then, *I* wanted to tell the world. *I wanted to tell you*, and all of our other friends… *I* wanted to!"

"So, you were both… homosexuals?" R.I.P. uttered quietly, and I could hear the disbelief in his voice. "I still am, Reggie! I haven't kept it a secret… but I did then… Thomas didn't want anyone to know."

"Is that why he went away?" R.I.P. asked, which elicited a pause followed by hearty laughter from Thornton. "Yes..." he continued to chuckle, "That was the cause; the *root* of his disappearance."

"But he failed out of school... he left. We didn't want him to tarnish the good name of Skull and Cross!"

"Reggie... do you believe that? After all of these years? After tonight and what I've just told you?" There was a break of silence, and I could picture R.I.P. nodding into his red bow tie. Suddenly, Thornton's mood seemed to shift, from manic to peaceful. "Reggie, Thomas didn't tarnish the reputation of our organization, I did! Don't you understand? Thomas didn't go away because he failed out of Asbury- *I killed him!*"

~~~~~

"What?" screeched R.I.P., and I could hear disbelief and fear in his voice.

"Yes... he didn't go away, I killed Thomas, and it's something that I've had to deal with all these years. No one knows..." There was another long silence as the news sunk in with the Professor, then finally, sounding hurt, he asked, "How?"

"I murdered him."

"But how? Why?"

"It wasn't on purpose. He was murdered accidentally."

"So you accidentally murdered him?  That sounds like an oxymoron." R.I.P. replied, regaining some of his usual fire.

"We were on the boardwalk… arguing.  I had just become involved with the Mattachine Society.  It was a part of the growing movement for gay folks in the fifties.  I was young, and wanted to tell the world who I was.  But Thomas felt differently.  He had political aspirations, and in the fifties, gays were targeted by many… including McCarthy.  McCarthy even accused President Truman of being lax in finding the gays in the U.S. government.  Thomas felt that if he came out, he would ruin his chances in politics."  Thornton paused, I couldn't tell if he took a drink of something, or was just taking a rest.  R.I.P. urged him to continue, "So you were at the boardwalk…"

"Yes… we were at the boardwalk.  It was night, well after dark, and we were going to walk on the beach… so no one would see us.  But we started arguing before we reached Ocean Avenue.  I was excited about Mattachine, and wanted Thomas to join me.  He was scared, and lashed out… he didn't want any part of coming out.  He couldn't take the names, couldn't bear the thought of being called 'faggot'.  So he told me to stop talking to him about it or he would walk away... from me… from us. I was so angry.  I had never felt love like that before… deep love, true love; the kind that takes your breath away.  He was standing below me on the stairs leading to the beach, and I pushed him.  He pushed me back… and I pushed him again; this time, so hard that he fell over the railing."

"In the darkness, I couldn't tell what had happened… all I heard was a thud and then nothing. I called to him, but he didn't respond. I ran down to him… and there he was… dead in the sand. He hit his head on a piling. He was dead." Another long silence ensued, as if in memorial to Thomas Moore. "So why didn't you tell anyone?" R.I.P. asked, which was exactly *my* question.

"I panicked. Although I wanted to come out to the world, do you think that anyone, especially the Police would believe that it was an accident? Two queers in a lovers' spat? Not then… probably not now. I dragged him underneath the boardwalk, and then returned to campus to find a shovel. I found one in the gardener's shed, and then went back to the beach… to bury him underneath the boardwalk."

"You dug a hole and buried him?"

"Yes… then told everyone that he had left… even his parents' believed it… never to be heard from again. Oh, I think people tried to find him… but then they finally gave up. Even *I* tried to erase him. That's why I decided that we should take a new S&C senior photo… replacing both Thomas and me in the picture. Now you know why… I didn't want to be linked to Thomas. You remember, right, Reggie? "

"Of course…" R.I.P. said, but then paused, "Artie, you killed Thomas?"

"Yes… and I've never forgotten it. I've thought about turning myself in a million times, but then always decided against it… I always thought that I could do more good repenting for my sins within society, than paying for them in prison."

"But what about people who cared about him? What about respect for his memory?"

"I tried to honor that as best I could. That's why I moved his remains to campus… every single bone that was left."

R.I.P. gasped loudly, "You did *what*?"

"I couldn't think of him under the boardwalk any longer… so, when I was back at Asbury to work on my Master's degree, I returned to the beach, uncovered him, and collected all the bones that I could find. Then, during one break when it was quiet, I put him back on campus, it took me a few trips, and draped him with one of our robes. I thought that he would like that."

"The skeleton found on campus was Thomas?" R.I.P. screamed, reaching a new level of exasperation. "Yes," Thornton said finally, "I'm surprised no one found him before; I've thought of that so many times." He stopped, and let out a cough, "I've tried to do the right thing over the years- turning my success into assistance for others. When you and Harold Farrow told me that the Dean was snooping around, I hoped that my last effort, the Langston Hughes Center, would finally appease my guilt… and show the world that I'm committed to Thomas and helping people… but I'm not so sure. I can't believe that I was guilty of defying the very thing that the Center stands for… for being who you want to be. Thomas wanted to live his life a different way than I did… and I didn't allow him the chance."

"So you think that Connors knows about what you did?" R.I.P. asked.

"I think someone does… someone knows… and put the poem I wrote on my speech. In a way, I'm glad. I might be ready to tell everyone what I did… or maybe not. Maybe I'll just take my secret, and Thomas' secret with me to the grave. You won't tell anyone after all of these years and disgrace the Society, will you Reggie?"

Suddenly, I heard someone behind me, "Lose a penny?" Chief Morreale said, coming up the stairs. I attempted to jump up, but being contorted on the floor for so long made me stiff… I crouched gingerly, being careful not to re-injure my knees or palms, and looked up. "Arthur Thornton just admitted to killing Thomas Moore," I whispered, struggling to stand slowly and meet the chief's gaze. Instead of shock, he just smirked at me, "So I hear."

"You knew?"

"Well, Barbara called me… she said that you had followed Thornton, and was worried about the confrontation. I see that the only one you've confronted is that crack in the door."

"So, what are you going to do now?" I whined, sore from lying on the floor for so long.

"I think I'll question Mr. Thornton," the Chief replied casually.

"But what if he denies it?" I beseeched.

"Well, if you found evidence, it shouldn't be too hard to investigate.  And now, we have a witness who heard it all."

"Right!" I said loudly, "Professor Preston is inside!"  The Chief looked at me quizzically, "Is the Professor inside?  I was talking about you."

-33-

I guess that I was louder than I thought, because when R.I.P. opened the door to find me and the Chief standing there, we all looked shocked. The Chief moved in quickly, and right to Thornton, "I hear that you have something to tell me?" he said without emotion, as I entered the room and stood next to R.I.P.

"I think it's time," Thornton said quietly, "I think it's past time." The Chief moved behind him, and led him toward the door, passing me along the way. As Thornton reached me, he stopped. Although I expected anger, the look on his face expressed gratitude and he smiled slightly. "Make good use of that Center," he said, and then moved out of the room, escorted by Chief Morreale.

The Professor and I stood in the empty room in awkward silence, neither of us knowing how to respond to the events that just occurred. I was surprised when it was R.I.P. who broke the quiet, "Well, there goes my ride... I came here with Arthur. I'm stranded here now!" A curmudgeon to the core.

"Do you need a ride?" I asked, feeling an awkward kinship with R.I.P. We had mutually been part of something both terrible and liberating, and although we experienced it from different frames of reference, the bond was real. He didn't reply to my offer, and instead turned his back, which sparked the anger that I had felt all day. "It's just a ride," I said, looking at his silver duck's ass on the back of his head, "You don't even need to consider it a truce. Just a ride home."

R.I.P. remained silent with his back to me, and I noticed his shoulders begin to heave up and down. Was he crying? Then finally squawked weakly, "I didn't know, Connors... I didn't know."

"I know," I said, trying to be reassuring, and then continued to let the silence hang in the air. He finally turned to me, and I saw the tears in his eyes. He looked away to hide his sadness, but the angle of his face only made the water in his eyes glisten more. "I feel like I covered for him," he said after a minute. "When he said that Thomas had left, we were worried about what it would look like. We had already taken the senior photo... a tradition still today... but Thomas was gone, and Arthur was going into the service, so it looked bad. I was one of the men who stood in for the replacement photo... the one that's in our Conference room."

I looked at him closely, with greater scrutiny than I ever had before, "You were the one with the beard..." I said hopefully. R.I.P. nodded, "I thought I was helping... I didn't know that I was causing more disgrace to our organization. I had no idea... just no idea." I felt badly for him; although I felt a sense of vindication, R.I.P.'s world had categorically changed. "So, what about that ride?" I asked again.

R.I.P. still didn't respond, but moved past me toward the door. As I followed behind him, I felt a sense of relief; the members of our Asbury community who had been lost were not forgotten. I thought of the photos of Thomas Moore, and Darcy

Green's dreams… I even thought about Ivory and Lacey.  Perhaps the truth was absolution for all of us.

Moving behind R.I.P., I sensed that he was having trouble with the stairs.  Without saying a word, I reached for his cane, offering to hold it for him while he held onto the banister.  "Thanks, Doug," he said… and for the first time ever, I knew that he meant it.

THE END

Don't miss Dean Doug's next lesson
Counterfeit by the Coast
Book 3 in the Ocean Grove Mysteries

When counterfeit hundred dollar bills start surfacing
at businesses around the Grove, it doesn't take long
for attention to fall on Asbury College.  As Dean
Doug and his staff investigate suspicious, and illegal,
activity on campus, the rest of the College prepares

for President Gwenyth Porter's anniversary celebration.  What no one knows, but everyone finds out, is that funny money isn't the only fake in town and even Dean Doug begins to question everything that he knows to be true.  Counterfeit by the Coast takes readers on another fantastic trip full of adventure, suspense, and an ending you won't believe!

And for more Ocean Grove fun
go to
www.101mysteries.com

Author, Heath P. Boice, in Ocean Grove, NJ

A college administrator for twenty years, Heath P. Boice knows about college life. He takes this experience and uses it as the foundation for his unique series of "cozy" novels. This most recent story, "Missing by the Midway" begins his exciting new Ocean Grove Mystery series, paying homage to his former home, Ocean Grove, NJ. This is a relaunch of his original, "Mystery 101" series.

Heath has received both regional and national recognition for his professional work in college administration, boasting over 50 publications and convention presentations on topics including: Higher education, service leadership and innovation in higher education, peer mentorship, and transition programs.

Heath holds a BA in Public Communications (radio/television) and a MS Ed in College Student Personnel and Counseling from the College of Saint Rose in Albany, New York. He also holds a Doctorate in Education from Rutgers University, New Brunswick, New Jersey. This has led him to a successful career as a college dean and college instructor at both private and public schools, most recently as the Associate Vice President for Student Affairs at the Rochester Institute of Technology (RIT). A lifelong learner, he earned an Advanced Graduate Certificate in Service Leadership and Innovation from RIT. Additionally, Heath serves as a faculty member for the School of Advanced Studies, University of Phoenix.

Before working in education, Heath worked both on and off air at radio and television stations as a news anchor, writer, producer, and feature talk show host. When not working with college students or writing, Heath enjoys spending time with his wife and daughters in their Rochester, NY home. He also enjoys gardening, cooking, and reading... mostly mysteries.

For more about Heath P. Boice, go to www.101mysteries.com

Made in the USA
Charleston, SC
28 June 2014